P9-DNC-501

Yester's Ride

Yester's Ride

C. K. Crigger

FIVE STAR
A part of Gale, a Cengage Company

Farmington Hills, Mich • San Francisco • New York • Waterville, Maine
Meriden, Conn • Mason, Ohio • Chicago

This novel is a work of fiction. Names, characters, places, and incidents are either the product of the author's imagination, or, if real, used fictitiously.

LIBRARY OF CONGRESS CATALOGING-IN-PUBLICATION DATA

Names: Crigger, C. K., author.
Title: Yester's ride / C. K. Crigger.
Description: First edition. | Farmington Hills, Mich. : Five Star Publishing, 2019.
Identifiers: LCCN 2018032029 (print) | LCCN 2018032087 (ebook) | ISBN 9781432849726 (ebook) | ISBN 9781432849719 (ebook) | ISBN 9781432849702 (hardcover)
Subjects: | GSAFD: Western stories.
Classification: LCC PS3603.R53 (ebook) | LCC PS3603.R53 Y47 2019 (print) | DDC 813/.6—dc23
LC record available at https://lccn.loc.gov/2018032029

First Edition. First Printing: March 2019
Find us on Facebook—https://www.facebook.com/FiveStarCengage
Visit our website—http://www.gale.cengage.com/fivestar/
Contact Five Star Publishing at FiveStar@cengage.com

Printed in Mexico
1 2 3 4 5 6 7 23 22 21 20 19

I'm dedicating this book to anyone who's ever felt
the ravages of discrimination
and had doubts about their self-worth.
Buck up, you guys. Stay strong. Prevail.

ACKNOWLEDGEMENTS

Thanks to my friends in the Red Ink Fictioneers Crit group. Your advice and camaraderie are invaluable to me. Shall I name you all? First and foremost, my mentor and the leader of our group, Pat Pfeiffer, as well as Carrie Stuart Parks, Bruce and Carrie MacBride, Joyce Nowacki, Jesse Steven Hughes, Kathryn Robinson, Karen Parks, Fred Jessett, and Randy Haglund.

Chapter One: Yester

Yester Noonan's butt ached. Not much to wonder at considering he'd been in the saddle since morning, and now the day was wearing thin. Hoping to ease the hurt, he stood in his stirrups and stretched. He was sixteen years old and hungry, and he'd been missing his ma's cooking. His gaze went toward the horizon and home, just one more hill away.

Squinting against the lowering sun, he jerked his hat brim down and stared harder. Flint, his horse, stopped. Dog Pony, the packhorse trailing behind him, stopped, too.

"Look ahead, Pa," Yester said to his riding companion. "Is that smoke?"

His pa only grunted. Big Joe Noonan, lulled by the smooth gait of his buckskin and the consumption of the better part of a fifth of whiskey, was about three-quarters asleep in the saddle. Drunk as an Irish lord, too, which made Yester nervous about waking him up. Liquor had an effect on Big Joe that made it tricky being around him.

But there was that billowing plume of smoke rising into the western sky.

"Pa, wake up." Yester spoke louder. "I see smoke. It's coming from our place."

His words had no apparent effect. Yester snatched up the reins lying slack on the buckskin's neck and drew the horse to a halt when it would've walked past him.

"Pa!" he shouted.

Damn Big Joe for being a sot and a drunkard. Big Joe needed somebody to make sure he got home all right from his monthly toot in town and Yester was elected. Which meant Ma and Yester's little sister, Ketta, were left at home to take care of chores.

The situation had a routine. When she saw them coming over the hill, Ketta, being plenty smart, ran and hid. As soon as he got in the house, Pa would smack Ma a couple times to "teach her respect" and to pay her back for Ketta. Then Yester would protest and try to fight Pa, which meant he'd end up with bumps and bruises in the attempt. Never failed. Once he'd even gotten a cracked rib. That had been a while back, though, when he was just a kid.

But meanwhile, in the here and now, smoke billowed into the sky where no smoke ought to be. The movement of air brought the odor of burned wood drifting toward them.

"Joe!" Yester hollered into his pa's ear.

He finally got a reaction. Big Joe awakened enough to cuff him alongside the head and call him a foul name.

Yester, being adept at ducking, wasn't much bothered. "C'mon, Pa," he said. "Get a move on. Looks like the barn is on fire. Or the house."

"Huh? Fire?" Straightening, Joe lifted bleary eyes and blinked. "Sonova . . . Smoke? Hope to Gawd it ain't the barn."

Not one word of concern about Ma or Ketta, though that didn't surprise Yester any. Setting heels to the buckskin, Big Joe crowded his horse to the front and, with a whoop, urged it into a dead run. Flint, being a small horse to begin with and old besides, didn't have a lot of run in him. Yester followed at a steady but slower pace.

When he topped the rise, his pa was already halfway to the buildings, flapping the loose ends of the reins against the buckskin's neck. Not all the buildings were standing, Yester saw, squinting to see through the pall of smoke. Not *everybody,* either.

"Ma." He drummed his heels against ol' Flint's side, the horse responding gamely.

Yester wasn't far behind his father when they thundered into the dooryard. Wisps of smoke came from the barn, although the corner where the fire'd started had already burned itself out before doing much damage.

The outhouse and the chicken coop had been overturned, both dragged a few yards off their rock foundations. Part of the outhouse's roof had been torn off, the wooden shingles scattered.

Over at the corral where the gate and the rails around it had been pulled down, the milk cow stood in misery, blood washing down from her hip as she dragged that leg. A few white Leghorn chickens ran loose, flapping their wings as they scooted from under the buckskin's feet. Several of Ma's prize laying hens lay dead.

Yester swallowed and looked away, then wished he hadn't as his gaze landed on the bundle of brown fur lying unmoving in the dust. Barney, Pa's ol' Airedale, appeared as dead as the chickens.

The house was still burning, flames shooting from the scorched roof and licking at the kitchen wall. That whole side of the house was charred, and only half of the porch remained.

And on the porch—

Pa dismounted before the buckskin even stopped. "Yester!" he yelled, like Yester was somewhere at a distance instead of only a few feet behind him. "Fetch some buckets of water. We gotta get this fire out."

Yester's eyes bugged. Fire out? To hell with the fire. Ma was his only concern.

"Fetch 'em yourself," he muttered, although not quite loud enough for Pa to hear. Ignoring Big Joe, he slid from Flint's back and dashed up the broken house steps. The smoldering fire was hot, searing his face as he dropped to his knees beside his mother.

Ma lay on her belly, her dress rucked up and showing her legs from ankle to thigh. Yester pulled the skirt down, although not before he saw blood there, between her legs. He hoped Pa hadn't seen. It was just like before. That time almost twelve years ago. He'd been awful young, but he remembered.

"Ma?" He didn't think she was dead, because her eyes were closed. Closed tight. Dead creatures' eyes almost always opened up because the muscles went slack, or so she'd told him once. Ma knew things like that. And for sure, as Yester put his hand on her shoulder, he felt her flinch.

"C'mon, Ma," he said to her, "it's me, Yester. I gotta get you off this porch before you get burned up."

Yester, a good-sized boy for his age and as tall as his pa already, got one arm under her knees and the other under her back and lifted. Good thing Ma was a small woman, he thought, grunting.

Still, he staggered under her weight as he started down the steps. With a crack of wood, the step collapsed. They both went rolling into the dusty yard. Ma cried out.

"Sorry," he said, near tears himself. "Sorry. I didn't mean to hurt you."

Now that they were out of the worst of the smoke, his eyes cleared, and he saw somebody had beat her up bad. Way worse than Big Joe ever did. He usually stopped with a slap or two—or three. A knot the size of a puffball mushroomed on the side of her head; both eyes were blackened, her lips split. Blood dribbled from her ear, while bruises in the shape of fingertips purpled a bare arm where the sleeve had been ripped away.

And on her legs. Blood on her legs. Fury ripped at him.

"Yester," she said, her voice a bare, raspy whisper. "Ketta. They took Ketta."

"Who did, Ma?"

"Him."

Him? Him who? Yester was confused. "She didn't run off and hide?"

"No. She stayed . . . tried to fight. Had . . . old pistol." She paused for breath. "Misfired. He laughed . . . took her. Find her, Yest—"

Yester's blood ran cold. "He?"

But Ma had passed out again, her breathing ragged.

Yester stood up, looking around for Big Joe. There he was, poking at the Airedale with the toe of his boot.

The dog stirred, lifted his head, and struggled to get his feet under him. Wonder of wonder, Joe stooped and lifted him until Barney stood on his own, shaky but upright. Maybe he'd be okay. Yester sure hoped so. And the cow, maybe she would be all right, too. Maybe the two critters were a good omen saying that his little sister Ketta had got away to her hiding place after all.

Big Joe's attention being elsewhere, Yester dodged around the corner of the smoldering house and took off up the draw behind it at a run. He had to make sure.

Ketta

"They'll be home today," Ketta's mother said, her mouth turned down at the corners. Ketta recognized the sad look. The look of dread. But then she should. Her own expression copied her mama's.

"Yes." Ketta forced a smile to turn up the edges, trying to act like she wasn't scared. Like Big Joe's arrival didn't mean she'd have to make herself scarce again. There'd be no hot supper for her tonight, that much was certain. She'd have to stay in her hideout until morning, hugging her arms around her knees to ward off the cold and shivering every time a coyote howled from the rocky ridge in back of the cave. *Her cave.* Yes, she'd be shivering, though it was summer, therefore warm even at night, and she knew the *coyotes* wouldn't hurt her. At least she'd have Barney, the dog, to keep her company and scare off any predators. He was good about staying with her.

Big Joe would've slept off the liquor by tomorrow morning. He'd be surly, but most of his mean would've gone away. Well, she amended to herself, Big Joe was always mean, but he'd keep his fists to himself. And he'd probably leave off turning his meanness and insulting words on Mama.

"Best have your picnic ready so you can grab it up on your way out the door," Mama added.

Picnic! There'd be bread and butter and maybe a hardboiled egg seasoned with salt and pepper, all tied up in a scrap of cloth. Some picnic.

Then, under her breath, Mama added something like, ". . . raging beast," and ". . . a child," and although Ketta heard very well, she didn't catch all of it.

Magdalene. That was her mother's name. Ketta still wondered over the sound of it. Two days ago, she'd found it written in the bible alongside Joseph Lincoln Noonan's on the page that had spaces for marriages, births, and deaths. Joseph Lincoln Noonan was Pa, she guessed, or at least the man she called Pa. To his face, anyway. In her mind she always called him Big Joe. Anyway, she saw Yester's name written in the bible, too. Her strong, tall brother, a little more than four years older than she.

Her own name, Ketta, wasn't in the book at all.

Born, get married, and die, Mama had said, and she hadn't been smiling. Then she'd said she'd almost forgotten she had a name. A real name besides Mama, that is. Or Woman. Pa usually just called her Woman, like she was a dog or a horse.

Even Pa's dog had a real name, Ketta had thought.

That was Ketta's fault, though, because Big Joe hated her, which somehow meant that after she got born, he hated Mama, too. Tears prickled behind Ketta's eyelids, so she closed them, just for a second, until they went away.

Ketta dawdled in making up her "picnic," first washing her hands, then taking out bread she'd baked this morning—she was a good baker, better than her mother, truth to tell—and cutting the heel off the end. She liked that piece best, although she seldom got it. Usually only if Yester, who liked it, too, would trade with her. Sometimes he did. As long as Big Joe wasn't paying attention, anyway.

With her supper packed up, Ketta went outside, where she found her mother standing on the porch. She was gazing off to the west. That was wrong, though. Big Joe and Yester, they'd ride in from the north.

"What is it, Mama?" Ketta asked. Her mother's shoulders were stiff and hunched, as if she was worried. Squinting a little, Ketta saw her mother's gaze fixed on a cloud of dust rising into the sky. In front of the dust were four horses with riders. "Is company coming?"

"Bring me the shotgun, Ketta." Mama's pretty face was pinched up tight. Her mouth, usually soft and relaxed when it was just she and Ketta at home, had drawn into a tight, straight line.

They kept the shotgun propped inside the house, just behind the door. Everyone in the family always said they wanted it handy in case of varmints getting after the hens, but a few years back, Ketta had figured out the varmints they talked about might just be of the human kind. And they had something to do with her.

With her and the reason Big Joe hated her.

"Hurry, child." Mama's voice was taut as a tightly strung wire fence. "And bring the box of shells. You know where it is."

"Yes, Mama." Ketta hastened to obey. But Big Joe stored the shells on a deep ledge above the dry sink, and she had to drag up a chair to reach them. Ketta was small for an almost twelve year old. Fine-boned and tiny.

"Typical for a Chink," according to Big Joe.

Whatever a Chink was.

Once up on the chair, she found Pa's old pistol at the back of the shelf alongside the shotgun shells. She spotted it only because she stood on tiptoe. The pistol was loaded, too, the cartridges visible in the revolving chamber. Not even thinking twice, she grabbed it down.

She didn't bother to put the chair back but raced out onto the porch, lugging the shotgun and shells and the pistol.

Mama and Barney were side by side in the yard, the dog baying his head off.

The men, strangers, were closer now. Close enough she could make out their faces. They did not look like nice men, unlike Mr. Fontaine, their neighbor, who, with his family, lived an hour's ride to the south. These men looked dirty, scowling, and evil. Even the one with eyes shaped like hers, except his were narrower and more slanted at the corners. One man had a raised scar over the bridge of his mountain of a nose. One had black skin, something she'd never seen before, and the other—Well, she'd never seen an uglier person.

Ketta shuddered as she handed her mother the box of shells. Her hands unsteady, Magdalene shoved shells into the shotgun's chambers and snapped it closed.

The men kept coming, spreading out as if to surround Ketta and Magdalene.

"Are they bad men?" Ketta whispered. "Are they outlaws?"

"Yes. They are. Get back to the porch." Mama spoke from the side of her mouth. "I'm going to shoot this gun. When I do, you run fast as you can, around the house and up the draw to your hideout. Can you do that?"

Ketta nodded, although her mother's instructions buzzed in

her head like a lost colony of bees.

"Do you hear me?" Mama said, very soft but fierce. "Run, Ketta. No matter what."

No matter what?

"Ketta! Do you hear me?"

Ketta found her voice. "Yes, Mama. All right."

They walked backward together, Ketta keeping her eyes on the men as she went. One of them pointed and laughed. The others laughed, too. All except the one with slanted eyes. His gaze was fixed on her.

Time froze. As if blown in on a gust of wind, the men were right there, not a dozen feet away. Their horses were worn looking, lathered and breathing hard.

Barney snarled, his teeth showing, sensing danger beyond the human's ken. He ran out, biting at a horse's ankles, until a shot rang out. The dog squealed once and fell. Ketta let out a little screech and lifted the pistol.

Then Magdalene's shotgun bellowed, too. Once, twice.

Almost blind with tears, Ketta pointed the pistol at the man who'd shot Barney. Using all her strength, she yanked on the trigger.

Nothing happened. A dry click and nothing more.

"Run, Ketta, run!" Mama screamed.

Ketta tried to obey—she really did—but then the man with slanted eyes stopped her. He'd dismounted and gotten behind her somehow, and he grabbed her up in a bone-crushing grip, squeezing her chest until she hardly had any breath left.

The useless pistol dropped from her fingers.

Dizzy as a speeding top, the whole world started spinning around and going black, like she was shut up in a box with no way out.

"Mama," she tried to say. But she just didn't have enough air left to force the plea for her mother to come help her. Her lips were frozen shut, cold as on a winter day.

Not that her mother could've helped anyway.

His grip never wavering, the slant-eyed man wrested Ketta away from the others. In Ketta's last moments of consciousness, she glimpsed her mother, Magdalene, lying on the porch, her skirt pushed up around her hips. The house was on fire behind her, flames licking at the window sill, Magdalene's blue calico curtains blazing up until they disappeared into charred rags.

All the men but the one holding her were fighting over Mama as she writhed and bucked against them. Innocent as she was, Ketta knew what that meant.

"No," she squeaked, so faint the word turned to wispy air. "No. Mama."

"I'm first," the scarred man said.

Another, the ugliest one, said a very bad word. "You're always first."

But they weren't really fighting. They were laughing. That was what Ketta saw.

Then Mama's scream was cut short, and Ketta's world finally went dark.

Chapter Two: Yester

Maybe Ma had been wrong. Maybe Ketta had got away.

The hope filled Yester's mind as he ran. His sister was a wily little fox. Had to be, ever since she was old enough to run.

Ketta's special place, her "HideFromPa" place, lay only a quarter mile from the house. Close enough that, if necessary, a feller could hear her scream. Could've if she'd been a screaming sort of girl, that is.

Which she wasn't. Silent most times to the point of being mute, Pa, maybe because of this, called her stupid. Yester knew different. He figured—no, he knew—she was smart, maybe even as smart as one of those geniuses. Smarter than him, by far. Smart enough to hide behind silence when around Pa. She could sure enough talk plenty when she wanted to. To him and Ma. And to Barney and sometimes the chickens, horses, and even the milk cow, one of Ketta's chores being to milk Ol' Bossy twice a day.

Yester, his long legs pumping, scrambled over the basalt boulder that guarded the cave's entrance from view. His ma said the boulder had been rolled here by an ocean of water headed for the big river but had left a crack behind it. That had been at the end of the last ice age, a long, long time ago.

His boots slipped in a patch of small stones and he fell, skinning a knee. The stones hadn't been here the last time he'd been around looking for his sister. They made a lot of noise, and he figured she must've scattered them as a way to hear anybody trying to sneak up on her.

Smart, for sure, if painful to the unwary.

"Ketta," he called real gentle-like, breathless from his run. What if those buggers who'd violated his ma were still around? "Ketta, you here? It's Yester. Come on out."

Nothing. No soft little voice replied.

Damn.

Ketta's cave was really only an indentation in the bank of a dry river, not really a cave at all. Big enough for a small girl and the boy Yester had been only a couple years ago, with Barney squeezed in with them. Now Yester dwarfed it. Which meant he needed only a glance to see the space was empty, the dust undisturbed for many a day.

"Ketta," he called again, louder this time.

But, though he called and searched around and about for several minutes, he found no trace of his sister.

Ma had it right. Ketta had been taken.

"Yester," his father's voice boomed out from down the draw. "Where the hell are you. Getcherself back here. We got work to do. Your ma needs you."

Ma. It was probably the only thing he could've said to bring Yester in as quickly as he did.

"I can't find Ketta," Yester said, running back into the yard.

"Don't matter," he said. "Got more important things to worry about than your ma's crossbreed."

Big Joe, shovel in hand, was busy flinging dirt over the last few flames still licking at the house's bottom row of cedar logs.

It seemed to Yester he was throwing most of it away.

"Outlaws opened the gates and ran the horses off." Big Joe stood up, breathing hard and canted a little sideways, like he still wasn't seeing too straight. "What they didn't steal. Another couple hours and the herd'll be scattered from here to hell's breakfast table. We gotta get them rounded up."

"How—" Yester began, but his pa interrupted.

"Found some loose nags that've been rode hard. I figure the fellers done this are on the run. We gotta get our horses back. Soon as you get the woman inside, I want you to ride over and fetch Fontaine and his boy. I need help, and I need it quick."

"What about the sheriff?" Yester asked.

"No time to ride back into town. Go on now. Do as you're told." Satisfied the fire was out, Big Joe wiped away the sweat rolling down his face with a filthy hand. "We gotta get a handle on this."

Yester figured that was no lie. "Yes, Pa," he said.

But Pa calling Ma *the woman* rankled. He hated when Big Joe spoke like she was some stranger. And Ketta? She might never have existed. Pa wouldn't lift a finger to help her. Shoot! Worse, he'd not mention her even if the sheriff did get called in. Probably not to Fontaine, either, whose wife most likely would come help Ma when asked.

The sheriff, though, he needed told what'd happened here. If the sheriff and a posse rode with Big Joe, they'd see no harm came to Ketta and that she was returned to her family. To Ma and him, he meant. But if nobody informed the lawman, then Pa would let Ketta go and say good riddance.

Magdalene Noonan, although a lightweight woman—she worked too hard to have a lot of meat on her bones—still proved more than Yester could carry far on his own. He fetched a blanket stinking of char from his ma's bed in the unburned part of the house and brought it out. Rolling Ma onto it, he tugged the makeshift travois inside. By then his mother was stirring, her wits slowly coming back. She was able, with his help, to crawl into bed, a single low moan escaping her clenched lips.

"Don't bother with me. I'm all right," she whispered. "It's Ketta . . ."

"You ain't a bother." He pulled the blanket over her battered arms, found a cloth and some water and wiped a smear of blood from her chin.

"You're wasting time," she said to him, turning her head away. "Go after her. Go right now."

"Me?" A little confused, Yester's mind whirled. "Who's got her, Ma? Where are they taking her? What do they even look like? Pa's—"

She hushed his flow of questions. "I heard your father. He won't look for Ketta. He's after his horses. It's up to you, son."

"I can't leave you here alone, Ma. Not when you're hurt and all. You need somebody to help you."

"Yellow Bird Fontaine. She'll come." Her skin shown as pale as the sun-bleached sheet pulled to her chin. "I'll be all right," she said again, although Yester didn't believe her. Not for a minute.

Taking in a shaky breath, his mother grabbed his hand, arresting it as he rinsed the rag and started to bathe around her ear where a thin trickle of blood had dried.

Magdalene winced. "It was her father who came for her. Oh, he didn't do this," a weak gesture indicated her battered self. "You can blame those three ruffians with him. But he didn't stop them. It was Ketta. He came for Ketta."

"Her father?" Yester could hardly believe it. After all these years? They—he and Ma—had talked about him once. They'd thought, hoped, he was dead. "Who is he, Ma?"

She winced when she tried to shrug, a quickly muffled moan escaping through clenched teeth. "A Celestial man with slanted eyes. You know that. God knows your father has raved about it often enough. Only his skin is much darker than Ketta's and has a yellowish cast. He's not all Chinese or whatever foreign land he comes from, though. I think he must be some white. He talks white."

Yester froze. He'd seen someone like that in town yesterday.

"Do you know his name?" Yester asked, an idea forming in his mind.

"No. Not really. I never wanted to. But one of the men, he called him Ko. I think. I'm not sure."

Ko? Or Kuo, like he'd heard? The idea hardened.

While Big Joe had been drinking and bragging and carrying on with a saloon girl, that foreign-looking man had been listening in. Pa had laughed about his woman at home taking care of the ranch and something about her abomination of a kid. The Celestial had been all ears. Yester knew because, drawn by some of the man's features resembling Ketta's, he'd been watching him. One of the rough group surrounding him had called him Kuo, pretty close to what Ma thought she'd heard. And, worse, the Celestial had known Ma and Ketta were alone and unprotected here at the ranch.

Pa's fault. This was Pa's fault.

Anger surged, white hot.

Ma raised her hand and touched one of her ears. "One of them hit me. I can't hear very well. Everything is muffled. You must go now. Right now, Yester, before they're too far ahead to catch."

"Aw, Ma—" Yester was torn.

She grabbed his hand, squeezing with surprising strength. "Now, Yester." Her bloodshot eyes swiveled to where Big Joe was still flopping a wet blanket over some embers outside the door. "Before he puts you to work chasing horses and stops you."

Yester didn't see that he had any choice. He just didn't know how he was going to get his sister back from four bad men. Not all by himself.

Ketta

Ketta came awake. She couldn't figure it out. Where was she? And why did her head hang down over the side of a horse, its front shoulder moving not three inches in front of her eyes? Powdery dust combined with the sweating odor of horse rose into her face, making it hard to breathe. And her stomach—oh, her poor stomach. A sudden lurch, and what little remained in there from her lunch spewed down the side of the horse.

"Uh," she said, halfway between a groan and an exclamation of disgust.

Memory came back like a brick falling. Hard, heavy, and terrifying.

The bad man—the man with the funny, yet oddly familiar eyes—gripped her tightly around the waist. It didn't make her feel any better. She'd just as soon fall off the horse and collapse onto the ground, burrowing in like a little old earthworm.

Such a respite was not to be. They didn't even slow down, the horse continuing at a fast walk, although she heard laughter from behind them, and someone called a raucous comment to her captor. He turned and made a rude gesture at them.

Ketta couldn't help it. She started to cry.

"Quit that," he muttered to her, then, low so the others couldn't hear, "No squalling. We'll stop soon. You'll be better." And even lower under his breath like he was talking to himself, "Knock you in the head if you ain't."

Ketta believed him about that last part, and since she sure enough didn't want knocked in the head, she fought back the tears and resolved to not be sick anymore. No matter what. Although if knocking her in the head is what this man had in mind, why'd he swoop her up in the first place? Why not leave her with Mama?

Where was her mother, anyway? Ketta didn't see her up ahead of them. Just one of those awful men. The black-skinned one, and he was alone. Carefully, to avoid having the man clutch her around the waist again, she stretched her neck to look behind them.

No sign of Mama there, either, which meant she was all alone with these men. But that ugly one with the paunchy belly, the one with the snaggly, yellow teeth and raggedy clothes, the one who'd been pawing at Mama no matter how hard she fought, he was there. The man with the scarred nose was there, too, slouched in his saddle, which had a missing horn. He looked like a sack of potatoes and just about as lumpy. They were riding two more of Big Joe's horses. In fact, she noticed now, they all were. Including the man who had her in a death grip. Beau was the horse's name, a brown gelding.

Oh, my goodness. Big Joe was going to be so mad.

"I want to go home," she announced in a small voice. "I want my mother."

The fellow's arm pinched her belly, although he didn't speak.

An awful thought occurred to her. "Where is my mother? Did you hurt her?"

He didn't answer, which she thought was an answer. They'd hurt Mama, all right. She knew they had. Tears seeped into her eyes again, but she blinked them away. She'd had a lot of practice doing that.

"Big Joe will be coming after his horses, you know," she said. "You're going to be in a lot of trouble. When he catches up, he'll hang you from the highest tree."

"Shut up," the slant-eyed man said. "I saw your Big Joe in town earlier. Feller drank so much whiskey this morning, it'll be a week afore he can ride."

"You don't know him." Her voice turned sepulchral, if a young girl's voice can ever be called such. "Big Joe can ride when he's asleep. Ask my brother. And a hangover always just makes him extra mean."

"What do you know about hangovers?"

"I know what they do to him," Ketta said.

Her captor seemed to be thinking it over. "You don't know nothing," he finally said.

His words just went to show *he* was the one who didn't know anything. She tried once to argue with the man, but he just squeezed her hard again. Without breath, she had to quit talking, which seemed to suit him better.

But they kept riding and riding, until Ketta thought she was being split apart. And still they kept going, on into the soft, purple evening, and into the full dark. Until the horse ahead of them stumbled over a broken tree limb and went to its knees.

The black man, invisible in the night except for the whites of his eyes, cursed. "I'm done in," he said, his voice a thick drawl, "and so is this nag."

Nag. Big Joe wouldn't like anybody calling his horse a nag, Ketta thought.

Her captor pulled up beside the black man. "We'll camp here for tonight, eat, and catch a little shut-eye. We'll hit the river tomorrow along in the afternoon and split up and meet again at the cabin later. Kid here says the rancher will be coming after his horses." He laughed. "Guess I ain't inclined to make it any easier for him."

Apparently, this suited them all. "I'm hongry enough my belly thinks my throat been cut," the scarred one said, seeming to think he'd just invented the phrase. He was wrong, though. Big Joe had been saying it all the years Ketta could remember. Another thing Big Joe wouldn't like Scar knowing, she reflected, seeing as he acted like it was brand new every time *he* said it.

Anyway, they pulled off into the trees, the black man leading his horse, which limped as if he'd bunged up his knee. Presently, Snaggletooth shouted out he'd found a little clearing, and they all converged on the spot, pine tree boughs forming a thick canopy overhead and shutting out the sky.

"This will do," her captor said, swinging down from Beau. He reached for Ketta, but she slid down Beau's shoulder by herself, landing in a heap beside the horse's feet.

"Here." The man grabbed her by the back of her dress and dragged her out of the way. "You lookin' to get trampled?"

She could've told him Beau never trampled anybody, that he was the kindest horse imaginable, but she didn't.

"Hey man, she stupid or something?" Scar asked. "Tell 'er to get cracking with our supper afore I start chewing my saddle."

Ketta stayed where her captor had dropped her, not sure she could move even if she wanted to. Her head drooped, and she noticed one of her braids had come undone. Loose hair fluttered around her face like an ebony halo.

"Get up, kid," her captor said quietly. "I'll build a fire. You fill the coffee pot from my canteen. There's bread and meat in my saddlebags. Check the one on the right. Took the bread right off the kitchen table."

Anger stirred, although she didn't let on. Bread she'd baked herself, this morning, in anticipation of Yester and Big Joe's return. Well, not anticipation exactly. Or not where Big Joe was concerned. But that didn't mean she wanted these . . . these . . . words failed her on what to call them, glomming down her good, yeasty bread, either.

She remained sitting where she'd landed and put her head on her knees while the man removed his saddle and tossed it down beside her. Leading the horse into the cleared area to graze, he glanced back at her.

"I said get busy, kid. There's plenty of wood around. Gather some up and drag it over there." He pointed to a spot under an enormous tree whose branches would absorb the sight and smell of smoke in case anybody chanced by.

"You gonna tie her up, Kuo?" Snaggletooth asked, whereby

Ketta finally learned her captor's name.

It was a strange sounding name, the likes of which she'd never before heard.

"She's scared," Kuo said. "And tired and weak. She ain't gonna run off."

"Probably get lost way out here in the wilds," Snaggletooth said, laughing.

"Well she better not be too scared or too tired or weak to fix me some supper." Scar scowled mightily. "Ain't no reason I can think of to keep 'er around if she ain't going to work. I suppose she ain't of a size to—"

Kuo, looking up from hobbling Beau, cut him off. "She'll work." He eyed Ketta. "She'll feel the back of my hand if she don't."

Huh! Nothing new in that, Ketta thought. Slowly, she stood up, grabbed a medium-sized chunk of old, dried tree limb, and dragged it over to the spot Kuo had indicated he wanted the fire. She'd rather have used the limb to give one of them a good whack upside the head.

Chapter Three: Yester

His ma's demand that Yester leave immediately and go after Ketta proved impossible when all was said and done.

Turned out Pa was waiting for him when he left the house, poor old Barney standing on three shaky legs beside him. "Your ma, how is she?" Big Joe asked with an uneasy glance toward the house.

Yester shook his head. "Not so good." He took a deep breath and prepared to jump in case his pa's fist started swinging. "Ma wants me to go after Ketta. She says those outlaws took her."

"You ain't going anywhere except where I tell you." Pa scowled. His fist knotted up, but he didn't strike. "Especially not after that crossbreed—" Seeing Yester's face, he stopped. "The woman say how many of 'em there was?"

"Four. Ma said four men."

"Well, then," Big Joe said smugly. "Just shows she's out of her head and don't know what she's saying. If she was in her right mind she wouldn't let you anywhere near them fellers. And I ain't going to turn you loose after 'em, either. A sixteen-year-old kid?" He snorted. "What you gonna do? Shoot 'em all with your slingshot?"

Anger burned the words in Yester's throat. "But, Pa—"

"I need you with the horses, you hear me, boy? And the first thing you're gonna do is ride over to Fontaine's cabin. Tell 'im I'll pay him to help round up our horses. He's the best tracker I know of. 'Sides, he's our closest neighbor. He's bound to help."

Yester shot his pa a look, knowing full well if Mr. Fontaine's animals had been stolen Big Joe wouldn't lift a finger. What's more, Fontaine would know it, too. He was Métis, which meant half Indian and half French-Canadian, and Big Joe Noonan never made any bones regarding how he felt about anybody with Indian blood. Yester reckoned it'd all depend on if Mr. Fontaine needed to earn some cash money. And on how persuasive Yester could be.

"All right," he said. For once, he was actually relieved to have Big Joe intervene with demands of his own. Truth to tell, he wasn't sure how he felt about going up against four outlaws all by himself. Then there was Ma, so beat up and frail.

One thing he could do is talk to Mrs. Fontaine. See if she'd come help Ma while the men were gone. Conscience eased, if only a little, he headed for Flint, hoping the old horse had rested up a bit, but Pa surprised him.

"Take the buckskin," Big Joe said, waving at the horse ground-hitched nearby. "We ain't got time to dally, and Flint is too slow. Use your spurs. It'll be dark before you get back as it is. I'll see if I can catch us up a couple fresh broncs while you're gone." He nodded out toward where trees provided a bulwark against the wind. "Some of 'em didn't stray far. I see Rory over there, and a couple more those outlaws missed. We'll be ready to start out as soon as you get back." Rory was the bay Big Joe rode when he wasn't riding the buckskin.

Yester didn't know what else to do. "Yes, Pa," he said and stepped into the saddle. To his surprise, the length to the stirrups fit him fine. His legs had grown as long as Big Joe's, maybe longer.

Once they were beyond the dooryard, he urged the horse into a trot, and then an easy lope. He didn't spur, though. It would take an hour to get to Fontaine's place. He wasn't going to run the buckskin to death.

Sorry, Ketta, he was thinking as he rode. *Hold on, little sister. You just hold on.*

Big Joe'd had his time a little mixed up, as Yester discovered. The sun was far down on the horizon, bathing the rolling hills of the Palouse with purple and blue before he reached the opening into the little valley where the Fontaines made their home. A hound dog bayed as he started up the trail to the cabin. Lights inside glowed yellow. By the time he got there, Fontaine was waiting outside the porch door, standing in shadows deep enough Yester knew where he was only by a slight stirring of the light.

It wasn't until Fontaine recognized Yester that he came to meet him.

"Hey, boy," he said, reaching for the horse's reins, "what you doing here this time of night? What you doing up on that horse? Ain't that one Big Joe favors?"

It was a well-known fact around the countryside that Big Joe didn't like to share, not even with his son.

Yester dismounted, his legs numb beneath him. It felt like he'd been riding all day, which, come to think of it, he guessed he had. If it hadn't been for grabbing onto the saddle strings, he thought he might've fallen.

"Big Joe sent me," he said, his voice breaking like it hadn't done for more than three years. "We got trouble at home."

"Trouble?" Fontaine flipped the reins around the porch rail. "What kind of trouble? Come on in, Yester, and tell me about it." His voice rose, but only a little, like he knew his wife must be standing right inside and hearing every word. "Bird, set another plate. This boy looks hungry."

Yester heard the pad of moccasined feet coming from the direction of the barn. Chirping crickets quieted all along the way. There was a rush, then the hound dog that'd bayed stuck his nose into Yester's open palm in a gesture of friendship. Nat Fontaine's dog. The dog and Yester were friends because Nat and Yester were friends.

"What's happened?" Nat asked, materializing out of the darkness like one of those haunts he told Yester about when they were trading stories. A half head shorter than his friend, he was wiry and strong and looked more French than Indian. "What did Big Joe do now?" He looked a little worried.

"Wasn't Pa causing trouble this time." At Fontaine's urging, Yester limped over and climbed the rounds of rough-sawn red fir that served as steps into the cabin. Once inside the aroma of venison stew and fried bread hit him, making his stomach growl. He paid the small fuss little attention.

"Me and Big Joe had gone to town and were coming home." He looked down, shame-faced. The Fontaines would know that meant Big Joe'd been on a bender, and he'd been along to see he got home in one piece. "Just before the last rise, I saw smoke. Turns out—" He had to stop a minute and swallow down a dry croak.

Without a word, Bird Fontaine filled a dipper from a bucket and handed it to him. Yester drank it down like he was parched, and he guessed he was, smoke from his home's burning caught still in his throat.

"You sit," Bird said. "Talk when you are ready."

It helped, not being pushed to explain the goings on at the ranch. Although he'd had all of the ride over here to think of what to say, nothing came to him now. Everything was jumbled in his mind.

After a minute, he said, "Some men, they beat Ma awful bad, and . . . and—"

Bird's dark eyes opened wide. "Someone attacked the ranch? They beat Magdalene?"

"Yes. They burned the house, killed some chickens, and shot

the cow and Barney."

Nat reared back. "Shot Barney?"

"Wounded him."

Fontaine, who'd settled on his stool at the head of the table, scooted it back, legs scraping on the plank floor. "Who did this thing, Yester? When?"

"Today. Some men. Four men. Outlaws."

Bird stopped what she was doing and stood, hands on hips. "Why did they beat Magdalene? Did they—" She stopped, her cheeks flushing.

"Yes." Yester answered her unvoiced question baldly. "I don't know why they did it, but they hurt her something awful." A sour taste filled his mouth. He hadn't yet said it all. "They took Ketta."

"Took Ketta?" Bird repeated, as if she couldn't believe it.

Nat struck at the heart of the matter. "We going after them?"

"My son," Bird said warningly, but Yester, relieved, nodded.

"Yes. That's what I'm here for. Big Joe sent me. He asked if you folks could help us out. See, they stole some of our horses, the ones Pa's been training for the army. Turned the ones they didn't steal loose so they ran off. He asked if you could maybe see your way clear to track'em down for us, Mr. Fontaine."

"Track who?" Nat wanted to know. "The thieves or the horses?" He'd seen enough of Big Joe to walk a wide circle around him.

"Both," Yester admitted. He looked to Mrs. Fontaine. "And he asked if you could come over and take care of Ma while we're gone." Or he should have asked, Yester thought to himself.

Bird frowned. "She needs care?"

Yester's face puckered before he could catch himself. "Yes, ma'am. She surely does."

Bird studied him. "Is she—" she started again, then stopped, probably guessing the answer to that particular question from looking at Yester's heated face.

"I will come. Take some things over there to help ease her." She lifted the pot of stew redolent of onions and venison from the stove and set it on the table, splashing a ladle into the thick conglomeration. "You eat. All of you eat."

Bird set about chores of her own, bustling around the room as she gathered things into a bundle. Medicinal herbs that hung from nails behind the stove were sniffed and approved or not approved. Contents of some purpled mason jars were separated out and put in twists of fabric.

"You got bandages?" she asked Yester.

"Don't know." He shook his head. "They burned the house. Tried, anyway. We put the fire out before it all went up. Looks like what's left can be rebuilt."

"Tch," she said and put a roll of clean gauzy strips of cloth into her bundle.

Fontaine's fist slammed down on the table, rattling spoons and bowls recently emptied of Bird's good stew. He still hadn't said if he'd help or not, and Yester began to fret. What would Big Joe say if he came back without Fontaine?

Worse, what would *he* do?

It was Nat, the one known to complain mightily whenever Yester's little sister used to try to follow the boys around, who brought up the elephant in the room. "What about Ketta?"

Yester pushed his bowl away, the food lying heavy in his belly all the sudden. "They took her."

"Yeah, you said."

"I promised Ma I'd go after her. Promised. Pa says no, but I'm gonna do it anyway. I should've lit out right away, but"—Yester's face hardened—"Ma needed help, too. And the one who stole Ketta. He's . . . well, he's . . ."

"He is what?" Fontaine's voice was soft.

"He's her pa." Yester forced the words out, though they stuck in his craw.

Fontaine jerked. "The Chinaman?"

So he'd known. Yester nodded. "But that don't mean he has any right to take her. She ain't anything to him. She's Ma's daughter, and she's my sister. Ketta, she even tried to shoot him, except she got hold of Pa's old .45 that don't work. I don't know why he'd take her after that. She's just a kid."

Bird's eyes filled with tears. "Punishment, of a sort. And because he could."

"Well," Yester said, stern as any preacher man, "he ain't going to keep her."

Ketta

Ketta's stomach still hurt, feeling bruised and twisted and as if a nest of writhing snakes crawled around in it. Regardless, she set herself to fetch firewood, haul water from a little spring the man with black skin had found, and even serve bread and beans taken from her mama's own kitchen. She didn't want anyone to be knocking her in the head like they'd threatened, for sure.

The men muttered among themselves when they thought Kuo wasn't listening. Ketta figured they were wrong. She was certain he heard every word they said. She also thought the way they tittered like school girls with a secret sounded remarkably silly for full grown men. Her model for a man's behavior being Big Joe, who seldom cracked a smile, let alone laughed, cued her to a whole different kind of man.

What really made her uncomfortable, though, was the way Kuo kept watching her. She planned on running away, hurting stomach or no hurting stomach, just as soon as these men settled for the night. Did he somehow guess her plans? If only he'd quit eyeing her. Intimidated by his scrutiny, she hardly dared move.

After a while, as the men sat around the campfire eating, nature called, and she slipped away to hide behind a bush. Tried to slip away, at least. She hardly got ten feet before he called out to her.

"Stay where I can see you, little girl," he said.

She said, "I've got to . . . go." In fact, the need had become desperate.

And he said, "Pee?"

She knew she turned red as a pie cherry but nodded.

Kuo pointed and said, "There."

Ketta nearly died. There was hardly enough cover to hide a rabbit, let alone a girl, even one as small as she.

Impossible to protest, though, when his narrow, slanted eyes pierced her like pointed sticks. Eyes so similar to what she saw in her own face when she looked in Mama's mirror. Which she didn't very often because she looked so different from everybody else in the family. Different from Yester. Brothers and sisters were supposed to resemble each other, weren't they? But Yester was a handsome combination of Big Joe and Mama, and she was—Well, she didn't quite know. But something about Kuo, and snippets of things she'd heard over the years, were starting to make her think. And what she thought made her tummy hurt all over again.

Settling as far away from the men as Kuo allowed, she resolved not to "think" anymore. Just "do." Starting the minute the men went to sleep. It was as far as her plan went.

Ketta managed to choke down a half slice of her own good bread spread with a spoonful of mashed beans. Her stomach, still tied in knots, balked at anything more, even if the men had been inclined to leave her any of the good stuff. Which they weren't.

Afterward, Kuo showed her how to clean the spoons and tin plates with sand and a bare cup of water. Disgusting to her way of thinking. The cleanliness didn't meet the standards her mother had taught her, that's for sure. But it was as she absorbed this lesson that she put in the question burning up her insides.

Setting her jaw, she glowered into Kuo's slanty eyes. "What did you do to my mother?"

He gave her a questioning look. "Don't you know?"

"I . . . no. You knocked me out." She set hands on narrow hips, a brave gesture of defiance. "You better not have hurt her."

"Or what?" He shrugged and almost smiled. "I didn't touch her."

That's right. Because he was holding on to me. Squeezing me until I couldn't breathe. Until there was pure darkness and nothing else. Ketta's narrow gaze fixed on the other men. "Them? They did. I saw . . ." She stopped again, unable to remember exactly what she'd seen.

He shrugged again. "She shouldn't have fought. Men get a little rough when a woman fights."

Ketta put what he said together in no time. "So, they did hurt her. You're all a bunch of dirty, weasel-eyed, low-down, sheep-biting . . ." She couldn't think of anything bad enough without using language more proper to Big Joe than to a young lady.

Kuo's fist bunched up. "Don't you go getting snippety on me, child. In fact, you keep your mouth shut unless I say you can talk. I ain't in the mood to listen to you. And take it from me, you don't want them to hear."

The "them" meant the black man, the scarred man, and the one with snaggly teeth.

Ketta eyed them in sudden fear as she watched for his fist to strike out, but, to her surprise, it remained at his side. Emboldened, she said, "You better let me go. My father and my brother will come for me, and you'll be sorry you ever saw me. They'll *kill you.*"

The slap came so fast she didn't have time to dodge any part of it. Pain stung her cheek. Her teeth sinking into her tongue almost made her convulse with the agony. But she didn't cry out.

"What's your name, girl?" Kuo demanded, his hand drawing back for another go at her cheek.

Silent, she glared back at him.

His hand raised. "Name."

"Ketta." She barely got the word out.

"Ketta?"

She nodded, inching backward. He didn't slap again but reached out and grabbed her skinny little arm, fingers clenched all the way around it.

"Well, Ketta. You talk mighty big, but we both know there ain't nobody coming for you. I seen your 'father' in town, and he don't care one cent for you. Besides the fact, he's got enough hootch in him to slow him down to a crawl. He'd probably even shake my hand for taking you. I heard him talking. As for your brother . . . huh. What's he gonna do? He's just a kid, too. Grown up tall, all right, but still a kid. He'll do what his pa tells him to do. Just like you're gonna do what your pa tells you."

Something stuttered to a stop in Ketta's brain but not because of the physical blow he'd dealt her.

"My pa?" she finally whispered.

The Chinese man's voice was almost as quiet as her own. "Your pa. Me."

Curled up on a bed of pine boughs and covered with the sweaty saddle blanket from Beau's back, Ketta tried to ignore her throbbing cheek. She couldn't sleep. Not even with a chorus of nighttime insects trying to sing her to sleep. Kuo's last three words still echoed in her mind. They were like waves on the shore of the little lake they sometimes went to when the summer sun liked to scorch them all to a crisp. Used to, anyway. Until Big Joe decided they didn't have time for such frivolous doings. She knew what his real reason was, though. Big Joe just didn't want to be seen in public with her and didn't want Yester tarred with her brush, either.

But, her father? This outlaw, Kuo? How could that be? Yet Ketta figured he didn't lie. All the half truths and hints and harsh words Big Joe, and even Mama, sometimes, had let drop proved the truth. This Celestial man was her father. Cross-breed. She really was a cross-breed, like Big Joe so often called her.

Yester knew all about it, too. He'd always treated her kindly, but what would he think now?

No. He wouldn't be coming after her, either. Her mother was the only one who ever loved her, and who knew if she was still alive?

Well, she had to find out. And, for that, she had to get back home.

A hiccuping sob escaped, and she quickly stifled a second one. She didn't think anybody heard, though. They'd decided a watch wasn't necessary, discounting Big Joe with a laugh. Now they all slept, the black-skinned man and Kuo quietly, their breathing soft and regular. Scar and Snaggletooth snored with a racket as loud as Mama's chickens in full cry.

Inch by inch, she pushed out from under the saddle blanket and got to her feet.

Ketta took care to move like she'd seen Yester's friend Nat Fontaine do when the boys were younger than she was now and they used to play cowboys and Indians—Yester truly being a cowboy and Nat truly being an Indian. Partly, anyhow.

She crept across the open space toward the horses. If she

could get Beau to stand still while she climbed onto the thick trunk of an old fallen tree she'd seen, she figured to clamber aboard bareback and run for it. Beau could outrun these other horses. He was one of Big Joe's best.

Chapter Four: Yester

Yester spent the night rolled up in a blanket on the Fontaines' cabin floor. He didn't drowse off for a long time; then the next thing he knew Fontaine was kneeling beside him shaking him by the shoulder.

Yester blinked his eyes open into a pre-dawn still lit by a waning moon.

"Better get up," Fontaine said softly. "Big Joe will be champing at the bit as it is. My wife will follow when she is ready."

"She'll be ready soon, won't she?" Yester threw off the blanket, the urge to act coursing through him.

"You bet. Not more than an hour behind us, she said."

Relieved, Yester got to his feet and stretched out a few kinks, put there by the hard floor and a long day yesterday in the saddle. By that time, Nat, who'd risen a while before him, had biscuits and cold bacon scrounged from the pantry ready to shove into his hand.

"Father says we'll eat as we ride," he said, eagerness showing in his voice. "I already saddled the buckskin for you. Let's go."

Go they did, horses fresh enough to cut an hour's ride down to forty-five minutes. Even so, they found Big Joe waiting for them with reins in hand and a scowl on his face. He nodded coldly at Fontaine, acted as if he didn't even see Nat, and said to Yester, "Where the hell you been? Think I sent you off on vacation? Them horses will be long gone by now, and it'll be your fault."

Yester's head hung, afraid Pa had the right of it. He should've come straight back last night to care for Ma, if nothing else. Even so, he appreciated it when Fontaine came down on his side saying, "Too dark last night to track anything. Just now it is light enough to see."

"Get off that buckskin and hand him over." Big Joe, ignoring Fontaine, spoke to Yester. "Rope yourself one of them others. A couple wandered in last night, looking for water."

So, Yester thought, dismounting, Pa hadn't gone looking for horses last night, either, but waited for them to come to him. His complaint about Yester being tardy didn't hold true.

Feeling a little better, he asked, "How's Ma?"

Big Joe shrugged. "She didn't get up to fix my breakfast, I can tell you that." He said it like he'd been slighted.

"I'll go see," Yester said and refused to listen when his pa told him to hurry up, that they didn't have time to coddle the woman.

The house stunk of burned wood and smoke. Looking it over now, Yester wasn't any too sure it could be made whole again. Part of it needed to be torn down, and new rafters, a roof, and framing put up. But at least the corner bedroom where he'd put Ma was still intact, if smoke-stained and the atmosphere noxious. Barney lay on a rug beside the bed, keeping her company while his own wound healed. At least, Yester trusted it was healing. Barney heaved himself to his feet and came over to lick Yester's hand, which made him think so.

Ma's eyes opened at Yester's soft-footed approach. "Did you find Ketta?"

He shook his head.

"He wouldn't let you go, would he?"

Yester knew who "he" was. He shook his head again.

She smiled a little. "Well, he was right. I don't know what I was thinking. You can't go up against those men, Yester. That's a full-grown man's job. The sheriff's job."

Yester felt like somebody had just yanked a weight off his back. "Are you feeling any better, Ma? Mrs. Fontaine is coming over to see if she can help."

"Bird is?" Magdalene smiled faintly. "That's real nice of her. Is that where you've been?"

Hadn't Pa even told her that much?

He nodded. "Pa says he'll pay Mr. Fontaine to track the horses. We're leaving right away." He frowned. Ma sure wasn't moving around much. And she hadn't answered when he asked if she was better. "Will you be all right?"

Her faint smile flashed again. Not a real smile, Yester realized, but something else. Something hopeless.

"I'll have to be, won't I?" she said. "Go then, son. Just take care of Ketta and see she gets home."

Big Joe, with single-minded intensity, had fixed the corral for the returned—and returning—horses and even daubed some purple concoction on the cow's wound. Hadn't done the morning chores, though, nor attempted to put the outhouse or chicken coop into workable condition. There was nothing Yester could do about those things now, what with Pa cracking the whip in the background.

Nat, complaining about all the practice he was getting saddling white men's ponies, helped Yester out by tacking up a nice black mare named Queenie for him. Yester fed the chickens, milked the cow, and made sure the critters had water. At last he was ready, and it was time to hit the trail.

In moments, Fontaine, taking the lead, had them all leaving the yard and heading for the hills to the south. Yester, though not a tracker, could see traces in the dirt where the outlaws had been pushing the stolen horses along in front of them. Big Joe whooped when he recognized Beau's track, notable for what looked like a question mark beaten into the shoe.

"This is easy tracking," he said to Fontaine. "Looks like I

don't even need you."

Fontaine's expression, though his face took on a darker hue, never changed. "You will," he said.

In another hour, his answer proved prophetic.

Big Joe, out in front and pushing the buckskin into a lope, swept around a bend and disappeared from sight. Fontaine, following at a distance far enough to keep himself and the boys out of the dust, stopped and held up his hand.

"Wait." Dropping out of the saddle, he walked from side to side of the narrow trail.

"What's he doing?" Yester asked Nat, who rode beside him.

Nat's gaze followed his father. "Trackin'," he said. "The job your pa is supposed to pay him for."

Yester thought his friend sounded a little doubtful about the pay part.

"Here," Fontaine muttered, as though to himself, then louder, "You boys hear that creek running?" He nodded off to the right.

Nat cocked his head. Yester followed suit, drawn by Fontaine's mention of the sound. "You thirsty, Mr. Fontaine?"

Fontaine grinned. "Well, I might be, but I can tell you a couple of them horses the thieves was trying to steal were. Two horses broke off here, heading toward the creek. I figure if you boys was to ride up on them nice and slow they'd be glad to get home."

Yester assumed responsibility and took the lead. Now that Fontaine had pointed it out, the evidence of the horses' passage was clear. Broken branches, a pile of turds, and, when they reached the creek, plenty of milling hoofprints in the mud at the edge. A few weeks later and he figured the creek would dry up, but for now the grass on the bank was lush and green. Hipshot and enjoying the day, a couple of his pa's horses stood in the shade of three or four cottonwood trees. They were one of

Big Joe's prize mares and her foal, a colt Big Joe had high hopes for.

Pa, Yester thought, should be pleased about the animals' recovery. Maybe it would put him in a better mood when he saw them.

Just as Fontaine predicted, the horses appeared glad to see him. In moments, he and Nat had rigged a rope halter for the mare and led the animals back to find Fontaine. The scout had already progressed a quarter of a mile farther on and had in his possession a young gelding with Big Joe's brand on its hip.

Yester held out his dripping canteen. "Fresh water, sir?"

Fontaine laughed, uncorked the metal container, and drank deeply. "My thanks," he said. "This is good water. Have any trouble?"

"Nah," Nat answered. "These horses are tame."

"They are," Fontaine said. "Well trained. Found this one over in that little clearing we passed."

Yester nodded. He'd noticed the place. "Thanks, Mr. Fontaine," he said. "I wonder why Big Joe passed him by?"

"Going too fast to see what's in plain sight." Fontaine shook his head.

"All guts and glory." Nat looked off into the distance. "Just like Custer."

Fontaine cast a quick glance at his son. "My son, show respect for your elders. That's Yester's pa you're talking about."

Nat's shoulders stiffened. "Sorry, Yester."

Yester figured out pretty quick when Nat said "sorry" he only meant he regretted Big Joe was such a wranglesome kind of feller. A fellow'd have to be stupid not to decipher the way his friend stifled all comment at mention of Big Joe. In fact, it was almost funny the way his mouth clamped shut. Yester, though, didn't see any reason to dispute Nat's opinion. He'd been on the losing end of Pa's fist often enough to know the truth.

They tied the mare and the gelding together and, leaving the colt free to follow its mother, they went on. Nat led the two.

"We'll trade off," he said to Yester. "Agreed?"

"Agreed." The pact sounded fine to Yester.

Though no tracker, he found it easy enough to follow the hoofprints left by Big Joe's horse even without Fontaine's guidance. They overlay the outlaws', the dust from his passage filling in and blurring the older tracks.

The quiet under the trees lining the trail gave an illusion of peace. It would've been a pleasant ride, cooler here in the trees than in the open. If it hadn't been for their objective, anyway.

Ketta had been gone for over a night, now. Those men wouldn't do to her what they'd done to Ma, would they? Yester was worrying himself sick over the idea. A young girl like her, and small besides? His fingers clenched on the reins, causing his horse to throw up its head and dance to a stop.

Nat, close behind, called out, "See something?"

Yester shook his head. Forcing himself to relax, he loosened his grip, and the horse plodded on.

Presently, they came to another of Big Joe's horses, a sorrel with one white sock. He'd been tied to a bush for them to find. Adding him to the string, the boys traded off, and Yester led the horses. In another mile they found two more of the Noonans' missing animals, and then Fontaine sent Nat after another whose tracks he spied when they were almost past. That one had acted like he'd been spooked, jumping a fallen log to get away.

Fontaine and Yester went on a couple hundred yards before the scout stopped again. "Look there," he said, pointing down.

Yester looked, and his nose wrinkled. "What's that? Uh. Is that dried puke?"

"Yes. But only a little. Your sister, she got sick, I think."

"Do you think they hurt her? Ketta don't hardly ever get

sick. She's little, but she's strong." Had to be, as Yester knew for himself, growing up around Big Joe. She was as tough as he was, and he considered himself pretty tough. Nevertheless, his earlier fear came back to haunt him.

Please God, she's just a kid and innocent as a flower in a field.

There was nothing to do but go on.

Ketta

Eyes wide, Ketta glanced all around into the darkness before loosening the lead shank used to tie Beau to the outlaw's makeshift picket line set up between two fir trees. Crickets chirped. A night bird cooed, undisturbed by her gentle movement.

"Shh, Beau," she told the horse, stroking his velvet nose. "You know me. We're going home."

To her relief, the horse whuffled his breath in her hair all friendly-like and agreeable. Maybe he remembered the small person who often fed him a misshapen carrot out of the garden. But just as she prepared to lead him away, he shied, nearly lifting her off her feet.

All that held her down was the heavy hand that clamped onto her shoulder.

"Where you going, little one?" The words sounded soft and slurry.

The black man, Ketta realized, her bladder an instant from giving way. The one Kuo called Tug. A cuddly sounding name for a man who wasn't cuddly at all. How had he found her, creeping upon her so quietly she hadn't heard a thing?

Her heart beat hard enough it like to came right out of her chest.

"I . . . I'm petting the horse," she said, the first thing that came into her head.

"The horse doesn't need petting, girl. You go back to bed.

And stay there." His teeth, very white in his dark face, flashed as he leaned in close. "Kuo'll have to tie you up, otherwise. Or I will. Understand?"

Mute, heartsick, and angry all at the same time, Ketta nodded.

"Then scoot." Tug gave her a push that almost sent her to her knees as she tried to think of a way to escape. Maybe her intentions showed on her face, because he grabbed her again and propelled her ahead of him.

Kuo rose onto an elbow as they approached, Ketta firmly in Tug's grip. They stopped beside Ketta's saddle blanket, where Tug pushed her down.

"Heh." Kuo glared at Ketta, then at Tug. "What's this?"

"Caught her trying to sneak off," Tug said.

Kuo's hand lashed out, catching Ketta on a forearm raised barely in time to save her face. It hurt, but Big Joe had hurt her worse, before she learned to dodge. Still, she knew from experience there'd be a bruise.

"Ow," she whimpered, her face puckering as if to cry. The act worked on Kuo better than it ever had on Big Joe. His hand hovered, then dropped.

"I'll tie the brat to me, Tug," Kuo said. "She won't be going anywhere 'less she drags me along with her."

The two men shared a chuckle. Tug found a piece of rope and formed a loop to put around Ketta's fine-boned wrist.

Kuo took the end of the rope and gave it a jerk, drawing her almost level with him. "That'll work."

He flopped back down and was asleep almost before Tug faded away as silently as he'd sneaked up on her.

Ketta, with her arm stretched as far as it'd go, didn't sleep at all.

The next morning, they went on. At times the men rode side by side, other times strung out single file. They got through the high ground beyond the Noonan ranch early and struck out across an area of steep, rolling hills. Patches of trees dotted the gullies where, in season, water ran. Now, with summer heating up the landscape, the gullies were mostly dry. Leaves on the few trees hung in parched and yellowed curls. The firs put out a strong resin scent, alternating with the dry aroma of sage in the open areas.

"Where are we going?" Ketta finally asked her captor in a small voice. She didn't think of him as her father. Not at all. He'd left the rope on her wrist, although he'd detached it from his own. It chafed, turning her fair skin bright red and leaving a welt. Surreptitiously, she worked the rope looser, until it hung over her hand.

"None of your business," he said. "But where I go, you go. Got it?"

"What are you going to do with me?" It came out an embarrassing squeak.

"A girl like you?" He shrugged. "You're a pretty little thing. Probably get a good price for you from the right man. If I took a notion."

Ketta's stomach turned, and she was sick again, the small contents of her stomach splashing onto Kuo's leg when she bent over Beau's side.

Kuo cursed and set her on the ground. "Walk," he said. Or maybe he meant run.

Kuo led the little cavalcade. After a while he took pity on Ketta, half-winded and puffing alongside Beau, and lifted her up again.

Or maybe, she decided, hot, breathless, and sweaty, it wasn't pity, but impatience from having to go slow enough she could keep up. Scar and Snaggletooth—well, she should properly call them Milt and Frank, although she didn't know which was which—kept to the center, and Tug rode last. When Ketta looked back, she saw the horse he was riding, the one that had gone to its knees yesterday, limping quite badly now and going slower every minute. Consequently, Tug, who stopped often to rest the horse, lagged behind. Every once in a while, Kuo stopped for him to come level.

Before long, the other two men began complaining, and even Kuo's aggravation showed. Tug knew it, too.

"Got to find me another horse," he said, lifting his floppy felt hat and wiping sweat from his forehead.

"Or else shoot that one and walk. If the girl can, I guess you can, too," Kuo said on one of their stops, although Ketta was riding in front of him again by this time.

Shoot one of Big Joe's horses? Horrified, Ketta, watching his narrowed eyes, saw Kuo wasn't joking.

Tug's face went blank. "There's a ranch over yonder." He waved a large meaty hand to the south. "They keep their remuda in a little valley about a mile from the house. We all could do with a fresh mount. What say we go help ourselves to a few?"

"How do you know about the horses?"

Ketta could tell Kuo was suspicious of any idea not his own.

"Worked there for a couple months. Long enough for me. The boss is a hard man to please."

Snaggletooth laughed. "I say yes. They got any women at that ranch?"

Tug lifted his shoulders. "Don't know. But I do know Ben Patton has a gun and ain't above shootin' trespassers. Might want to use a little stealth, if you know what I mean. Should give us a few hours head start."

Afternoon found the black man walking, limping almost as badly as Big Joe's horse. Forced to slow down, they paused frequently for Tug to catch his breath. It had taken them several hours to circle around the ranch and find the valley, tucked away as it was between two hills formed of rocks and soil blown in from the Palouse country. Sure enough, just like Tug'd said, there were several horses to choose from, blocked from escaping by a wide rail gate and a well-built fence.

Tug collapsed onto a chair-height rock in the shade of a cottonwood and huffed out a relieved sigh. He looked more gray than black, Ketta thought, covered in dust kicked up by the others' horses.

"Son of a bitch," he said. His shirt was wet with sweat from his effort to keep up.

Kuo lifted Ketta down, giving the rope on her wrist a shake and rubbing the raw spot enough to make her wince.

"You stay put," he said and went on giving orders. "Frank, take the saddle off Tug's horse. And hurry it up." He spoke over the snaggletoothed man's protests. "I don't like it here. It's too open. You, Milt, shake a loop. Select a horse and get saddled up."

"What'll we do with these here horses we're riding?" Milt asked.

"Turn 'em loose," Kuo said. "Who cares?"

"Well, I ain't shooting the lame one," Tug said.

" 'Course not." Kuo sent him a scathing look. "A gunshot'd probably bring a dozen men down on us."

Ketta realized that Kuo, *her father*—the sickening reminder shot through Ketta like a lead ball—was the leader of this group of outlaws. Furthermore, he didn't like the black man. Sometimes, he stopped just short of making fun of him. Well, that was all right. She didn't like Tug, either. Hated them all and *him, her father,* the most. She had to get away, escape and get back to her mother. The memory of Mama fighting those awful men flashed through her mind.

But how? Her mind scurried like a mouse between two cats.

She needed to make a plan, that's how, and carry it through quick, before Kuo took her any farther.

Ketta looked around and almost burst into tears.

She didn't know where she was or how to get home, but even so, an idea was forming in her brain. The rancher Tug talked about would know what to do. And chances were, he'd take her home, too, when she told him her story. She just had to escape first, that's all. Disappear until the outlaws gave up looking for her.

The men were busy, their attention on selecting and saddling fresh horses. Inch by inch, Ketta crept backward. If she made it as far as those rocks a couple hundred feet off to the side, she'd hide. She was good at things like that, hiding almost in plain sight. She'd had a lot of practice in her short life.

She felt sure Kuo, being in a hurry to leave the ranch behind, wouldn't take the time to look for her. Not for more than a few minutes, anyway.

Would he?

CHAPTER FIVE: YESTER

For all his pa's bragging about not needing Fontaine's scouting abilities badly enough to pay for them, Big Joe had cause to eat his words before much more time elapsed.

Fontaine, along with Yester and Nat and their string of horses, caught up with Big Joe in an hour or so. They found him dismounted and gazing around, slapping his hat on his leg and making the horse fidgety at the motion. He stood at the edge of a campsite empty of everything except scrapings of food and the lingering odor of charred wood. The surrounding grass had been eaten down by the outlaws' horses. Big Joe's horses.

"About time you got here. You're letting these thieves get away." He sent them a scathing look. "See you managed to find a few of my horses, at least."

He didn't sound particularly grateful, to Yester's way of thinking. According to the look on Nat's face, he didn't think so, either. But then, Big Joe wasn't known for a generous attitude or for saying thank you under the best of circumstances. Of which this wasn't one.

Fontaine grunted, which could've meant anything. He paid Big Joe no attention, but paced the area, his searching look going everywhere, his nose sniffing, even his ears pricked, if such a thing could be in a man. He reminded Yester of a tracker hound.

"I think this is all of the stolen horses, Pa," Yester said, counting the animals they'd gathered, "except for the ones they're riding."

"One of those is limping," Fontaine said. "It will slow them down."

"Limping," Big Joe repeated, then cursed, like it was somehow Fontaine's fault. "Which one?"

Fontaine smiled, a faint twitch of his lips. "The one carrying the heaviest of the men. I do not know the horse's name."

Yester started to smile until Big Joe scowled. "Well, let's get after them," Pa said.

They mounted up, his pa once again pounding off in the lead ahead of Fontaine, Nat, and Yester.

"He will make tracking harder by destroying the signs of their passing," Fontaine said, his censure mild in view of Big Joe's head-up-his-butt attitude. He pointed to scuffed marks in the forest duff where the only traces they saw belonged to Noonan.

Embarrassed for his father, and embarrassed by him, too, Yester found it impossible to meet Fontaine's gaze. Well, this wasn't the first time, he thought, remembering their time in town just yesterday. He made a sound low in his throat.

Nat shot him a look that spoke of sympathy.

Big Joe kept on until he broke out of the timbered hills into the flatter, drier prairie lands that would eventually take them down to the Snake River.

They caught up with him at a spot shaded by a single tree where the outlaw party had stopped and milled around for a bit. Even Yester could tell there might've been some confusion going on between the outlaws. And it was he who found their target's prints in the dirt. The heel of a boot, regular as could be, about a yard apart. Fontaine nodded approval at Yester's find, although Big Joe said nothing.

But then the tracks traveled across a dry creek bed and vanished into the hard-packed earth.

"The horse is still limping," Fontaine said, "The man is walking and leading him. Soon the others will either abandon him and go on without him, or they will find a way to get more horses."

Big Joe sneered. "Where? This country is empty as a broke eggshell."

"I have been this way before," Fontaine said. "There are ranches."

"Yeah? Where?"

"There." Fontaine pointed south. His finger moved. "There." Again, "And there."

"You're the scout. Which way did they go?"

Fontaine shrugged. "We will fan out. Don't get too far apart. Watch the ground; eventually there will be sign. Be careful not to destroy it. When one of us finds something, wave or holler, and we will join together."

"Takes time," Big Joe growled. "Meanwhile, they're spoiling my horses. And these here could use water." He indicated the string of recovered animals, patiently following at the end of Yester's lead.

"Then take them home," Fontaine said. "The boys and I will go on. Find the rest and free the child."

Yester saw the look on Big Joe's face. He'd forgotten all about Ketta.

For a moment he appeared to consider Fontaine's suggestion, then his jaw, unshaven in days and dark with stubble, tightened. "We're all going on. I ain't turning back without all my property, and Yester ain't, either."

He didn't say a word about Ketta. Yester's heart sank.

It was Nat who picked up the trail, yodeling an attention-getting cry and waving his arms to signal the discovery. Yester, being nearest to the others, passed the signal on. Gigging his horse into a trot, the recovered animals followed on their leads as he headed over to Nat.

He reached his friend's side first. "You've got good eyes, Nat. This sign is hard to see." As far as he could tell, the scant traces consisted only of a few blurred marks, a couple overturned stones, and a crumpled branch of sage.

Pushing out his chest, Nat's face lit up. "My father is a good teacher."

Yester nodded, his gaze going to Big Joe, who'd nudged his horse into a lope, cutting ahead of Fontaine in his rush to reach them. Then, his impatience clear, he had need to wait for the scout to make sense of the sign.

Fontaine dismounted, plucked a bit of the sage and sniffed. Scanning the hills rising before them, he shook his head. "They are headed for Patton's Rocking Box P, I think. The closest place to find a horse to mount the man afoot." He switched his gaze to Yester's pa. "And they are miles ahead of us."

"Patton, eh? I've heard of him." A scowl furrowed Big Joe's forehead as he took off his hat and wiped sweat. "You know where to find this Patton's place?"

"Yes."

"What're you waiting for then? Let's go."

Fontaine lifted a hand. "Cautiously, Noonan. Patton is known to be quick with a gun."

"Good. Then maybe them thieves are already dead," Big Joe said.

"As you may be if you barge onto his land like some kind of war party and without his say-so. Especially if these outlaws have already been there."

Big Joe, not being one to hide his feelings, glared, although Yester noticed he slowed down and let Fontaine take the lead.

They went on, sure now of their destination.

Although slowed somewhat by the string of recaptured horses, within a couple hours, Fontaine had guided them to a rutted wagon road. In the distance, a group of ranch buildings nestled in the lee of a small grove. Yester figured the trees had been planted some years ago for a windbreak. They were only slightly stunted, so he guessed there must be a good spring to keep them watered.

But before they got to the buildings, they found the road blocked by a gate. The gate wasn't connected to a fence, which struck Yester as strange. The land alongside the road was wide open. A hand-lettered sign hung on the gate. YOU GOT BUSINESS HERE, COME IN. YOU DON'T, RIDE ON. IF YOU ENTER, CLOSE THE GATE BEHIND YOU. SAME WHEN YOU LEAVE, UNLESS I'M SHOOTING AT YOU.

Not exactly welcoming, but kind of funny, in a way.

"Huh," Big Joe said. "Who's that sonofagun think he is?"

Fontaine's lips twitched.

Yester figured this Patton and his pa should get along fine. Unless they didn't.

Big Joe rode around the gate. Fontaine gestured for Nat to drag it open since Yester was leading the horses.

"But, Father," Nat protested. "Why not . . ."

"Open the gate," his father insisted.

They politely entered the property and, like good guests, meticulously closed the gate behind the last horse.

By the time they were a quarter mile from headquarters, two people came out of the house and stood on the front porch watching them come. A spotted dog stood beside them barking loudly. As they got closer, they saw the craggy man with salt-and-pepper whiskers held a Winchester lever-action rifle. The woman, wrinkles making a map of her face, clutched a double-barrel shotgun. Both wore grim expressions. Yester believed either would shoot if they thought it necessary.

Fontaine drew rein a short distance from the hitching rail. Taking a prudent course for once, Yester's pa followed suit.

The rancher, whom Yester assumed must be Mr. Patton, cocked his head and studied them.

"Fontaine," he said, acknowledging the scout. Sharp eyes examined Big Joe, the boys, and the string of horses before finally sliding away. "Pleased to see you again. You're some way off your stomping grounds."

Fontaine crossed his hands over the saddle horn, his reins loose and relaxed. "Yes. On the trail of four horse thieves and kidnappers. Yesterday they stole this man's horses and his twelve-year-old daughter. We aim to get them back. They headed this way. Thought you might have seen them."

Big Joe muttered something, causing Patton's gaze to shift toward him before the rancher looked back at Fontaine.

While Patton might not have heard him, Yester had. "Not my daughter," is what his pa had said. Ornery old sonovagun.

To his surprise, Patton's face flushed a bright turkey-wattle color. "Seen 'em, no. Seen what they did, yes. Appears this feller here"—his nod indicated Big Joe—"and me got something in common. They got into my remuda and stole several horses. Bastards stole my prize Percheron. Well, Percheron mix." He shook his head and breathed deep. "Then they ran off the rest, probably to hide their own tracks. What they did," he turned to face Noonan and pointed at Rory's hip, "is leave the wore-out ponies they were riding behind. Horses with the same brand that one there is wearing. They're taking up space in my pen as we speak."

He didn't sound all that pleased about it, either.

"Only reason I'm to home right now is I've got my hands readying to go after them," Patton continued. "We'll be gone directly."

"Penned, you say," Big Joe breathed. "Then we got no more business here. I'll pick up my horses and get 'em on home."

"You do that," Patton said with a short nod.

"Pa?" Yester said, meaning to ask after Ketta. But Mrs. Patton, if that's who the woman was, got in before him.

"Horses!" she snorted. "What about the girl? They've still got her. A *twelve-year-old girl.*"

Yester had a sick feeling in the pit of his stomach. He knew what she meant.

KETTA

Ketta crouched low.

Tiptoeing light as a fairy and fairly flying across the dry ground, she'd made it to the boulders scattered at the right of the barrier where the horses were corralled. When she'd decided on the rocky area as a place to hide, it had looked ideal. But now she was here, she regretted her decision. The rocks grew into a solid bluff behind her with no way out. They formed a barricade as much to keep her in as to keep others out. It wasn't a bit like her hideaway at home, where the entrance was hidden from view and had a way for a wily kid to slip out of sight.

Still, she thought hopefully, these men were in a hurry. She'd heard them talking, even as she pretended to pay no attention. They wanted to put miles between them and the law. Horse thieves and robbers were bad enough, but what they'd done at her home was worse. What if Mama—

Her mind stuttered. She didn't want to think of that. Better to get herself out of her own predicament.

If the men were unable to find her right off, she expected they'd abandon the search real quick. Those men—Tug, and Frank, and Milt—they had no use for her. Her father—*her father*—had no use for her, either. Did he? He wouldn't really sell her—would he? Even Big Joe hadn't threatened such an awful, frightening thing.

No. He'd rather she were dead.

All these worrisome thoughts made her stomach hurt again.

Swallowing down nausea, she risked a glance over the top of her rock.

Kuo stood beside his selection of mount, a dun that stood twitching his tail as the man tightened the cinch. Tug was already astride the biggest horse she'd ever seen. It was black, with such huge feet it could only be a mixed draft/saddle horse. The other two men were ready to ride. Each had chosen a nondescript bay, and they were passing a jug and swallowing deeply of its contents.

Ketta recognized the jug's shape. She had a feeling Kuo wouldn't be pleased if the pair imbibed so much they slowed the getaway.

Kuo finished with his horse and put his foot in the stirrup. Once settled, he looked around, spun his horse in a circle, and looked again.

For her.

Ketta barely stifled a shriek of fear. Without thinking, she took a step backward. And another and another, until the rock bluff at her back put a stop to any retreat. Frantic, she turned around, searching for any small place to hide. The only possibility she found was a crevice, more a fold in the stone than a real opening. She pressed herself into it, not even feeling the weather-honed stones slashing at her arms, or the blood starting from the small wounds.

"Ketta," Kuo called. "Come out. You can't hide. I'm your father. You belong to me."

Did he hear her heart beating? So fast, so loud the rocks around her seemed to vibrate.

"Ketta." He walked his horse back and forth in front of the gate. "Come out now, and I won't punish you." He stared into the remuda pen where the remaining horses milled, disturbed by the strangers' intrusion, as if expecting to find her there.

Go away. She was willing him with all her might. *Go away.*

But he didn't.

With an angry gesture, he yanked open the gate and let it fall as he rode into the pen. "Hiya," he yelled at the first few horses. They began trotting in a circle, closer and closer to the downed gate.

"What're you doing?" Milt asked, gaping at Kuo.

"Looking for the girl. Where is she?"

The men looked at each other and shrugged.

"Leave her," Tug said. "We need to go."

Yes, leave me. Go.

"The rancher'll see the dust these horses are stirring up." Tug scowled, eyes flashing in his dark face. "I'd just as soon not be around when he comes after us. No sense in making it easy for him."

"Scared?" Kuo sneered.

"Not scared. Just trying to be smart. Unlike you. Leave the girl go, and let's get out of here."

Why, Ketta thought, doesn't Kuo listen to him? *Oh, please.*

He acted as if he hadn't heard. Within moments he'd cleared the pen, sending the horses off across country with the dust Tug had mentioned flying up from under their hooves.

Frank uttered a curse lost in the tumult of galloping horses and blowing dust. He and Milt exchanged wary glances and, without a word spoken between them, set spurs to their mounts and charged after the escaping horses.

Tug didn't stir, just sat on the huge black horse he'd chosen to steal and waited.

Why Tug? Ketta wondered, taking a quick peek. Kuo doesn't like him, so why is he the loyal one? Why does he stay?

Kuo—she couldn't bring herself to call him her father—gave up examining the pen where the horses had been. Evidently deciding she hadn't been trampled into the ground, he reined the dun close to Tug's giant horse. The men spoke softly, beyond her hearing.

Tug pointed toward the rock bluff. Right toward her hiding place, if just a couple degrees off center.

"Ketta," Kuo called again. "I see you. Come out. Now."

She jumped a little. He didn't really see her, did he? He was trying to trick her.

"Now," he repeated.

A stone turned under her foot and twisted her ankle, painful enough she gasped just the least little bit.

She closed her eyes. If she couldn't see him, he couldn't see her. Right?

But even with her eyes closed she knew when he approached. Felt the sudden cooling as his shadow drifted over her. Sensed as his arm came down to snatch her from her hiding place.

Ketta screamed. Right up until Kuo smothered the sound with a hand that stunk of horse and dirt and maybe death. And still she fought, wriggling and twisting and garnering scrapes and bruises from beating herself against his saddle. The stone cuts bled again. Once she grabbed for the pistol in his belt and got roundly slapped for her pains.

In the end, none of it did any good. She was still his captive.

They rode out at a gallop, passing several of Patton's loose horses that had stopped to graze on the sparse yellow grass. Chasing them into a run again, after a mile they slowed down, angling toward the conglomeration of tracks Frank and Milt had left. Those tracks now headed toward mountains rising blue in the distance.

"Stupid muck-eaters," Kuo said. "They don't even know where they are. Or where they're going."

Tug laughed. "Good riddance. We headed for the river, boss? Maybe we gonna catch a steamboat out of this country?"

Steamboat? Fresh terror shook Ketta. Nobody would come after her if Kuo took her away in a steamboat. Nobody would guess where she'd gone.

She hiccuped on a small sob. Probably nobody would even care. Except her mother, if Mama was still alive. And maybe Yester. Yes. She thought Yester would care, too. But not Big Joe.

"I'll think on it," Kuo said after a time, finally answering Tug's question.

They abandoned the trail when they found a gully that led downhill over ground so dry and hard even Tug was confident no tracks would show. Some distance later they found a low point and climbed out of the gully. They went faster then, horses loping over even spots, slowing when gopher holes and erosion broke the earth. It didn't take long to come upon Milt and Frank's trail again.

Ketta's whole body hurt from riding crammed between Kuo and the saddle. The sun beat down on her bare head. She was thirsty, too, and dirty, and hot enough to melt. Silent tears ran down her cheeks, tears she angrily brushed away.

"I don't want to go on a steamboat," she announced.

Kuo snorted; Tug guffawed.

"You go where I tell you, girl." Her father gave her a shake that wrenched her neck.

"Take a switch to her," Tug advised. "A few lashes will cure her argumentative nature."

Kuo stiffened against her back. "She's got spirit," he said, almost as if he were defending her.

"She's got sass, and that ain't a favorable trait in a girl child. Need to beat it out of her. It's a father's duty."

Ketta felt Kuo's breath on the back of her neck. Hot and heavy. Angry?

At Tug? Or at her for embarrassing him in front of Tug?

"You know so much about being a father?" Kuo asked the black man.

"Hell, yes." Tug grinned. "Got eight children."

"Eight?" Even Kuo sounded a little shocked. "Where are they? I didn't know you had a wife."

"Who says I do?" Tug, riding slightly ahead, turned in his saddle and winked. "The children, they're scattered here and there. It ain't like I'm a man satisfied to stay in one place with one woman. Not for long."

Kuo grunted.

Ketta despaired.

Chapter Six: Yester

Big Joe swung Rory around, acting as though he hadn't heard Mrs. Patton's question about the girl. About Ketta.

"Hurry it up, son," he said to Yester. They all understood the message was meant for Fontaine and Nat, as well. "We'll gather my horses and get them out of these good people's hair."

He turned back to the Pattons and tipped his hat. "I'm obliged to you for holding our stock in your pen. I take it kindly. If you're up our way, stop by anytime. My missus will fix a fried chicken dinner for you."

Patton nodded, but *his* missus tapped the stock of her shotgun on the porch floor. "The child?" she repeated. "What are you doing for her?"

"Why, nothing to speak of, ma'am. She's my woman's daughter, none of my concern."

The rancher leaned down to whisper something to her, not that it had any apparent effect. She shook her head, as if disagreeing with him. Her lip curled as she eyed Big Joe, her sweeping glare taking in all of them.

Fontaine sat his horse, his expression placid, while Nat made faces at Yester. Yester pretty well guessed what Nat's faces meant, too. His question was the same as Mrs. Patton's.

"That isn't right." Her voice rose over whatever her husband was saying. "Any child is more important than horses. Even one . . ." The rest trailed off, inaudible.

Yester guessed he knew what Patton had said to her. Neither

Ketta's mixed blood, nor the way she'd come about, was much of a secret in this section of the country. People, when they got together, talked, and the account of the attack on the Noonan ranch all those years ago had been spread mouth to mouth all over the Northwest. He suspected there were some folks around who sided with his father. They didn't know Ketta, though, how she was smart and funny and brave.

Big Joe glowered at the woman who dared question his actions. To Yester's apprehension, his pa appeared to be swelling up like a toad frog. A sure sign of his temper rising. Finally, some modicum of common sense took over, and, avoiding the woman's accusing stare, he reined his horse in a needless circle.

"Yester," he said, all sharp and demanding. "Git." At the last moment, he paused and spoke directly to the woman. "The girl, I'm telling you . . . she's an abomination and none of mine. Ain't any of my business, either. Anyways, we don't even know she's with them. For all I know she might've took fright and run off somewhere. She's prone to doing that."

Mrs. Patton took a step forward. "And I would ask why?"

"Why? I don't reckon that's anything to bother yourself over," Big Joe said.

"A child is everybody's business."

Patton laid his hand on his wife's shoulder. "The girl is with them," he said to Big Joe. "I seen tracks. Looked like she'd tried to hide herself away, but it didn't work."

Big Joe shrugged and set spurs to his horse, making it dance in place. Over at the barn, two men poked their heads around the wide-open door. Tacked up horses showed inside.

Yester didn't move except his breath going in and out and steadily deeper. "She's my business," he announced in an angry burst. "She's my sister, and I ain't leaving her with no damn Celestial outlaw."

"Half sister." Big Joe came near to shouting. "And a half-wit.

Nothing to be proud of. Leave her with her own blood."

"She's *my* blood." Yester's own came near to boiling. "Mine and Ma's. And she's no half-wit. She's smarter than any of us."

"Smarter than you if she's got you wound around her finger."

Patton stepped off his porch. He motioned with his Winchester. "Your horses are just over that hill. Get 'em and go. I ain't having my wife upset any more than she already is, and I ain't mixin' any in a stranger's family matter."

"Good enough." Joe Noonan's voice turned hard. "Hurry it up," he ordered Yester and cantered off.

Patton eyed Big Joe's retreating figure as he headed in the indicated direction. "He your neighbor?" he asked Fontaine as the scout turned his horse to follow.

"Yes." Fontaine paused.

"Bet he ain't a good one," Patton said.

Fontaine's lips twitched.

Yester hung his head as he and Nat fell in behind Fontaine, their horses plodding at a more restful pace. Why'd Big Joe have to be so damn mean and argumentative, anyhow, setting everyone against him without half trying? He'd been different once upon a time, or so Yester thought. He remembered his father playing with him, held in the saddle in his pa's arms being taught to ride. Of Big Joe laughing and swinging Ma around like they were dancing. Until the day that man took his ma and bloodied her. He never played like that again.

And then Ketta was born.

Ketta, who was afraid to even cry.

He turned in his saddle. "I'm going after her," he shouted, but he was too late. The Pattons had gone inside and shut the door.

When they got to the remuda pen, Pa was already on the ground, examining hooves, rigging halters, and checking the overall condition of the recovered horses. All were well, except the one with the limp in its right foreleg, even if the sweat dried on them indicated hard use.

Big Joe was cussing up a storm. Overhearing, anyone who didn't know him would've thought every animal ruined.

Fontaine shook his head. "He shouts to hide his responsibility for Ketta from himself," he said to Yester. "Maybe he thinks he hides it from you."

"I'm going after her." Yester set his lips. "Don't matter what Pa says."

Fontaine nodded. "I understand."

"I'm going with him, Father," Nat said, looking worried.

At this, Fontaine hesitated. "Your mother . . ."

"He's my friend." Nat glanced at Yester. "And he doesn't track as well as I do. He might get lost."

"Will not," Yester said.

Fontaine gave a little huff. "Have you supplies, Yester? Money? Ammunition for that rifle?" He indicated the beat-up old rifle in a scratched scabbard attached to Yester's saddle.

"Got five dollars," Yester said. "Got some ammunition, so I guess I can shoot me and Nat our supper." He glanced at his friend. "Maybe I can't track as well as you, but I sure can shoot better."

Wisely, Nat avoided that trap. "You have five dollars?" He allowed surprise to widen his dark eyes. "Where'd you get it?"

Yester glanced at his pa, who was winding a piece of dirty white cloth tightly around the limping horse's cannon. "I had two dollars, and Ma gave me three more before we left. Egg money, she said, to help me find Ketta." He spoke low, so Pa wouldn't hear.

Fontaine nodded. "Then you must do as your mother says. Mothers are to be obeyed."

Except, to no one's surprise, that didn't quite jibe with Big Joe's opinion.

Yester had dismounted and worked hard helping his pa prepare the rest of the horses for the trail home. Not until they all were ready did he broach the subject of Ketta's abduction again.

"Ma asked me to," he reminded Big Joe. "And I promised."

"The woman is out of her head," Pa raged. "Been that way for some years now. Ever since . . . Well, she ain't thinking straight, and that's for sure, otherwise she wouldn't dream of sending her son, a kid, after a no-account abomination like a mixed-blood Celestial brat. Like to get him butchered, is what. Fellers killed those Chinks down on the Snake thirteen years ago had the right idea. Too bad they missed the one that showed up here."

"What fellers?" Yester was confused. "What Chinks? What are you talking about? What's this got to do with Ketta?"

"I'm talking about the one they didn't shoot."

No more enlightened, Yester shook his head, whereupon Big Joe pointed a dirt-encrusted forefinger at him.

"Never you mind. Get up on that horse, and head for home where you belong." His voice gritted like sand on rocks. "Now. You're not too old for me to take a strap to where it'll do the most good."

Unfortunately, and Yester knew it for himself, he'd been born with a stubborn streak. Maybe something he'd inherited from Big Joe. He shook his head. "We're close behind them now. I figure on catching up by tonight. We'll be home right behind you."

"You ain't going anywhere without I say so, sonny, and I'm saying get on that horse and head for home." Big Joe's face grew darker and more sullen by the minute, and even his nose seemed swollen, as though stung by a bee. His muscles flexed. "Now, afore I beat the tar outta you."

Yester's guts trembled, though he hoped none of that showed

on the outside. "No, sir," he said. "I can't do it. Me and Nat, we're going. Ketta, she's my sister, even if only half, and that's what counts."

The blow to his face came so fast he hadn't a chance to duck or, better option, to skip out of the way. He landed on his butt in dust made powdery by the churning of many horses' hooves. Big Joe made to reach down and pull him up by his shoulder but hadn't counted on Yester's weight, added to in the last couple months. Yester easily twisted aside, scooting away as his father lifted a booted foot ready to thud into his backside.

"Cut it out," he yelled at his father.

Pa affected not to hear, following as Yester scuttled out of reach.

Until Fontaine took a hand. Literally. "Enough," the scout said, his arm catching Big Joe across the belly and holding there. His dark face was drawn down tight. "You make a mockery of fatherhood," he said to Big Joe. "Your son honors his mother and his sister. You should be proud of this boy who vows to do a man's job."

The implication seemed to Yester as if Fontaine were saying Big Joe should be going to Ketta's rescue. And maybe that he wasn't much of a man.

"You stay out of this." Big Joe wrenched at Fontaine's arm like it was a bar of steel. "Ain't none of your business."

"It is my business when *my* son honors his friendship with your son by going along to help. Do I like it? No. I fear danger for both of them. But they will soon be men, maybe by the end of this quest. They have the right to choose their path. I will help you get your horses to your ranch and that is that."

The two glared into each other's eyes, Big Joe's falling first.

But if Yester expected a blessing at this point, he was sadly mistaken.

"Don't bother bringing the abomination back," his pa said.

"Don't come dragging yourself home, either. I won't have you, and I won't have her. You take her part over your own pa's, then you can have the keeping of her."

"I don't want to come back," Yester choked out. "Except to see Ma. I'm sick of your meanness."

"Don't count on seeing the woman," his pa said. "Could be she won't be there, either."

And with that, he stomped over to his horse and swung astride. "Hiya," he shouted at the horses in his string and yanked on the lead.

Fontaine shook his head and touched his son's chest above his heart. "Take care," he said. "And take care of him." His nod included Yester.

But Yester couldn't see on account of the dust irritating his eyes and somehow filling them with moisture hard to blink away.

Ketta

Ketta's insides trembled as the miles wound out behind them. And though she tried her best to remain upright and proud, she felt herself shrinking down smaller and smaller until she drooped over Kuo's arm like a wilted flower.

Hours ago, not too long after they left the ranch where the outlaws had stolen the horses, Kuo had sent Tug on ahead to find Milt and Frank.

"Tell them we'll meet at the cabin." Kuo had sounded tired and angry. "Day after tomorrow."

Tug eyed him with what Ketta judged to be suspicion. "Day after tomorrow? We could make it sooner. Why don't we catch up with them and ride to the cabin now?"

Kuo shifted in the saddle. "I don't like riding with them, that's why," he said. "And I've got something else to do first."

Ketta lifted her head, relieved to hear Kuo say so. She didn't like riding with them, either. Them, most of all, even more than with Tug.

A loud snort from Tug's broad nose made her jump, but he was only laughing. "Kuo, you ain't thinking. We get to the cabin, it'll only be worse. They'll be worse. They're white. They don't like men who got black or yellow skin. What you got to do is run 'em off. Otherwise, one of these days you're gonna have to kill 'em. Or they'll kill you."

Ketta guessed Kuo couldn't argue. At least, he didn't, and after a moment he simply said, "Go on, now. Do like I told you."

So, Tug, slapping the Percheron with the reins, galloped on out ahead, leaving her and Kuo to take a slower pace. After a while, Ketta noticed they were ambling in a different direction.

A long time later, or so it seemed to Ketta, Tug appeared again, and he was in no good mood.

"Just about didn't find you," he said, taking off his hat and wiping sweat from his brow and the side of his face. The Percheron was lathered. "Where the hell you think you're going?"

"I told you. I've got some business to take care of," Kuo said.

"Business? What kind of business?"

"Mine. In Lewiston. It don't take us much out of the way."

"The hell," Tug said, settling more comfortably in his saddle. "Lewiston, eh? I like Lewiston fine. Like Portland better."

Finally, as dusk cast out fingers of dark so that they rode first in shadow and then in light, they reached the top of a tall hill covered with low sage, rabbit holes, and sharp shale rocks. Kuo called a halt, then. Possibly because even Tug had started grumbling.

"Get down," Kuo said to her. "Stretch your legs. Pee." He handed her a metal canteen covered in a thick cloth. "And drink."

Ketta looked around as she took a sip of water almost as hot as though it'd been heated on the stove and whimpered, "There's no place to hide."

"Go over there, on the off side of the horse." He looked over at Tug, who was already unbuttoning his britches. "We will stand on the other side." And louder. "With our backs turned."

Tug snorted. "Reckon she'll get used to looking at men soon enough."

Kuo didn't answer.

What did Tug mean? Ketta wondered. She often saw men, but she didn't pee in front of them. Nor did they, she reflected, pee in front of her.

It was hard, turning loose, although from the sound of things the men had no such problem. Eventually she got the job done, and then there was nothing to do but go around to where the men paced slowly along the top of the knoll, scanning back the way they'd come. She watched them, staying close to the horse, who nuzzled her hair as if he might find it tasty.

Was Kuo looking for signs of someone coming after them? Her heart took a little leap. Maybe someone looking for her? But who would that be? Not Big Joe, for sure. Maybe the sheriff? Or maybe Yester?

But no. Yester, her brother, undeniably tall and handsome and strong, was only sixteen. Big Joe would stop him if he tried. Anyway, she didn't want him harmed. The black man and Kuo, they were bad men. Scar and Snaggletooth were even worse. She had no doubt that if they got the chance, any one of them would hurt Yester and take pleasure in the doing.

She forced away a sudden vision of Mama, fighting and screaming. Until she stopped.

"See anything?" Tug asked as he and Kuo met up after each taking a half circle around the knoll.

"No. You?"

"Nah. From what I hear, Noonan ain't going to waste time looking for the girl."

"No," Kuo agreed. "But Patton is a different story. It's best not to forget these are his horses we're riding now."

Tug patted the pistol dragging at a worn old holster riding his hip. "I ain't forgot."

"He will come for the horses," Kuo said.

The black man shrugged and grinned over at the Percheron. "Well, he ain't found them yet. Turn 'em loose when we reach the river. We can find more. Or," and here he took to an argument he'd been making off and on during the day, "we can take the riverboat up to Portland. Ain't anybody gonna chase us there." He gestured at Ketta. "Not on her account."

Ketta's head, like an overly heavy flower on a stem, sagged low. He was right.

Kuo deemed it too dangerous to take the steep, winding trail down to the river in the dark. They'd make camp where they were, he declared, after a short argument with Tug. And so, under his direction, once again Ketta found herself in the servant's position, gathering bits and branches of dry, woody sage for a small fire.

"Better warn her about the rattlesnakes," Tug said, laughing as she jumped back from a crooked stick that seemed to her to wriggle and twist.

"Keep your eyes open," Kuo said, so she knew, or guessed, anyway, that Tug's warning wasn't all a tactic simply meant to frighten her.

Presently, after gathering enough sticks, she sat in the sand by the fire watching some potatoes burn in a skillet. Scorched or not, Ketta still managed to eat a share of the spuds, and a rasher of thick, meaty bacon, too. Then, though far now from home—too far for a girl to walk—Kuo poured the remains of their coffee on the fire and once again tethered her wrist to his.

After a while, as she lay with her eyes wide, staring up at the starry sky, his voice came to her. Soft, perhaps so Tug wouldn't hear.

"Have you been to school?" he asked, a question that surprised her.

"No. But I've been schooled. Mama taught me. She was a schoolteacher, before she got married and had Yester." Ketta lifted her head proudly. "She says I'm an excellent pupil. Better than Yester."

"Yester is your brother? The young one I saw with Noonan?"

"Yes."

"He treats you good? Or bad?"

Ketta smiled. "Good."

He went silent, then said, "Go to sleep" and rolled over.

The rope tether burned her wrist, but, at last, coyotes yodeling eerie cries from their rocky dens in the boulder-strewn hills, sang her to sleep. A few hours later she awakened to silence. Chilled through and through, goose bumps puckered her skin.

Ketta sat up, ceasing all movement at the first tug on the rope tying her to Kuo. He didn't stir, and she took the opportunity to study his face, lit by a full, silver moon. His eyes didn't look so different from anyone else's when they were closed. Now she had a chance to think on it, she didn't really look much like him. Her eyes were more brown than black and not as slanted. Her skin was not as dark or as yellow. Pinker. Her skin was pinker. Actually, she looked a lot like her brother. Her heart swelled with relief. She didn't want to be a Chink.

Across from them, Tug snored with a racket fit to frighten the coyotes. Perhaps, she thought, that was why they'd ceased their yipping a while ago. Unless they were creeping up on the camp and making ready to carry her off.

Coyotes don't do that. Do they? It's wolves people have to look out for.

On the off chance, she moved a little closer to Kuo and lay down again. Immediately, cold crept through the dirt, permeating her thin dress and chilling her to the bone. She shivered. Get up, she told herself. Run. Now. Before he carries you away on a riverboat and sells you to . . . somebody. Some awful somebody.

Ketta believed Kuo when he said he was her father. Though slight, their resemblance to one another proved that. It was enough, especially when put together with the things she'd heard Big Joe—and others—say. But Kuo wasn't family. He'd never be family. She didn't doubt he'd be glad to sell her to the highest bidder. But then, so would Big Joe if he got the chance where people wouldn't talk.

Very carefully, she sat up again, a plan of sorts taking hold. Pieces of shale peppered the ground all around and were sharp. Really sharp. Ketta sucked on a finger bleeding from a cut acquired when she'd picked up sticks.

She could cut through the rope with a shard. She was sure of it. And if she stored a couple pieces in her pocket, if she didn't manage tonight, she could try again tomorrow or the next day, or every day until she won her freedom.

Sitting cross-legged in the dirt, she started sawing.

Chapter Seven: Yester

Yester and Nat, taking care for their weary horses, hadn't gotten far when riders thundered up behind them. Patton rode in the lead, followed by four of his hands. All five wore grim expressions and packed pistols on their hips. Saddle guns were stowed in scabbards.

"Seen where two horses headed out trailing them outlaws," Patton said, taking off his hat and wiping his forehead on his shirtsleeve. "Knew it for you two young fellers."

"We won't get in your way, Mr. Patton," Yester said, hoping the rancher didn't plan on putting the kibbosh on his plan. Trying, anyway. He didn't figure he was beholden to the man, even if they were on his property. For now. He glanced at Nat. "Me and Nat Fontaine, we're just going after my sister. I don't care," he added, his head tilting proudly, "if she does have some foreign blood."

Nat, backing him up, nodded.

"Well, son, you go right ahead, and more power to you."

To Yester's surprise, Patton sounded approving.

"I figure since we're all riding in the same direction for now, we might as well join forces." The rancher scanned their gear, which consisted of a thin bedroll behind each cantle, a canteen apiece, and Yester's old rifle. "Looks like you're a bit short on vittles. My missus packed up some trail supplies for me and the boys in case we're out overnight. Reckon she's made enough to share a morsel with you two. I don't reckon you'll want to turn it down."

Yester, who'd been a little worried about going hungry, smiled. "No, sir. I don't expect we will."

Of one accord, they urged their horses on. The trail here was easy enough to follow, although Nat and one of the Patton crew each took a side looking for any tracks separating from the main band.

Patton's runaway horses soon started showing up, heads down grazing bunch grass turned brown under the hot sun. Much as they'd done at the Noonan ranch, the outlaws had run off the horses to wander and confuse the trail for whomever was tracking them.

A futile ploy, and not particularly effective in either case. Yester, for one, thanked them for that. After an hour or so, Patton had a couple of his riders herd the recovered remuda mounts back to the ranch. Not him, though. He stayed on the trail.

"They still got four of my best," he growled. "And they've got my Percheron." He kept going with his other two hands closing up ranks behind him.

Yester, watching the rancher's set face, figured blood and the shedding of it was on his mind.

They camped together that night. Patton posted guards to stand two-hour intervals, leaving the boys out of his schedule. Yester made a token protest, although he was so tired his eyelids closed once or twice of their own accord before he was done eating.

Even then, he forced himself to his feet and went around gathering tin plates and frying pans from everyone and cleaning them in a nearby creek. It wasn't much of a creek. One dried over the summer to a thin trickle.

Patton tossed the dregs from his coffee cup over his shoulder into a clump of the bunch grass and handed the empty cup to Yester.

"You're a tough kid," he said. "Both of you are." Smiling faintly, he pointed his chin toward Nat, still upright but nodding with his head hanging. "He's a fine tracker."

Yester smiled. "I know."

"You've got a good friend in him."

"Yes, sir, I do," Yester said.

"You know what that means, don't you?" Patton stared into the fire.

Confused, Yester shook his head.

Patton nodded. "Means you must be a good friend to him, too, or he wouldn't be with you now. You ain't paying him, are you?"

Yester shook his head again.

"Didn't figure so. I wager Noonan keeps money out of your hands, having need of it himself."

At first Yester didn't catch on to what the old man implied, then he did and felt his face heating up. Nat'd told him he looked plumb devilish when that happened, so he was glad the darkness hid his features. Seemed everyone in the country knew about Big Joe Noonan. And none of it was good.

"I got some money," Yester said through gritted teeth.

"Yeah? How much?"

He took in a couple breaths through his nose, then said, "I reckon that's my business."

To his surprise, Patton laughed. "I reckon it is. I'm glad to see you ain't one of those young fellers who talk real loud but roll over at the first challenge."

Yester glared at the old man across the fire, wondering if the question had been a test.

It was Nat who took it on himself to answer. "Yester don't talk much at all, mister. He just does what he sees needs done."

Patton shifted his attention to Nat. "And you help him."

Nat ducked his head. "Sometimes. This time."

"Why?"

"Because he needs my help. Because he is my friend. Because Ketta is my friend and needs help from us both."

Patton sat back and poked a half-burned stick into the fire. "You remind me of your father, youngster. Loyal. Honest." He nodded. "That's a compliment."

"Yes," Nat said. "I know it is. I wish to be like my father."

If Yester had a wish, it would be that he could say the same.

Nat's brow furrowed. "How do you know my father?"

"He worked for me a few years. Saved up his money 'til he figured he had enough and then quit." The rancher chewed on a twig, rubbing it over his teeth. "We didn't always see eye to eye, but I was sorry to see him go."

He didn't say what it was they didn't see eye to eye about.

In the morning, Patton had them all up before dawn. They saddled their mounts and started out as soon as they could follow the outlaw's tracks. Tracks growing fainter by the hour as a stiff breeze blew dust over the imprints, changing the few that remained into indistinct and confusing blurs, and obliterating many entirely.

Within half a mile, the trail divided into two.

Patton sat with his arms crossed over the saddle horn, eyes on the ground pondering the scant evidence. After a moment, he looked up and gazed into the distance.

"Well, young feller," he said to Yester after a bit, "looks like they got smart and split up. I believe that's what we ought to do, too. Thing is, which of these has your sister?"

Nat answered before Yester got his mouth open. "This one, I think." He pointed at the set of tracks veering off in the general direction of Lewiston. "This is the same horse and rider that picked Ketta up at your pen when they stole the horses."

"Sure about that?"

"Yes, sir. There is a mark in the shoe, and I found one clear print. As far as I can tell, three riders went that way," Nat pointed, "and the one with Ketta went this way."

"That's how I had it pegged, too, son."

"So we must follow the trail of one horse," Nat added.

Patton sat a moment, then appeared to come to a decision.

"One of these fellers has my Percheron," he said, indicating the group of three. "He's a black gelding, and his name is Dusty. I want him back. I'm posting a reward for whoever returns him or any of the others." Patton, smiling a little, reached behind him and untied a gunny sack. He handed it to Yester. "Supplies for the trail. You boys take care. Watch out if you catch up with any of these fellers. If you run on to my horse before I do and can recover him without getting shot, bring him home, and you'll earn the reward. But your first job is to fetch your sister and get all of you back safe."

He turned his horse and gestured to his men. "Let's go." But he had a couple last words for Yester and Nat. "Good luck."

Yester nodded, then said, "You, too."

The boys waited until the dust from Patton and his men's horses settled to earth before following their chosen trail.

Yester grinned. "A reward, Nat. Hope we're the ones who finds Patton's horse. If he doesn't, I mean. That Percheron critter has feet about the size of my ma's supper plates. Happens those outlaws get back together, he should be easy to track."

"Yes. Even you can track that one, if we find his trail again. I wonder what sort of man would ride a Percheron," Nat mused as they struck out.

Yester was afraid he knew. A large man had to ride a large horse. Just as he'd noticed the Chinese man in town the other day, he'd noticed the man with black skin. The two had been together then, just as they were now.

KETTA

Ketta blinked sleepy eyes open. Kuo—*her father*—yanked her close with the rope binding her to him. He slid the point of his knife under the loop around her wrist and sliced it through with a simple flip.

"Rise and shine," he said, tossing the rope remnants into the dirt. "Get ready to go. We're moving out."

The message repeated for Tug, only Kuo wasn't as gentle with him. He booted the black man in the ribs with the toe of his boot. "Wake up."

Tug winced and raised onto an elbow, rubbing his ribs. He scowled at Kuo. "What's the rush? It ain't even daylight yet."

Ketta said a little prayer of thankfulness for the lack of light as she kicked dirt over the length of rope, hiding it from view. Weariness had demanded she give up after an hour or so trying to cut it during the night. The spot where she'd hacked at the strands had weakened but refused to break, the rock shards proving useless after all. It'd been for nothing. Too late now, to escape. Hadn't Tug said they'd reach Lewiston today?

But there was tonight, she reminded herself. She'd try to make her getaway then. *Somehow.*

"I'll tell you the rush," Kuo said. "I saw the light of a campfire last night, over there on that ridge." He pointed back the way they'd come. "I figure the rancher is coming after his horses. Loose ones ought to slow him down some, but if he's like you described him, he'll want a piece of us, too."

Tug tossed his blanket aside and rose to his feet. "Could just be some hands watching livestock," he said on a hopeful note.

"Yes, and maybe it isn't. Saddle up."

Tug did as Kuo told him, lifting the saddle onto the tall,

broad back of the Percheron and grunting with the effort.

Their provisions, scant in the first place, had run out. Not only was she cold in the dawn hour, but Ketta's stomach squeaked a protest as once again Kuo hoisted her onto the horse. This time she rode behind him, where the saddle skirt pinched her thighs with every stride the horse took.

"I'm hungry," she whispered, mostly to herself, misery making her brave.

"So'm I," he murmured. "It ain't far to town. Maybe we'll eat there, in a restaurant. If you're a good girl. If you ain't, I'll leave you tied up with the horses."

A restaurant? Ketta's breath caught. Imagine that! She'd never, in all her twelve years, been to town, let alone to a restaurant. Yester had told her about eating there, when he accompanied Big Joe. He'd also said Ma—and Ketta, too—were better cooks.

Tug, whose ears must be as long as a mule's since he always managed to hear what Kuo was saying, like it or not, had an opinion. "Best leave her tied up with the horses, anyway, boss. It's dangerous to show her off around town. She's a pretty little thing, and people might notice. Can always bring'er back a biscuit."

Kuo touched the pistol at his side. "Let them notice. She is my daughter."

"Yeah, well, she's that woman's, too, and word's apt to have got out by now. Hell, they got telephones most everywhere nowadays. Seen the poles, ain't you?"

Ketta saw a small smile touch Kuo's thin lips. "I saw them."

They rode a few strides more.

"Remember, I did nothing to the woman," Kuo said at last. "You did, and Milt and Frank did. My daughter knows." He twisted in the saddle to look down on her. "You know, yes?"

His eyes, narrowed to slits, were so deep a brown it seemed

he had no pupils. Like a demon Nat had told her about once, when he and Yester were teasing and trying to scare her with tales of ghosts and evil spirits. Nat hadn't really frightened her, although she'd cried out in an effort to reward him, but Kuo did.

Her own eyes, tilted at the corners, widened. All thought of a restaurant meal faded.

"You know, yes?" he said again.

What else could she do? She nodded, head almost too heavy for her neck. Her mind seethed, though. *This time,* she was thinking. *You didn't hurt her this time.* But now she knew the circumstances that caused her to be born and Big Joe to hate her. Maybe she couldn't even blame him.

The horses plodded on. Cresting the hilltop, their hooves dug in as they started down the steep slope. The sun rose shining golden, promising another day of heat. Birds—hawks, or ravens, or maybe even vultures—wheeled through a sky that changed from milky gray to brilliant blue.

Off to one side, Ketta saw what must be a wagon road, switchback following switchback around boulders, scab rock, and large, woody sage. She bit her lip as she noticed parts of wrecked wagons strewn about and, in more than one case, the picked bones of the horses or mules that had drawn them.

They took a less circuitous route than the wagon road, one even more dangerous. Kuo's horse slid, too, sitting back on his hocks and snorting.

Her thigh pinched yet again, Ketta let out a stifled cry.

"Do you wish to walk?" Kuo asked. Then added, as she started to nod, "There are rattlers here, hiding in the rocks."

"I'll ride," she said, not being fond of any kind of snakes, even the harmless garter snakes that lived down by the pond and kept vermin out of Mama's garden.

"Hang on," he said. "Grab my belt."

The advice was all that saved her as the horse plunged forward onto his knees. Miraculously, he regained all four feet. They went on, turning to slant downward on a diagonal route.

The Percheron, with the black man aboard, plowed on without much trouble, his large feet adding purchase. At this rate, Ketta thought he'd reach the bottom of the grade well before them.

At about the halfway point, Kuo called a halt and dismounted while the horse took a breather. Ketta was happy to stand close beside him, hoping any rattler would select him as its target. Far below, a wide river, which Kuo told her was the Snake, undulated in a serpentine shape down the center of a canyon. A city spread out on either side of the river, one city in Idaho and one in Washington.

Ketta had good eyesight. Even from here she could see boats on the river. They must've been enormous boats, she thought. Steamboats, like the black man had spoken of? She didn't think she wanted to ride on one of them. No, she knew she didn't want to ride on one.

Tug had a different idea. "The Whyte Line's *White Queen* is leaving port today. Saw the advertisement for it up in Pullman. Go down to Portland, boss, and get ourselves lost. You can do something with the girl there. Bigger market, better price."

"You take the boat," Kuo said. "Do as you wish. If you are afraid of the rancher, or of Noonan, go."

The careless remark drew a scowl. "I ain't scared. Leery, maybe, of Patton, but that drunk Noonan don't bother me none."

Eyebrows raised as if questioning, Kuo said, "Don't worry, then. I, too, am finished with Noonan and won't be going his way again." He snorted. "Wouldn't have gone there, anyway, if I hadn't heard him talking in the saloon, and that was accidental. I was headed for Grangeville next with Frank and Milt when I met you there. Milt's sons, too. Come along if you want. Take the steamboat if you don't."

"Was?"

"Was what?"

"You said *was* headed for Grangeville. That mean you're not now?"

Slowly, Kuo shook his head. "I'm not. Fact is, after this last meeting I'm done with Milt and Frank. I'll tell them then."

"Because of the girl?" Tug didn't sound happy. "They ain't gonna like it."

Kuo shrugged.

Meanwhile, Ketta's forehead puckered in a frown. What was he talking about? she wondered. What did he mean, he was finished with Big Joe? Finished with Milt and Frank and Milt's sons? That awful scarred man had children? What did any of it have to do with her? She wished she dared ask.

But she didn't.

After what seemed hours, they reached level land. They clomped across a wide wooden bridge spanning the river, the horses' hooves sounding hollow underfoot, and stopped on the edge of town. This was the Idaho town of Lewiston, Kuo informed her. But he was too wily to just ride in directly from the trail. Instead they took back ways and alleyways and roundabout twists and turns, until Ketta knew she'd never find her way back to the road going up the long, steep hill they'd just come down.

Hill? It was next door to a mountain.

She gawked around at the many buildings, trembling with excitement. It was so noisy! And busy. Her ears roared, ready to burst with the cacophony of squeaking wagon wheels, neighing horses, barking dogs, a piano being thumped with an enthusiastic hand, hammering, and a dozen—two dozen—other sounds.

But it was the people who made her mouth round in wonder.

People rushing here and there. People, both men and women, pedaling tall-wheeled bicycles in the streets, and dogs of all sizes and colors dashing out to bite at the tires. And talking. Lots and lots of people talking.

And the smells. Mercy, how the place smelled.

Her nose wrinkled. Actually, the place reeked.

They stopped outside a rundown barn where she could see a huge manure pile at the back. A pile so tall it was higher than the lean-to in front of it. A broken-down corral ran along one side. In front, a door hung by a single hinge.

Big Joe would never tolerate such a mess, Ketta thought scornfully and, strangely enough, felt a sudden little thrill of pride.

"We're here," Kuo said. He dismounted and lifted Ketta down, too, depositing her on the beaten ground just short of the pile of horse manure.

"Ah," Tug said. "It's good to be home."

Ketta stared at him in wonder. *Home? This filthy place?* Her stomach churned. "I'm going to be sick," she announced.

Chapter Eight: Yester

Trailing the outlaws as far as the city limits was easy. Yester made no bones about saying he didn't need Nat's expertise, having eyes in his own head. For instance, when the horse with dinner plate–sized feet rejoined the single horse they'd trailed for a good part of the day.

"Patton's Percheron," Nat had said, as if he were happy about it and, at first, Yester agreed.

"We've got a chance at the reward money," he said.

But having second thoughts, Yester wasn't so sure. The negro he'd seen with the Chinaman had been huge as well as fearsome looking.

Early this morning, having started out as soon as it was light enough to see, they'd come upon the outlaws' camp. Yester, leading the way over a sleepy Nat, had a little thrill of accomplishment.

"Yep," he said to Nat, "it's them all right." He pointed at the ground. "Here's the feller we've been following." He placed a booted foot next to a clear print beside the campfire. "Look at this, Nat. He's almost a giant."

The print was half again as large as his own.

Nat, not to be outdone, shoved Yester aside and put his own foot there. "Twice the length of my foot."

"Yeah, but you're one of them dwarfs."

"Am not."

"Are."

It was true Yester had gotten a growth spurt and was tall as a full-grown man—taller than most, actually—while Nat was a half head shorter. He probably always would be. Sad to say, when it came to shoe leather, Yester's feet had even outgrown his height.

The argument being nonsensical even to the pair of them, they next picked out a second man's tracks. Kuo's tracks. Yester named him, remembering again the name from their time in Pullman. The Celestial who'd taken his sister.

As for Ketta, they found her tracks, too, in the mud close to the trickling creek. She'd left them a sign.

"Look there," Nat said, pointing down.

Yester, Ketta had printed. *Help me.*

Yester had a notion she was running out of hope. His throat closed, and for a second, he couldn't speak.

"She trusts you to save her," Nat said.

"Dang it, I'm trying." Yester swallowed. "We're trying."

"You'll do it. I'll help." Swinging aboard his pony, Nat looked up at the sky, where red streaks colored the sky. "Wind is coming. It'll blow away their tracks again. We'd better get along."

Heart heavy, Yester spared another glance at Ketta's message before stroking across it with the toe of his boot. "Yeah, all right." Mounting up, Queenie had taken quite a few strides before he trusted himself to speak again. "Wonder how she's holding up."

Nat remained silent.

Neither of them had traveled the Lewiston grade before. Nor viewed the Snake cutting through the canyon. It was the widest and deepest river Yester had ever seen, although Nat said he'd traveled with his mother to visit relatives on the Columbia once, and it made the Snake look almost small. Certainly, neither had visited a town with even half the population of this one. Awed, Yester didn't even try to subdue his excitement at the sight, and, judging by Nat's face, he felt the same.

They'd found it simple enough to follow the traces the outlaws had left. At first. Wind, blowing harder as the morning wore on, hadn't completely obliterated the gouges where Kuo's horse had gone to its knees. Or where the Percheron, weighing in at almost eighteen hundred pounds, had dug holes in the earth all the way to his hocks.

But as soon as they cleared the hill, the trail mixed with freighters' teams of heavy draft horses, wheel ruts, and animals driven to market. Dismayed, Yester knew there was no way to tell which way the outlaws had gone, carrying Ketta with them. Or even which town they'd end up in, Clarkston on the Washington side, or Lewiston on the Idaho.

"What we gonna do, Yester?" Nat stroked his cayuse's neck, trembling just a little.

Yester, hoping he didn't look as bewildered as his friend, tried to think. What would he do if he were an outlaw?

Stay out of sight? Hit the seamier side of town? Having Big Joe for a father, he knew all about the red-light districts almost every western town sported. A town like this one was bound to be right lively, with many such places to choose from.

All of which begged another question. Did the outlaws have any money? Were they the ones he and Big Joe had heard about that had been robbing travelers along the roads? Or that farmer bank over in the Odessa area? And if they weren't the thieves, how else would they get money?

An idea hit.

"That Percheron we been tracking? Let's ask around and see if anybody has seen him. He must be pretty noticeable. Ain't too many folks use a critter his size for a riding horse. Or even have a critter his size."

Nat's face lit up. "Yeah. Good plan." Then he frowned. "Who we gonna ask?"

Yester thought. "Everybody. Anybody. Anybody who'll talk to us. Ask at the hotels maybe, or livery stables. You take one side of the street, and I'll take the other."

"Think they'll talk to me?" Nat brushed his black hair, flowing loose around his face, behind his ears. He had no hat.

"Club your hair back," Yester advised him. "Sit up straight, and don't slouch. Shoot, you ain't all Indian. Maybe you can pass for an Eyetalian. Seen one the other day had darker skin than you."

Nat straightened, all right, but it took only a minute for Yester to figure out it wasn't because he'd told his friend not to slouch. It was because he'd taken offense.

"I am not ashamed," he said. "I am who I am."

"I know that," Yester said, the voice of reason. "No reason you oughta be. But you know how people are around here. Some people."

Nat's scowl would've scared a dog. "Yeah. Dirty Indian. I've heard that before. Guess they don't notice my shirt is cleaner than yours."

Yester glanced down at himself. Nat was right. His shirt cuffs were black with grime, thanks to poking around the campfire the last couple nights. And an obvious spill of food—he thought it was drippings from the bacon they'd had for breakfast—streaked the front of his shirt. His britches would practically, as Ma often said, stand in a corner by themselves.

And Ketta, he remembered, would always laugh at the thought, nod, and say, "Almost."

He brushed at a shirtsleeve. Shoot, nobody ever looked at britches anyway, did they?

When he looked back at Nat, he knew he wore his shamed face. "So, you want to stay together and let me do the talking?"

Nat sat his pony as erect as the spit-and-polish cavalry officer (or so Big Joe described him) Yester had seen once. "Too slow. I will take the north side of this street," he said.

Relieved, Yester nodded. "So, I'll take the other. We'll meet at the next crossroad in a half hour."

"All right. One question."

"Yeah?"

"Are we looking for the Percheron, or are we looking for your sister?"

"Find one and we'll find the other," he said. "Stands to reason."

Yester started his search by stopping just about every pedestrian on the street. Those who'd linger a moment, anyway. All these city folks rushed about in a tearing hurry. He didn't know why, since most of them just headed into the various saloons or the storefronts. Why would anybody be in such a hurry to do that?

With the women, his inquiries were about Ketta. "She's yea high," he'd say, measuring off about mid-chest on himself, "with black hair and brown eyes. Eyes got a funny little tilt to them. She's pretty." He couldn't quite bring himself to mention the part about her foreign antecedents.

"What is she to you?" one crusty old woman asked, eyeing him suspiciously like he might be a crass villain.

"She's my sister," he said, "half sister, and she's been kidnapped."

"Harrumph," she said. "Kidnapped, you say. Well, I've seen only one girl child today, and she was with her father."

"Were they on horseback?" he asked.

"No. On foot." The woman's wrinkled face puckered like a dried apple. "She was very dirty, and not pretty at all. A real sad sack."

Yester's head drooped. Discouraged, he toed a circle in the dusty road. "Oh," he said. "That's not her. She never gets dirty."

"Well, that's the only girl I've seen." The woman stepped

around him and passed on into one of the little riverfront stores, one that sold rope and cleats and gadgets Yester thought must be used on boats.

The next woman he stopped wore paint on her face and a frock with a skirt kind of short in front to show her ankles, and kind of low on top to show her . . . uh . . . show more of herself than she ought.

She looked him over with a calculating eye and had a question of her own before she attended his inquiry. "How old are you?"

"Sixteen." Yester didn't know what difference his age made.

"Got any money?"

"Money?" For a minute he didn't know what she was talking about. Then he did. Sweat trickled down his ribs as embarrassment sneaked up on him, but he stood his ground like a trouper. "I just want to know if you've seen a young girl. She's got black hair and is real pretty. Kind of foreign looking." Foreign looking was as close as he could come.

She eyed him disapprovingly and said, "What do you want with a young girl?"

"I want to find her. She's my sister and—"

A hand grabbed him by his elbow and swung him around. "Taking up one of my girls' time is going to cost you, pal. You ready to pay?"

"I . . . I . . ." Yester's mouth dropped open. It took him a moment to gather his wits, and he jerked away from the seedy looking character who'd accosted him. What did he mean, anyway, one of his girls? "I was just asking if she'd seen a girl."

"Well, she ain't," the feller said. "Move on."

Yester's jaw jutted forward. "How do you know what she's seen and what she ain't?"

Unmoved, the feller said, "I know. Now git along." He took the girl's arm and started towing her in the opposite direction.

At the last second, she turned her head and winked at him. But then she shook her head slightly, too, which Yester figured was her way of saying she hadn't seen a young and pretty black-haired girl. Or not that she noticed, at any rate.

By this time, a couple men had stopped to listen in and laugh, though whether at him or at the situation, Yester didn't know. He was ready to "move along" like he'd been told. Worse, there was Nat, standing under the overhang of the boat supply store, listening and laughing, too.

Yester stomped over to him. "You shut up," he said.

And Nat said, "I . . . I . . ." like some kind of jackanapes, whatever that was.

As it turned out, Nat hadn't found anybody who'd seen Ketta or any other little girl, either. What he had found was a man who admitted to having spotted a big black horse he was pretty sure was a Percheron go past the saloon where he'd been carousing. When? He wasn't just sure, but he thought it'd been sometime this morning. Although it might've been yesterday. But, no. He was almost positive it was this morning.

Yester sighed in disgust. "So, you've found a feller who don't know what day it is who thinks he saw a black horse, and I've found one old biddy who saw a dirty, ugly little girl with her daddy. We're never going to find Ketta at this rate."

"Or the Percheron." Nat made a face.

The long, sad, and loud toot of a steamboat whistle sounded over all the other noise of a busy city.

"Want to go look at the boat?" he asked Nat.

"Sure. I never seen a steamboat before."

"Me, neither."

They walked out on a dock over the water, where Nat almost got knocked into the Snake by a fellow pushing a heavy barrel of something toward the steamboat's gangplank. A couple men and women strode up the plank behind him, to settle along the rail and wave to someone still on the dock.

That's when it struck Yester.

Why would a Chinese horse thief be on the waterfront where the boats tied up, anyway? Except . . .

His mind stuttered. Except if he intended on getting on board one of these paddle-wheelers tied up along the docks. Or even one of the smaller boats. The ones propelled by muscle and bone. If the Chinaman did that and took Ketta with him, Yester didn't know what he'd do, or how he'd get her back.

Ketta

Ketta, totally preoccupied by so many people, strange sights, and even stranger sounds—almost unbearable noise, she meant to say—tripped over an uneven plank in the boardwalk.

All that stopped her from falling was Kuo, who had a firm hold on her hand as if he expected her to run for it if she got the chance. He jerked her upright before she fell.

"Whoa up. Watch where you're going," he said. "I don't need you skinning your knees and busting out crying."

Offended, she tried wrenching her hand out of his. To no avail, since he only gripped her tighter, pinching her fingers together almost to the breaking point.

"I don't cry," she said, "and I can walk by myself."

"No."

"Why not?" She pondered a moment. "I promise I won't run away. Where would I go?"

"Probably to the—"

He broke off, which provoked Ketta quite a lot.

"Never you mind," he said.

If he'd finished that sentence, she might've guessed what to do, in case she did break free. As it was, she had no idea. Surrounded by so many strange, hurrying people, she was afraid to speak to any of them. She'd never in her life been to town, or even seen the children at the school where Yester went when he wasn't working alongside Big Joe. Big Joe forbade her being seen in public. The only other youngster she knew was Nat, and he was Yester's friend. If Nat hadn't been Métis, she'd probably never have met him.

As far as speaking to, for instance, that old woman who'd looked her over and shaken her head . . . well, the woman had terrified Ketta. So disapproving. Ketta knew what that look meant. She'd seen it often enough in Big Joe's eyes.

And in Tug's. She was glad he'd broken off from their little group and entered a saloon.

"Where are we going?" she nerved herself to ask Kuo.

"You said you were hungry."

"Yes." She said it slowly, drawing the word out. What did he mean by that? It almost sounded like he would see she got food. But from where? They hadn't made a camp. He didn't have his saddlebags, and, besides, they'd emptied them last night.

An exciting thought struck. "Are we going to a store? To a mercantile?" She saw one up ahead. The building said so on a sign right out front. What wonderful things might be inside? When Mama went on one of her rare trips to town, she always brought something delightful back for Ketta. Candy, sometimes. Or just a few months ago, as Ketta got older and grew several inches, enough material for a new dress. She supposed it must've burned up. She'd seen the smoke rising from the house in the distance after she woke up.

Her beautiful new dress.

"Bought from my egg money," Mama had told Big Joe, her mouth set and defiant. "It's no expense to you." And mercifully, Big Joe had said no more.

"No store," Kuo said now, drawing her from her memories and dashing her hopes. But then he said, "I told you. There's a restaurant. A Chinese restaurant. It's time you learned a little of my culture. Your culture now, too."

A restaurant? Shock sizzled through her. He truly meant she was going to a restaurant? Indeed, she felt a little faint. And what did he mean, "his culture"?

A half block farther on, he stopped in front of a very narrow storefront. One window, with some peculiar characters in black drawn upon it, faced the street. Ketta, with a little skip, stuck her nose into the air and sniffed. A most delicious scent overrode other, more noisome odors, and her stomach rumbled.

"This is it," Kuo said.

"The restaurant?"

"Yes."

But then he looked down at her as if in doubt about something. His black eyes narrowed to tilted slits.

This time when Ketta jerked her hand, he let her go.

"You're dirty," he said, his disapproval as clear as Big Joe's ever was.

Glancing down at her dress, she shivered. Would he beat her now? Take her away without anything to eat?

Ketta straightened her thin, narrow shoulders. "This is the only dress I have. Of course it's dirty. I've been cooking over a campfire and sleeping on the ground."

Expecting a blow for sassing him, she was surprised when Kuo blinked and nodded.

"There's a trough over there. Go wash." He pointed at a galvanized iron watering trough set up for the few horses standing outside the stores. Mostly, people walked in this section of town.

Ketta's eyes widened. "Where horses drink?"

"There's a spigot. Turn it on, child, and wash your face and hands." He squinted. "And your arms. Here." Fishing a comb missing a few teeth from a shirt pocket, he handed it to her.

"Comb your hair, while you're at it. It looks like packrats have been nesting there."

Mortified beyond words, Ketta took the comb, running it fiercely through her hair, careless of a snarl that broke another tooth from the implement. And pulled several fine strands from her head in the bargain.

When she'd done the best clean-up of herself possible under the circumstances, Kuo took her hand again.

"Better. Now let's eat." He sounded almost cheerful.

The suggestion suited Ketta. She was too hungry to care about anything except food. Even the constant worry about her mother faded into the background. Her stomach growled again as Kuo opened the door and pulled her inside behind him.

She hardly knew what she'd expected, but it wasn't this dark, pokey little place. Ketta had seen from the outside that the building was confined between two larger ones. All of them needed paint. Inside, counters ran along each side of a narrow aisle. Every couple feet a stool was pushed under the counter—unless it was occupied, which most were. At the back, a tiny kitchen was filled with several bustling people who pushed past each other, all the while chattering in loud, high-pitched voices like a bevy of chipmunks. Ketta couldn't understand a single word they said.

Following Kuo, she was aware of these people staring at her. She stared back. To a man—and they were all men—they stopped eating as she passed. Stopped talking, too. Finally, Kuo found two stools next to each other. He lifted her onto the one that butted up against the kitchen, putting himself between her and the other customers.

"Don't look at them," he muttered to her. "Mind your manners."

Ketta gulped. "Yes, sir."

A woman, and Ketta didn't know how she knew it was a

woman since the small person was dressed just like the men in baggy black pants and a long tunic, charged from the kitchen and spoke to Kuo in that strange language.

He answered in the same tongue. They spoke for a long time, gesturing, voices loud, then whispering soft. The woman, her eyes as black and hard as obsidian, eyed Ketta up and down and nodded. Kuo's mouth compressed, and he frowned, then also nodded. He didn't look real happy, though, at whatever they'd discussed.

Smirking, the woman turned to her. "What you want?"

Ketta's hand came up to cover her mouth as she cowered on her perch. Not knowing what to say, she looked at Kuo. He grimaced and rattled off something more to the woman. She nodded with a sharp flip of her pigtails, darting back into the kitchen to start what sounded like another argument with the other two or three people in there.

Apparently, the cook, a man, prepared the meals on the top of the stove without pans. Ketta watched as he dumped some tiny meat strips, chopped vegetables, and several different kinds of seasonings on a pile on the stove and spread it around to mix it all up.

"What did she say?" Ketta nerved herself to ask her captor . . . her father. "What did you say?"

"She asked if you liked chicken or pork. I said to give you pork. There were many chickens around your house. You must eat chicken often."

"They're laying hens," Ketta said, astonished. "For eggs."

He shrugged. "Pork is cheaper."

Ketta nodded. She knew all about cheaper. But she had a notion it hadn't been food, cheap or otherwise, Kuo and the woman had argued over. What she was certain of is that she'd heard an argument.

Swinging her legs as they dangled from the stool, she glanced around. Apparently, the others had lost interest in her, for which she was glad. So many eyes watching her every move made her nervous.

Within moments, it seemed, the woman set a plate down in front of first Kuo, then one for Ketta, and a small jug of some brown liquid between them. Her plate was piled with barely less food than the man's. Two round sticks stuck up out of the pile.

Ketta looked at the mound, delighting in the smell. But there was a small problem. She didn't know how to eat it!

"Where is the fork?" she whispered to Kuo. "Please, will you ask her."

He shook his head and picked up the sticks from his own plate. Somehow, to her amazement, he managed to catch the food between the sticks and place it in his mouth. All without dropping a bite.

"Chopsticks," he said, as if that explained anything. "Try it."

Just as Ketta was on the point of grabbing up a fistful and stuffing it in her mouth, Kuo finally took pity on her and demanded a fork. The woman gave her a glance of disgust. Even though embarrassed, Ketta loved the food. The salt and tang of the strange brown sauce that Kuo dumped over everything. The different vegetables. The funny crisp little bits of what Kuo called noodles. The whole experience.

Just think, she told herself. When next she talked to Yester, she'd tell him all about eating in a restaurant. A Chinese restaurant.

If she ever saw Yester again.

The reminder brought a lurch to her heart and came close to spoiling the whole experience.

Chapter Nine:
Yester

Yester, with Nat on his heels urging him on, tromped up the gangplank to the deck of the paddle wheeler tied up at the pier with its steam engine chugging softly. The whole affair—dock, plank, and boat—rocked gently. The motion was a whole lot different from riding a horse. It made him a little dizzy. Looking down at the waters of the Snake roiling beneath them made it even worse.

A heavyset feller wearing a folded bandana wrapped around his forehead stopped them before Yester could raise a foot to step onto the boat's deck.

"Where do you boys think you're going?" he demanded. "Got a ticket?"

Yester cleared his throat. "No, sir. We're . . . I'm trying to find my sister. I just needed to ask if you've seen her."

"Yeah? You can do that from a distance. No need to come on board."

The man studied him to the point Yester felt a sort of itching discomfort at the nape of his neck. What did the man think as he stared unblinking into Yester's eyes? And Nat's, for he came under the man's scrutiny as well.

At last he said, "Your sister, eh? What makes you think she'd be on my boat? She wouldn't be a stowaway, would she? I don't allow no stowaways on the *White Queen.*"

Yester and Nat exchanged a worried look. Nat shrugged. "Guess we don't know what a stowaway is," he said.

"Think it's somebody who sneaks on a boat or a train or whatever to catch a ride and doesn't pay." Yester spoke from the side of his mouth.

The man was nodding. "You've got it just right, sonny. So, this sister of yours the sneaking kind?"

"No, sir. But the man who's got her, he might be. And my sister is just a kid. She wouldn't have any say in it."

The man's eyebrows drew together, causing the bandana to slip a little lower. "Suppose you tell me what's going on. If your sister—your little sister—ain't a stowaway, is she a runaway?" He seemed to enjoy his play on words, but when neither Yester nor Nat got the joke, he yelled around them at a stevedore wheeling a crate of fruit up the gangplank from one of the farms along the river.

"Be careful with that. Them melons ain't a box of rocks—like your brains is." Then to Yester and Nat, "You boys step aside and make room. We're taking on cargo and got to keep to the schedule."

The whole conversation was getting away from him, Yester thought. He'd better speak up fast, before the feller got any more impatient.

"My sister, she's a pretty little girl. She's twelve years old and small for her age. Dark hair, tilted dark eyes. Looks kind of . . ." he hesitated. "Looks kind of foreign. She's with a Celestial man. He kidnapped her off our ranch. She's probably scared."

"But not crying," Nat added. "She don't cry."

Pushing the slipped bandana back in place, the man looked from one to the other of them. "Sorry, boys. I not only ain't seen a little girl in any way, shape, or form, but I ain't seen any Celestials lately, either. Only passenger ticket I sold today is to a negro. He had cash money, and I didn't see any reason to deny him."

Yester's shoulders slumped.

"Seen any black draft horses go by?" Nat put in. "Maybe a Percheron?"

The man grinned. "Sonny, I can't tell one kind of horse from another." He patted the boat's gleaming, white-painted rail. "This beauty is what holds my attention."

"Shoot, Nat," Yester muttered as they retreated down the narrow gangplank, "we're getting nowhere fast."

"You're not giving up, are you?"

"No. Hell, no." Yester stepped onto dry land with a sense of relief. He didn't think he liked boats, bouncing around the way they did. Too different from a horse's easy rocking motion. "I just wish I knew where to go next."

He looked around as if seeing the town for the first time. Spread out along the river, Lewiston was larger by far than the town where Big Joe went on his toots. Everybody knew his Pa there, and, by association, they knew him, too. The Noonans were *somebody* in their own territory. Here, he was just another kid too young to be on his own. Too young to bother with paying him any mind and answering his questions.

Yester drew a deep breath. "How's your feet holding up?" he asked Nat, who sent him a questioning stare. "Feel up to walking up and down the next street?"

"Sure. And the one after that, too, if we don't find Ketta beforehand." Nat puffed out his chest, acting like he wasn't tired after three days on the trail and an afternoon of poking his head through doorways searching for his friend's little sister. The thing is, Yester knew differently, because he was tired to the bone himself.

They set off again, Yester on one side of the street, Nat the other, setting up to meet at the end in another hour, or maybe sooner. By then it would be time to scout up some supper, Yester's treat, and see if they could sleep in their horses' stalls. Tomorrow they'd have to buy camping supplies. Five dollars—

four after paying the livery—wouldn't last long, and it sure didn't stretch to eating in cafés.

Speaking of which, he passed by a pokey little eatery that was so dark inside a fellow'd have to carry a barn lantern to see what he was eating. Could be worms, for all he could tell. Worse, the voices he heard chattered away like a flock of screech owls carrying on a monumental argument, and he couldn't understand a word of it. Fine with him. Two steps and he was beyond the place anyhow.

Besides, a man was sweeping end-of-the-day dirt out the front of the store next door, and Yester hurried to catch up with him.

"Say, mister," he started, taking off his hat and spinning it around and around in his hands, "I'm looking for a little girl and wonder if you might've seen her."

The man didn't glance up. "Doubt it. Little girls don't generally wander into this part of town."

Yester stared around. *This part?* It didn't appear all that different from any other part to him. Kind of dirty, kind of smelly, definitely loud. "Well, she's probably with somebody. A Chinese man. She's my sister, and he kidnapped her from our ranch."

"You got a ranch?" the sweeper put all his doubt into those few words.

"Yessir, my family does."

Broom action ceased. "A Chinese man, you say?"

Yester nodded.

"I haven't seen any little girls," the man said, putting a stop to Yester's sudden rush of hope, "but you might ask next door at that restaurant. It's run by a Chink, for the Chinks. Men mostly, no women. Good luck finding somebody you can talk to, howsomever. I don't think they speak English."

Yester had already begun to turn but stopped at that. No English? No women? Not a place, then, worthwhile spending his time on.

"Thanks, mister," he said and, jamming his hat over his sweaty hair, moved on.

At the end of a frustrating hour, the boys met at the end of the street, once again finding themselves near the docks and fairly close to the livery where they'd left their horses. Nat had gotten there first, and, even at a distance Yester knew his friend's search had come up as empty as his own. Nat stood with an arm wrapped around a red-and-white-striped barber pole and was digging his moccasined toe in the crack between the sun-dried boards of the shop's stoop.

"No luck?" Yester asked, wanting to make sure of his first impression. He added, as Nat gave a disgusted shake of the head, "Me, neither." His shoulders slumped. "I don't know what to do, Nat."

"You want to go home?"

"Not without my sister." He paused. "I don't *want* to, but what if we can't get a lead on her? I don't have enough money to stay here long."

"Go see the sheriff, or the marshal, or somebody," Nat advised. "Get some help. It's what you figured on doing before we left home, isn't it?"

"Yeah. But now we're out of our home territory. Whoever's in charge here ain't going to care about a little lost girl—a little lost Chinese kind of girl—like Sheriff Zeigler does."

"You don't know that." Nat grinned. "Sheriff Zeigler cares about your ma, is what."

If Yester hadn't been so tired, he might've taken offense. But why? Nat was right. And there didn't have to be anything fishy about the caring. Most everybody liked his ma. Why wouldn't they? She was a fine woman who treated everybody well. Yeah, and even he could tell she was a pretty woman.

He nodded, even as he gazed down the street. "There's an

eatery over there. How about some chuck?"

"Yeah," Nat replied with enthusiasm. "I've only eaten in one other restaurant in my whole life, Yester. How about you?"

"Plenty of times. When Big Joe . . . well, when he goes to town and I go with him. Molly's Place. It's pretty good chuck. But Ma's is better." Yester thought a moment. "So is Ketta's—mostly."

Unfortunately, that wasn't the case at Pete's Eats. But at least it was cheap with plenty of it.

As Yester and Nat made their way back to the livery and their horses through the purple shadows, they caught sight of the quay where the *White Queen* had been tied during the afternoon. An empty slip marked where she had been.

Yester stopped in his tracks, struck by an unwelcome thought. "One of us should've stayed there and watched that boat," he said.

Nat sent him a darkling look.

"In case that Celestial bought tickets at the last minute. He's trying to get away after kidnapping Ketta, burning the ranch, and attacking my ma. That's what I'd do."

A worried expression creased Nat's face. "You ain't him. Hard telling what he'd do."

"Yeah." Yester took a long shuddering breath. "I know. And how would we even find out?"

Neither boy slept well that night, curled up in mounds of loose hay like a couple of abandoned puppies. Dawn was a long, restless time coming.

KETTA

Ketta had never been so tired in her life. Not even on the nights she fled to her little cave, hiding from Big Joe and his fists. Being kidnapped, then staying awake for three days and nights running, had brought her near to exhaustion.

Finished with her meal, which had tasted as good as it smelled, although it was like nothing she'd ever eaten before, she slumped on the stool, head bobbling. Kuo noticed finally, although he'd been deep in a conversation with the man sitting next to him. Ketta had no idea what they were saying, as they spoke in that odd sing-song way of the Chinese. She was half-asleep when his hands on her waist lifted her from the tall seat and stood her on the floor.

"Come, girl," he said, nodding to the man and giving Ketta a push.

But not outside into the night, she found, stumbling along behind him as he kept hold of her hand. Instead, they passed through the tiny kitchen into the alley behind the eatery. A rickety lean-to, so badly built she thought even she could've constructed a better one, jutted from the side of the building.

The woman from the café was waiting for them, a dim lantern in her hand. "Here, girl," she said, gesturing to a pallet of what looked like a pile of rags spread thinly over some splintered planks. "You sleep here."

The area, to Ketta's eye, was quite dirty. It stunk, for sure, with strong odors of stale cooking, sweat, grease, and unwashed humans.

She backed away, horrified, as in the darkest corner, a body moved. And, as the lump moaned, backed even farther, straight into Kuo's knees. Unmoving, they kept her from fleeing altogether.

"No," she said. "I'm not staying here. This place is dirty."

The woman glared first at her, then at Kuo. "What she say?"

"I said it is dirty. And it stinks." Ketta didn't compromise, making her feelings plain. "And who is that?" She pointed at the barely seen human form, now sitting up and watching.

Kuo gripped her shoulders, giving her a shake. "Mind your mouth, girl. You're staying here."

"No," she said again, but he wasn't listening to her. He directed more of that Chinese chatter at the woman, causing her to nod. Bending down, she rooted among the detritus on the floor and pulled forth a cloth rag about two feet long.

"There," she said on a note of satisfaction and, grabbing Ketta's hands, swiftly tied the rag around her wrists. Tight, but maybe not too tight. She ignored the struggles as Ketta wriggled and twisted for all she was worth, even crying out more than once when the woman pinched between her tendons to reach a tender nerve.

Ketta wasn't helped as Kuo quelled her endeavors with an arm like an iron band around her middle. She was soon trussed up like one of her mama's chickens, whereupon the woman cast her down onto the mess of rags covering the floor.

Finished, the woman glared at Kuo, her black eyes glittering in the lantern light. "This one cost you," she said.

"Just don't let her get away." Kuo's expression was equally as hard. He turned to go but had one more word for Ketta. "Behave and you'll be all right." He walked off into the evening as though he hadn't a care in the world, leaving Ketta behind.

The old woman fluttered her hands at Ketta, making smacking sounds. "You be quiet now, little girl. I beat you, you make too much noise."

Ketta kicked out at her, a glancing blow that—to her utter satisfaction—almost knocked the woman off her feet. The satisfaction didn't last long since she received a kick in return, only harder than the one she'd dealt. Satisfied, the woman clacked at her, clacked at the form stirring in the shadows, and had the last word. "You a bad girl. Better not be a bad girl more." A telling glance at the shed's other occupant indicated her meaning. She retreated, disappearing back into the restaurant and taking the lantern with her.

"Old biddy," Ketta said. But maybe not loud enough for the

woman to hear.

Without the lantern the lean-to was terribly dark, the only light coming through the cracks in the sun-dried boards. Ketta didn't really like the dark. She didn't like the scratching sound she heard, either. It made her think of rats or bears or maybe wildcats creeping up on her where she couldn't see.

Or maybe the other person here, the one she'd hadn't really seen, was after her. Who knows what the old woman said for him to do. Maybe kill her? Was it a monster?

Like it or not, and Ketta didn't like it, not one bit, a few tears leaked between her eyelids. A single sob escaped.

"Shh, shh, shh." The sibilant sound reached across the shed.

Ketta froze. "Who are you?" she whispered and brushed angrily at her eyes.

"No cry," a whisper answered. "She come."

At first Ketta thought the answer was a name, perhaps in that strange, strident tongue of the Chinese. *No ki Shee kum.* That's what she'd heard. It took a few moments for her brain to sort the words into something she understood.

"Oh," she said in surprise. "Oh, you're speaking English." Not only that, but the person speaking was female. Some of her fear drained away. But not all. "I'm not crying," she added stoutly, a blatant lie.

"Shh, shh," the girl said again.

"Why should I 'shh'?" Fresh anger roiled in Ketta's heart. "I guess I can make noise if I want to." And to prove it, she let out a little scream. Then, because that felt so good, she screamed again, louder.

The other girl's protest became more pronounced. "No, no," she said. "Shh. She come."

"Let her. She's not my boss. Is she yours?"

"Boss," the girl replied. "Owns me."

"Owns you?" That annoying touch of fear clawed at Ketta

again. "People can't own people. There was a war."

Mama had been Ketta's schoolteacher, and she'd been a good one. Ketta read better than either Yester or Big Joe and knew more math, as well. She knew all kinds of things, having read about the war between the states, and slavery, and freedom. She knew slavery had been abolished years and years ago.

But, she wondered now, what about Mama, and what about herself, confined to the ranch like they were. All because Big Joe said so. What would've he done if they'd disobeyed? Would it have been any worse? Doubt filled her.

What had the black-skinned man, Tug, said? Something about Kuo selling her? Had he sold her to that awful woman who ran the restaurant?

She was a prisoner, wasn't she? And what did prisoners do?

They escaped, that's what. Exactly what Ketta had in mind.

She went mum after that, acting as if she were too terrified to scream or speak anymore. Acting as though the other girl's warning to "shh, shh, shh" had meant something to her. Well, it had. Warned her she'd have to work on loosening those rags around her wrists where the girl couldn't see. And when she crept out of the lean-to, she'd need to wait until the girl slept and then be very, very quiet.

Ketta, working in the dark, stifled a crow of satisfaction as the bonds dropped away. That evil old Chinese woman wasn't so smart after all, she thought, delighted. Using rags to tie her wrists had worked right into her plans. She'd had lots of practice in escaping as Yester and Nat used to take her prisoner all the time, back before they'd all gotten too old to play. They'd tie her up, and she'd regularly get loose. They never did figure out how she did it.

She felt a giggle rising and tamped it down. Escape had been a matter of tensing muscles and stretching just far enough to go unnoticed. Who'd ever expect a five-year-old to figure that out? Her brother never had. The old woman hadn't, either.

Over in the corner, soft puffing breaths indicated the other girl had finally gone to sleep. Ketta rose to her feet, piling the rags into a person-shaped form before inching toward the door. Everything went fine until she got there and tugged the latch.

The door didn't budge.

Locked in!

Ketta quivered. They'd locked her in like an animal. Her and the other girl. Now what was she to do?

Rage lent strength as she fumbled with the door latch and yanked again. Unfortunately, with the same result. The door remained closed.

But it wriggled. At the top and the bottom.

Ketta wished she'd been paying attention when Kuo and the woman brought her out here. A vision of the way they fastened shed doors at home came to her. All they did was get a block of wood and nail it into the door jamb. Not all the way. Secured, but leaving it loose enough to pivot on the nail until half of the block held the door closed.

If they used the same method here, maybe she could manage to get the door open. Not so easy, though, from the wrong side and without tools.

Squatting down, she patted the dirt floor of the shed. It had once been a wood shed, she thought. In fact, part of it still was. Just this area had been turned into a . . . what? A prison for girls? A bedroom of sorts for the other girl? A storage area to lock in slaves? Ketta hadn't forgotten the girl told her the old woman "owned" her.

She finally found what she'd been searching for, a slender stick narrow enough to fit through the crack between door and jamb, that she hoped would prove strong enough to shift the block of wood.

Reaching upward almost to the limit of her height, she pried at the block. At her wits end, she pressed on the stick and jumped. The door creaked open, two inches, then six.

Perfect.

Ketta started through, then froze as the other girl's cry pierced the air.

No soft "shh, shh, shh," this time, but something loud and Chinese.

Ketta darted outside and ran.

Chapter Ten: Yester

Hay rustled. An animal snorted, and droplets of something splattered on his face.

Rubbing the dampness away, Yester opened one eye and then the other, both still blurry with uneasy sleep. Nat was standing above him, pushing at the nose of his cayuse, who appeared to wonder why two boys were sleeping atop his breakfast.

"Uh," Yester said, and sat up.

"Yes. That's the same thing I said." Nat laughed. "I'd rather camp out, Yester. Leastwise there ain't drunk people coming and going all night long. And this hay itches."

"It does. Tonight," Yester promised, scratching at a red welt, "we'll camp, even if it's only a grassy spot down by the river." He turned his boots upside down and shook them in case a mouse or a spider had taken up residence—which it hadn't—before pulling them on and lurching to his feet. "You hungry?"

"Yes. Empty as if I'd been working all night."

"Me, too."

Pausing only briefly to finger-comb hayseeds from their hair and splash a little cold water from the outside pump over their faces, the boys sauntered from the livery.

"Wonder if there's a better place to eat than that café from last night." Yester lifted his nose and scented the wind like Barney when he scented something good.

Nat smelled it, too, and pointed with his nose. "This way."

He led them down a narrow lane between buildings until

they came out behind some little hole-in-the-wall businesses. A barber shop with a single straight-backed chair and a table holding scissors and a couple razors. An office with a lady offering to read or write or post letters for the illiterate. An eatery composed of two tiny tables with two rickety stools each, and an exceedingly stout woman baking biscuits in a dutch oven over a campfire. Ham and grits cooked in pans resting atop a funny little stove barely the size of a child's toy.

One of the eatery's little tables was occupied. The other not. Yester and Nat moved to remedy the situation.

"I got biscuits, ham, grits, and gravy." The woman reeled off the menu in a gravelly voice. "And honey for the biscuits. Breakfast is ten cents, all you can eat. Take it or leave it."

"We'll take it, ma'am," Yester said, smiling widely.

The boys each eased onto a stool, careful how they placed both feet and butt. One wrong move, Yester figured, and they'd land in the dirt. Within minutes, the men at the other table finished and paid up. Another two men took their place. One of them scowled at Nat, who looked away, his eyes wary.

"I ain't eatin' with that Injun," the scowling man announced to the cook.

Nat breathed out hard through his nose. It was up to Yester to scowl back.

"Shut up, Orin Richards," the woman said. She didn't glance up from her cooking. "A paying customer is a paying customer."

"Not to me, it ain't," the man said.

"This is not your business. It's mine."

The argument went back and forth. Yester grew more and more uncomfortable, even as Nat's brown skin paled.

At last Nat stood up. "I'll leave, ma'am, but," he said, gaze fixed on the man, "I am not 'that Injun.' I am Nathaniel Fontaine. I am Métis."

The woman slapped slabs of ham onto tin plates and added a

heaping spoonful of grits. "Sit down, boy. Nathaniel Fontaine who is Métis. Whatever that is. Sounds like a Frenchy, to me. Your breakfast is ready. You, too," she added to Yester, who'd gotten up when Nat did.

The woman was so firm about it, Nat sat back onto his stool, apparently not noticing the way it rocked beneath him. More slowly, Yester followed suit. In view of the plates of steaming food she set before them, it didn't take much to persuade them to ignore Orin Richards. Not even when he emitted grumbles when the stout woman's back was turned.

The boys didn't linger over their breakfast, although the cook's friendly way encouraged him to ask his hopeful question about Ketta.

"Nope. Ain't seen her," the woman said and cocked a thumb toward Richards. "Chinamen don't come here. Reckon you can see why. Got a lot of customers like him, 'specially when it comes to Chinks."

Downcast, the news didn't stop Yester from gobbling his food. In truth, he'd expected her answer.

"Mighty good grub," he told her shyly as he added a nickel to the total bill. It's what he'd seen Big Joe do after a good meal in one of his few generous moments.

She patted his shoulder. "Thank you, son." Bending closer to his ear, she added, "You boys clear out. If you see Richards in the distance, head off the other way. He's a real sour feller, and you don't want to mix with him. You or your Métis friend."

Yester sighed but nodded. He'd figured as much for himself. The problem was, he still had to find Ketta, and that meant asking questions. He needed Nat's help, but from what the woman said, maybe they'd better stick together.

Bellies full, they waddled off down the narrow back street until the two-table café faded from sight. From there, they fetched their horses and mounted up, ready to take up the search again.

They soon reached a sprawling section of town where the blocks were not so delineated as they followed the winding river bank. It was here they cut their first sign of the outlaws.

Nat saw him first. A big black horse looking trail-worn and thirsty. "Whoa," he told his cayuse.

"Yester," he said, surprising Yester and jerking him out of a low mood brought on by what was beginning to strike him as a hopeless task. "Look there."

"What?" Yester stopped, too, and straightened in the saddle, his gaze following the direction of Nat's pointing finger. He stared. "Hooie, Nat. That's a Percheron if I ever saw one."

"Yes. And how many black Percherons are we going to see in Lewiston? Not many, I bet."

Yester nodded. "Most people, they own a horse like that, they either got him out working, or he's slicked up and ready to show off. Not all dirty and full of dried sweat. Looks like he ain't seen a brush for a week."

"Rode hard," Nat agreed.

"Gaunt," Yester added. "Like he needs water." Chirping to his horse, he headed over to the rundown pen where the horse was confined. As they neared, they saw an empty water bucket kicked over and laying on its side. Grunting, he dismounted and reached into the pen to pick up the bucket. There was a spigot out by the street. He filled the bucket there and lugged water back to the horse.

With a dry snort, the Percheron immediately ducked his nose in and slurped. In seconds, it was gone, and Yester went back for a refill. This time the horse paused long enough to shake back his mane and receive a pat, which is when Yester spotted the brand.

"Look here," he said to Nat, who patiently held Queenie snubbed up close to his pony.

Nat peered. "Yeah, and see there," he said, pointing at the ground. Tracks showed clearly where the bucket had tipped over and the horse had walked through the mud, dried now. The tracks were familiar, seeing as they'd followed them for miles yesterday. "This is Patton's horse for sure. I don't need to see the brand."

The brand consisted of a quarter circle on the bottom with an open square sitting on it. The inside of the square contained the letter *P.* Rocking Box P, Yester remembered Mr. Fontaine naming it.

Yester grinned at Nat. "Finally." He eyed the hovel sitting only a few feet from the pen. A smudge of smoke came from a lopsided chimney. "Maybe Ketta is in there." Even to his own ears the comment didn't exactly sound like he hoped for it.

Nat raised his eyebrows. "If she is, she won't like it. That place looks hog dirty."

"I know." Yester took a deep breath. "I'm gonna go see."

"Should we get the sheriff? Or the town marshal?" Nat appeared a little worried by Yester's brash intention. "What about those outlaws? You and me, Yester, I don't think—"

Yester nodded. Reaching over, he drew his rifle from the saddle scabbard. "I'm going in armed. If anything happens, Nat, you tear on out of here and fetch the law."

Nat shook his head. "We'll go together." He slid from his cayuse's back, flipped the reins around one of the rickety rails forming the pen, and did the same with Queenie's. "I'm ready."

Setting his lips, Yester leaned the rifle over his shoulder. They'd each taken a step when the door of the hovel slammed open, and a man stepped out onto the porch. Yester was sure he'd meant to appear tough, but since the man stepped on a rotten board and sank through to his ankle, he was not impressed. Or maybe he meant intimidated.

The man, an old feller with a white beard and runaway hair,

pulled his foot out, cussing roundly. When he got his breath back, he hollered, "You boys get away from that horse. He's a killer."

Yester almost laughed. Almost. "He's no killer," he said as he approached the old man. "What he is, is stolen." As far as he could tell, the other man wasn't carrying a gun, but who knew but what he had one hidden in a pocket or behind his back. Yester figured it was best to take no chances.

"This horse belongs to Patton's Rocking Box P, and his name is Dusty." He glared at the old man. "Outlaws stole him from Patton's ranch two days ago, and we been following him ever since. You one of those outlaws?"

The man's jaw dropped. "The hell you say. I ain't no outlaw. I ain't no horse thief, either. I paid for this here nag fair and square."

Nat broke in. "Did you get a bill of sale?"

"Bill of sale? Bill of sale, you say? Why, why . . . what's it to you young hooligans? You ain't the law. You ain't nothing but a couple of kids, one of which," he added, peering closely at Nat, "is an Injun."

Nat sighed audibly.

"We may not be the law," Yester said, "but we sure enough can turn you over to the sheriff for a horse thief. Mr. Patton, he's gonna be here soon. He's a quick man with a gun. He sees you with his horse he'll shoot you down in the twitch of an eye." Yester poured it on. "He won't have any trouble finding you, either, because I'm gonna send my partner over to the bridge to report to him. And I'm gonna sit right here with you and wait. I never saw anybody get shot before. It'll be interesting."

If it hadn't already been white, Yester was sure the old feller's hair would've lost all color in that moment.

"See here," he said, then apparently lost track of his words.

"Unless . . ." Yester drew it out.

"Unless?"

"Unless you can tell me where to find the girl that came in with this horse."

Ketta

Scared almost witless by the other girl's cries, Ketta sped down the alley, careless of any noise she made. Freedom beckoned at the end, down where flashes of light shone from lanterns hung outside the few businesses, mostly saloons, still open.

Forgetting to breathe, stumbling over bottles and tin cans and other trash dumped there as if to deliberately impede her, Ketta gasped as she burst from between buildings.

Straight into Kuo's waiting clutches.

She started to cry out, managing only a squeak before it was too late. Kuo's hand covered her mouth, muffling all sound.

How had he come to be here at just this time? The wrong time. The question roared through Ketta's mind. How? Why?

"I expected you to try something," he said, as though he'd read her mind. "I thought I'd have to wait longer. You figured it out fast."

Ketta wrenched her face away. "Let me go. I want my mother."

His expression turned hard. "You're mine now. Her time is done."

"No," she cried, but he ignored her protest. Gripping her thin arm, he frog-marched her back the way she'd come, until she once again stood in front of the shed door.

"Go in," he said. "Sleep. We'll leave in the morning. Don't try to run again. I'll be here, and I'll catch you. Or she will." A gesture showed the restaurant woman's approach. The threat was clear. He pushed Ketta inside before he turned and walked off.

To take up his post at the end of the ally, ensuring she remained his prisoner?

Figuring she didn't have a choice at the moment, Ketta stumbled across the shed's earthen floor and sat down, her head on her knees. She turned away from the woman who followed her in. The respite didn't last long. Only until the first thwack of a whip across her shoulders.

More surprised than feeling the hurt, Ketta scooched backward.

"Stop it!" she shouted. "Stop it. You get away from me."

Her protest served no purpose. Looming above her like a fairytale witch, the woman brought the whip down again. And again, harder. And then again and again.

Ketta lost count of the lashes. Pain washed over her with each new strike, even though she didn't cry. And she didn't scream, either, aside from that first surprised shout.

At last, the woman did stop. Breath ragged from her strenuous efforts, she bent down and hissed at her, "You be good now, or I come back with a club."

Shock held Ketta silent, believing the old woman's every word.

Somewhere out of sight, the other girl, the one she hadn't even really seen yet, made a rustling noise.

The old woman whirled. "You. No speak."

The rustling stopped.

The woman, showing a cautious nature, retreated without turning her back on Ketta. The door slammed shut, throwing the shed into ebony darkness. Outside, she heard the latch turn, then a hammering sound.

The shoddy door and walls couldn't muffle voices from outside. Shouts. Some cuss words in English. Jibber-jabber impossible to understand. The old witch woman and Kuo renewing their argument.

So he hadn't left, but only absented himself while the woman beat her. Ketta listened with a heavy heart.

This father was as bad as Big Joe. The only difference seemed to be that Big Joe slapped her himself, and Kuo left the beating to another.

At last, footsteps faded into silence.

After a while, a soft, a very soft whisper reached Ketta. "I said, 'Shh, shh, shh.' "

"Why did you scream when I left?" Ketta asked over pain that spread like fire across her back.

The other girl's snort was the loudest and most eloquent thing she'd spoken to Ketta. "She beat me, I don't. I no want beating."

Ketta guessed she couldn't blame her for that. "You should've run away with me," she said, not caring about her accusatory tone. "Together we both could've gotten away."

"Not me. Cannot run," the girl said, and now Ketta heard sadness in her voice.

"I would've helped you," she said.

"No. No help for me," the girl replied.

In the morning, as the first fingers of sunlight drove away the darkness, she found out why. The girl's feet were malformed, curled into tiny clubs on the ends of her ankle bones. She was barely able to hobble to the privy, let alone run anywhere.

Ketta stifled a gasp, hands over her mouth. "Oh, my goodness," she whispered. "Does it hurt?"

The girl nodded. "Many years. Not so bad now. At first, yes."

"At first? You mean you weren't born this way?"

The girl's head drooped, like a flower too heavy for its stalk. "No. *Mu qin* do it. Wraps my feets, always, always. They grown round, not flat, like you."

"Moo cheen?"

The girl hesitated. "Mother."

"But why? Why would she do such a thing?"

"Worth more. Men like." Her eyes closed. "Some men like."

"But—" Ketta couldn't go on. What kind of people would deliberately cripple a child. Their own child. Even Big Joe would draw the line before that.

Ketta decided she didn't want to be Chinese. She *wouldn't* be Chinese.

And that was final.

Kuo came for her just after dawn. They went into the pokey little restaurant before it was even open. The old woman and a male cook were already there, chopping and roasting and preparing for the day. The stove was already hot. The cook stirred up a batch of eggs with rice and vegetables mixed in, and poured a brown sauce over it. That was breakfast.

Her father lifted her onto the stool, giving her a sharp look as she winced away, but he said nothing to the old witch woman. Ketta, feeling a little braver, glared at her.

The witch woman glared at Kuo and smiled evilly at Ketta, revealing several broken teeth. Ketta hoped someone had knocked them out for her, and that it had hurt.

Kuo shook his head. "Eat," he said.

So, she did, and although Ketta wouldn't have said so for the world, the food tasted good.

Finished with their meal, Kuo paid the woman, several coins passing from his pocket to hers. Avoiding his touch, which had hurt, Ketta slipped from the stool while his back was turned.

He grasped her hand as they left, holding it tightly enough that she had no chance to wrench away. A horse waited at the rail outside the café, twitching its tail against flies. Not the dun horse, she noted, that he'd stolen from the rancher, but a bay. Ketta spared a thought for Beau, left so many miles behind. She figured Big Joe had probably already gotten Beau and his other horses back. And that meant he'd have no reason to pursue

Kuo or any of his men any further. It also meant Yester wouldn't be coming. Maybe the other rancher would, but even if he caught up, what difference would she make to him? He'd have no reason to care about her.

She was doomed. She knew it.

"Ride behind me," he said, swinging into the saddle. "That way I won't be rubbing your back." He grinned a little. "Yes. I know it's sore. I knew she'd beat you. But it won't happen again." Inexplicably, he added, "I'm not leaving you here. You're worth more."

Reaching down, he offered his hand. Ketta ignored it.

"Mad at me, child? Your own fault. You must learn to obey. Chinese girls learn early to do as they're told, as their fathers tell them. Come. Let me help you up."

I won't be Chinese. I won't.

But the old witch woman's sudden presence behind her made her straighten and shy away. The woman flourished her whip at Ketta and smiled.

Slowly, ever so slowly, Ketta extended her left hand to Kuo, allowing him to pull her onto the horse behind him.

Another kind of punishment coming her way, she thought, trying to settle. Pinched by the saddle, for one. The welts left from the old woman's whip, for two. And for three, the pain in her heart. Her courage was seeping away like water after a rain.

Chapter Eleven: Yester

The white-haired old man was full of bluster and shifty-eyed as he looked from Yester to Nat and back again. "What little girl?" he said. "I ain't seen any little girls. What would one of them be doing down here by the river? What did she do? Steal this horse?" His guffaw sounded like a donkey with a throat infection.

Yester knew he lied, the problem being to force the truth out of him. This, he thought, was the hard part of being young. Old blowhards like this one didn't try very hard to hide their lies.

He turned to Nat. "You want to go wait for Patton or should I? Either way, one of us needs to stay with the horse. Make sure he doesn't disappear again. Better go tell the sheriff, too."

Nat put on his fiercest look. "I will stay. Be glad to. I'll watch this one, and the horse. Can I borrow your rifle? I might need it to shoot any marauding varmints."

"Sure." Yester handed the rifle over. Nat took it with a grin.

"Now see here," the old fellow started, but as Yester made a move to mount Queenie, he changed his attitude. "Wait just a minute."

"You got something to say?" Yester figured Nat's fierce expression must've worked well. That and the rifle, which seemed to accidentally point in a certain direction. He stopped with his left foot in the stirrup.

"There was a kid," the man said. "Not right here. But Tug McClure, that's the feller sold me this horse, rode in with this other feller. That one, a Chink who goes by the name of Kuo, had a kid perched on the back of his horse. They didn't come close. I can't say whether it was a shemale or not." His eyes shifted back and forth and finally rolled upward. "McClure said he owned the horse. Why wouldn't I believe him? Just 'cause he's one of them negroes?"

Kuo. Yester felt a leap of excitement. He knew that name. But he said, "A negro?"

The riverboat captain had talked about a negro, too. The same one he'd seen in Pullman? It seemed likely. Did that mean Ketta was on a steamboat heading down to Portland?

Yester felt like pounding himself on the head. The boat. Where the captain had said he'd sold a ticket to a black man. Would there be more than one negro taking a boat on any single day? Yester doubted it.

"Yeah, negro. You heard of them, I suppose," the man said sourly. "We fought a war over 'em."

Yester had no reply to that. "Did you 'buy' the other feller's horse, too? When you 'bought' the Percheron?"

"Nope. He didn't offer it up for sale."

"Where'd they go after you 'bought' the horse?"

The old fellow grinned. "Well, the negro got on board the *White Queen,* and away it went, downriver. Guess you'll have a hard time catching up with him."

Yester tensed. Looked at Nat. "Remember, Nat? Captain said he sold only the one ticket. That means Ketta and . . . and her kidnapper are still around. Somewhere."

"We'll find her," Nat said. The rifle, the point of aim having lowered a bit during all the talk, raised into shooting position again. "Where did the friend and the kid go?"

"How would I know?" The old fellow was back to bluster. "I weren't keeping track of them. My business was with McClure."

Nat poked the rifle barrel into his chest. "Make a guess."

The man batted at the rifle barrel and backed out of reach. A shrug prefaced words. "Dunno. Maybe Chinatown."

"Chinatown?" Yester's heart dropped. "Where is that?"

This time the man sounded almost satisfied. "No place you want to go, sonny. We burned that damn heathen Chinatown to the ground back in '83. But they're like vermin. They come right back." Then he added thoughtfully, "We keep 'em penned up pretty good in there, and they don't take kindly to whites coming in."

But he went on to tell them which street and precisely where to find it. Yester figured he hoped they'd find trouble there.

If he hadn't spotted the sheriff's office right on the way to Chinatown, the old fellow and Patton's horse might've gotten away free and clear. But he did spot it, a pokey building with a deputy sitting right out front in the sun, so that Yester felt duty bound to stop. Given Patton had been good about supplying him and Nat with food for their journey, it didn't strike him as neighborly to simply pass by. If all went well, the Percheron would find its way home in the next day or two.

The worst part was the search for Ketta being slowed for a half hour or so while Yester explained the circumstances.

"Yeah, yeah, I know who you mean. I'm acquainted with Ol' Pa Reilly," the deputy said. "This isn't the first time he's 'bought' a horse with a questionable bill of sale. Rocking Box P, you say? A rancher by the name of Patton? Reckon that would be Horace Patton, with a spread about thirty miles west of here. Seen that black Percheron of his before. About twice a year his missus hitches it to a carriage and drives into town."

Apparently able to supply his own identification of man and horse without their help, Yester and Nat continued on toward the street Ol' Pa Reilly had identified as Chinatown. Oddly enough, Yester had walked through a bit of the street the day before, but now it seemed strange and wicked to him. Whether he imagined so or not, he fancied he caught the odor of burning opium. Not that he knew what it smelled like. But everybody knew Chinamen regularly frequented opium dens, so that's where Yester began his search.

The people here lived in hovels. Or so was Yester's impression as they reached the street Reilly had called Chinatown. Hovels, with garbage dumped in the streets and bodies slumped in the alleys. Opium addicts, he surmised. He'd read about them. Sometimes they were dead. His nose turned up.

"Do I hear hogs?" Nat asked. Keeping a careful lookout on a pigtailed man walking about wearing what looked like a black nightshirt, he kept his pony's nose right up beside Yester's mare. The man's eyes were fixed on Yester, and only Nat's close proximity kept the Chinaman from coming between them.

"I think so." The grunting came from behind one of the more rundown buildings. One whose roof sagged right to the point of falling in. Smoke rose from a crumbly chimney, fragrant with what might've been apple wood. As if on cue, a sudden shrieking squeal rose over the other noise, then abruptly shut off. Yester shuddered. "Yep, you hear porkers, all right."

"Don't think I want to try the bacon off that one," Nat said. Then, "Look out!"

Yester, startled by Nat's yell, dug his heels into Queenie and twisted in the saddle. The quick maneuver was just in time to avoid the blade of a small knife slashing at the ties holding his bedroll on the back of his saddle.

"Hey," he yelled, as, thwarted, the knife wielder darted away. "Thanks," he said to Nat.

"Saw him looking at you funny."

"I wouldn't've wanted to lose my blanket."

Nat nodded soberly. "Guess I'm glad I'm Métis. Pa told me Chinamen don't like Indians. Not even half Indians." He paused. "And Indians don't like Chinamen."

"Can't say as I care for them myself." Yester was still looking over at the alleyway where the almost-thief had disappeared. "Why do you suppose he picked on me? Shoot, I don't hardly have anything worth stealing."

"Yeah, but you're white. And a kid."

Yester snorted. "Easy pickin's—or I reckon he thought so. Guess I would've been if it hadn't been for you. I didn't notice him coming."

Once past the first couple cross streets, as they delved farther into Chinatown, the buildings took a slight turn for the better. Here, too, were a few whites. But no white women. At one store, they heard English spoken. A queer sort of English, but understandable when Yester took time to ponder on it. The speech came from a man passing a bundle of some sort to a white customer.

Here, too, Yester sniffed at the odor of strong lye soap. A laundry. This was his chance to ask about Ketta. Since the proprietor did business from a counter set up right on the street, he didn't bother to dismount but just leaned down a little.

"Yes, yes?" the Chinaman said.

"You seen any little girls? I'm looking for my sister. She's part white . . . mostly white . . . and part Chinese."

The man gave him a doubtful appearing stare and shook his head. "No see."

"She'd be with a man." Yester grimaced. "A man like you. A Celestial."

"No see," the man repeated.

The conversation, such as it was, ended there. Frustrated, Yester moved on, Nat trailing after him and holding his horse whenever Yester entered a business to provide his description and ask his question. Slow going with no response, until, finally, he seemed to have hit pay dirt. A slant-eyed devil, as he'd named these foreign people to himself, leaned against the outside wall of a tiny storefront chewing on some sort of straw. He wore the ubiquitous black pajama outfit and a small cap on his head. A thick pigtail reached all the way to his hips, like his hair had never been cut. Behind him, the building's interior was so dark Yester could barely see the great many jars and canisters lining some shelves. Not that he cared about them, or the potent odors arising from inside.

Yester open his mouth to speak, but the Chinaman beat him to it.

"You look for little girl?"

"Yes." Apparently, the news had spread.

"I know of little girl," the feller said.

"You do? Where is she?" Yester tried not to show his excitement.

The Chinaman made a motion with his head and stood erect. "You come." He cast a baleful glance at Nat. "Not him. No Injun. No horse. *Mu qin* say no."

Yester and Nat exchanged a look. "I don't like it," Nat said softly. "I don't like *him.* He looks shifty to me. I don't trust him. He's as likely to stick a knife in you as not."

"I don't trust him, either, but Nat, I've gotta take a chance. If he knows where to find Ketta—"

"Yes. I figured you'd do it. I'll hold your horse, but if you aren't back in ten minutes, I'm gonna take your rifle and come after you. And I'll be riding horseback." He darted a glance at two Chinese men who had stopped and were scowling at him. "If I live so long."

Yester grinned. "You do that." Dismounted, he stood a good six inches taller than the Celestial. He figured that should give him an advantage if it came to a tussle.

"Where's the little girl?" he asked, but, instead of heading off to show him, the man stuck out his hand, palm up. Yester shrugged.

"He wants money first," Nat informed him, like Yester was some kind of rube who didn't know up from down.

Yester reached into his pocket.

"Don't let him see how much you've got," Nat said.

"I won't." He fumbled for coins and found what he figured was a dime. Pulling it out, he dropped it onto the extended palm. Fingers immediately closed over it.

"You come," the Chinaman said and started off in a shambling trot.

Yester followed, aware of Nat's worried eyes on his back.

Ketta

Sunlight blazing down on Ketta's back burned through her thin dress. It felt like she was on fire, the welts from the old witch's whip growing more painful with every degree of heat. The very air around the moving horse seemed to spin, making her dizzy. She clung to Kuo even though from the way he swayed in the saddle she thought he was half asleep.

When the horse they were riding stumbled, it caught her unaware. Kuo, too. When he slid forward, she slid forward, the saddle skirt pinching a bit of skin on her thigh between leather and horse. Unable to stop herself, Ketta squeaked.

"What the devil is the matter with you now?" Kuo groused. "Sit up and watch where we're going."

As if he weren't as guilty as she. Stung, Ketta said, "How—" catching the rest of her words back just in time. She wanted to ask how she was supposed to watch the trail ahead when her view was blocked by his body. Thankfully, prudence stopped the retort in time. She knew what would happen if she said such a thing to Big Joe. Kuo was probably no different. But then, she thought, she already hurt so badly, what difference would a few more bruises make?

"How what?" Kuo looked over his shoulder at her, even though he probably couldn't see much of her. She was small enough to be hidden.

"I can't see around you," Ketta said. It came out much more meekly than she intended.

"Huh. I suppose not."

Ketta's eyes opened wide at his agreement. And because he'd sounded almost amused.

"We'll stop soon," he said. "We're almost through the shortcut. The river is just ahead. We'll rest a while and eat before we go on."

"Eat?"

"I had the old woman pack us some food."

He couldn't know how much this relieved Ketta, who welcomed even a small respite from the constant motion of the horse. She'd be glad when they crossed the area between bends of river, too. It was cooler by the water, and she liked hearing the sound as the stream tumbled over rocks and rills.

"Where are we going?" she asked after a while.

He shrugged, body moving under her hands as she gripped.

"My home."

"You have a home?" She froze, thinking he might take offense.

"Of sorts," he said after a pause. "I thought we might ought to hole up for a while. Until the hurrah dies down about what happened at the Noonan place. And the other."

"Stealing horses, you mean?" Ketta knew she dared punishment with the question but couldn't hold the words back.

Kuo's answer was slow in coming. "Yeah," he said after a while. "Among other things."

Ketta wanted to ask, "What other things?" but on second thought, maybe she didn't want to know.

They plodded on.

Her legs were unsteady when at last Kuo lifted her down. "May I go down to the water?" she asked, gazing longingly to where the river bank sloped in a steep pitch.

"Go. Fill this while you're there." He handed her his canteen. "I'll water the horse."

"All right." Ketta's heart lifted. He was letting her go by herself. No one to watch as she relieved herself. She'd wash, while she was there. Maybe cool her feet and clean the pinched part of her legs. If only she could take off her dress and bathe her back. But no. She didn't quite dare do that.

Searching out the path of least resistance, she found a way to the river. While still some distance away, she squatted behind a rock, then went on. Remembering something Big Joe had said, she filled the canteen where she saw no trace of animal tracks and where she was certain the water was clean. She secured it in a shallow eddy to stay cool while she washed.

Removing her shoes and stockings, she waded out a little, hanging on to an overhanging bush in case the bottom suddenly dropped off beneath her. Farther and farther she went, until the water closed around her waist, and then, when she was sure of her footing, dipped down until her shoulders were covered.

Ketta shuddered with relief and pleasure as not only the dirt of four days travel with outlaws washed downstream, but all—well, some—of her collective pains went along with it. She wished she could stay there forever. Closing her eyes, she splashed water over her face and scrubbed.

"Ketta."

Kuo's voice roused her.

"Ketta? Child, where are you?"

"I'm here," she called.

"You're taking too long. Get up here. We need to eat before we go on."

"I'm coming." Already? The habit of instant obedience being ingrained, Ketta stood up, water sheeting from her body and shivering a little in the sudden cold.

That's when she saw it, coming right at her.

Horror froze her. She wanted to move. Wanted to move in the very worst way, if only her limbs hadn't refused to take action.

The thing bumped into her.

Ketta opened her mouth. Opened it far enough for a noise such as she'd never made before in her whole life to come rushing out.

She screamed. Caught her breath and screamed again and splashed wildly at the water.

Kuo's shout answered. She didn't know—and never did learn—what he answered. But there he was, plunging down the steep embankment toward her.

"Ketta," she heard him say. "Child, what—"

And then he reached her, and he saw it, too, and, after a brief moment, pushed it away to continue turning and tumbling down the river.

"Come," he said, taking her hand and giving a little pull.

She didn't budge. Couldn't. Her feet remained planted in place.

"Child." He picked her up, and, for the first time, she was glad of his arms around her. He didn't hurt her, not even her back unless she had lost all feeling, but he seemed gentle even when he stumbled on the way up to the trail and almost fell.

He didn't even get mad when he had to make another trip down the slope to retrieve the canteen and her shoes and stockings. Meanwhile, she rested her head on her knees and trembled.

After a while, the shaking stopped, and Ketta found her voice. "That was him, Snaggletooth, floating down the river."

"Snaggletooth?" The corner of Kuo's lip turned up. "Yes. It

was Frank."

"He'd been shot," Ketta said.

"Yes."

"In the head." She shuddered again. "He only had part of his head."

He nodded.

Ketta thought Kuo appeared kind of sick himself, just like she did. "Why was he so white?" she asked.

Kuo hesitated. "His blood all drained out, I guess."

"Would I turn white like that if all my blood drained out?"

He hesitated even longer. "Probably. Put your shoes on. We need to go."

She did as told, fumbling with the laces so her usually precise bows were all scraggly looking with a bigger loop on one end than on the other.

Looking up, she asked, "Do you know who shot him?"

Slowly, he shook his head. "I can guess." And then, as though talking to himself, "This calls for another change of plan. He's bringing those witless bastard sons of his. I can't take—"

Sons? Ketta wondered. Who did he mean? Milt? Did he mean Milt had killed Frank? His partner?

But he didn't say, only closing his mouth and looking grim.

When it came time to mount, Kuo flapped his coat a few times and made a pad for under her thighs before they started moving again. The relief to her abraded legs was immediate, though she found the coat a bit scratchy. But at least it didn't pinch.

It was only some time later that Ketta remembered they hadn't eaten.

Before traveling many miles down the trail, Kuo changed direction. He avoided speaking to the few travelers they met. At a cutoff only visible if one knew where to look, they traveled away from the river and higher into the foothills. His unhappy expression grew more pronounced.

My fault? Ketta wondered, afraid to ask.

Kuo wasn't forthcoming. A long silence passed before he spoke again.

"Here we are," he said.

CHAPTER TWELVE: YESTER

The Chinaman led Yester between buildings, in his opinion shacks being a more accurate description of the rundown structures. They dodged garbage and avoided mangy dogs and rooting pigs, until they came to an overgrown woodshed. Overgrown, because instead of a simple open lean-to, it had boards covering the sides and boasted a door. A new padlock hung loose on a freshly installed hasp.

"What's this?" Yester's voice slid up a tone. "She's locked in? I want—"

"You want? Girl here." The man was firm.

Yester glanced around. The area smelled of hot grease and frying food, all mixed up with the rot of garbage. An unsavory place, for sure, even aside from the man lying up next to one of the buildings. He couldn't tell if the man was dead or not.

Wishing he had more than Pa's old jackknife folded up in his pocket, Yester called out, "Ketta? You in there?"

Nobody answered, but a rustling noise indicated somebody was inside. Figuring he didn't have any choice, Yester stepped to the door, pausing with his hand on the latch. "Don't you lock me in. Try anything, and my friend will come in shooting."

The man flipped his long braid, "queue" Yester guessed they were called, over his shoulder, barred the door with an arm, and held out his hand. "Twenny-fi cents."

Clamping his jaw with the thought that searching for his little sister was an expensive proposition, Yester dropped the coin into the other's palm. Taking a deep breath and receiving a whiff of the wood stored in there, he sidled inside.

"Ketta?" he called again. A broken ray of sunshine touched upon a small form sitting atop a pallet. She was struggling to rise. *Ketta.* Intent on helping her, Yester stepped forward. The door slammed shut behind him, shutting off the light.

"Dammit," he said. At least he didn't hear the click of the padlock, so maybe he'd be all right. But the dark was intense. "Where are you?" he called out.

A girl's small voice answered. "Here."

Disappointment . . . more, make that anger . . . swept over him. That wasn't Ketta. He'd been suckered.

"Who are you?" He peered through the gloom at the girl. "Where's my sister? Where's Ketta?"

"Don't know," she said. "Father take."

"Father?" What did she mean? Confused, Yester wondered how in the world Big Joe had gotten here before him and found this place. Then he realized this couldn't be. Did she mean . . . "Ketta's father?"

"Yes. Kuo."

Voices spoke outside, drawing his attention. The Chinese man protested something, and there were a series of grunts. The door opened. Sunlight flooded in.

"What's taking so long?" Nat demanded from outside. Yester's rifle was tucked under one arm in a position where he'd be able to snap it up in a hurry. "You find Ketta?"

"No. But I found somebody who's seen her." He turned back to the girl. "Where—" He got not further as the girl rose from her pallet.

She was tiny, but not as tiny as Ketta. Older, too, and—Yester's breath caught in sympathy—crippled.

The girl didn't seem to notice his dismay. She shuffled past him into the sunlight, picking up a bucket on her way out.

"Need water," she said to the Chinese man standing outside, at which he nodded.

Yester followed her as she clumped out, glad to escape what was evidently her crib. Not an entire innocent—he'd accompanied Big Joe on his toots too often for that—he realized the girl's place in life.

Nat stared at her as she went past him on her way to a water pump placed in the middle of the street behind the houses. Her stilted gait proclaimed what an effort it was for her to walk. She couldn't have run away had it been her dearest wish.

Glancing at Nat, she sniffed in disapproval.

"What happened to your feet?" he asked baldly.

The Chinese man started forward. "No talk," he said, adding, "Injun."

Nat faced him, eyes narrowed. "Chink."

Yester stepped forward. "When did Ketta and her . . . father . . . leave?"

The girl, he observed, was careful of her answer. She shrugged. Gripping the pump handle, she started levering it, best she was able, up and down, to start the water flowing. Both Yester and Nat, who pushed the Chinaman aside with the rifle barrel, trod over to help.

"When?" Yester persisted, taking the bucket from her.

"Morning," the girl shook her head but muttered, mouth hardly moving, "One, maybe two, hours."

She called it "mowing, and wan and ows." Funny.

The news made Yester mad enough to chew leather. Close. They'd been so close. If they'd gotten here just a little sooner they would have had her. Providing he could've taken her away from the Chinaman who'd kidnapped her, anyway.

Well, he just would've. That's all.

"Where'd he take her?" he spoke softly, too. With his back turned, he was sure the Chinaman couldn't hear. It was obvious the girl was scared of the man and didn't want him listening to what she said.

She made another of those tiny shrugs. Her eyes swiveled, and her head, topped by shining, blue-black hair, tilted a mere half inch toward the east. "There. Somewhere there. In hills."

"Is she okay?" he asked.

The girl hesitated. "*Mu quin* beat." Then she added quickly, "But okay. Father good to her."

Yester's eyes opened wide. "What?"

But apparently their conversation was over, his twenty-five cents used up. The Chinaman grabbed the girl and pushed her toward the shed. He started speaking fast and loud, drawing other men from the shadows. Yester thought maybe they appeared out of the cracks in the very boards of the houses, kind of like termites.

"C'mon," Nat said, tugging on Yester's arm. "Let's get out of here."

Figuring he'd probably heard everything relevant, Yester took out his jackknife and snapped it open. Shoulder to shoulder, he and Nat bulled their way out of the alley, leaving a few disgruntled slant-eyed devils behind. He'd had to scratch one of them with the blade of his knife, drawing a tiny trickle of blood. Guess he hadn't been as cowed by the odds as they'd expected. He'd never been so glad as he was right now that his height made him imposing. Even though he was only sixteen years old, he was man-sized on a man's quest.

He and Nat mounted up and rode out, their horses kicked into a fast trot.

"Where should we go next?" Nat asked when they'd left the furor behind.

"East. Into the hills."

"Any place a little more specific?"

Yester shrugged. "A few Chinese still mine a little along the

Snake. Some of the tributaries, too. We can look there. But mostly, I think—" His heart almost failed him at the idea of their next adventure. Those men who'd taken his sister, they were bad, bad men. Look what they'd done to his ma. What would they do to him and Nat if they got the chance?

The sad face of the girl from the woodshed haunted him.

Worse, what would they do to Ketta if the Chinaman didn't protect her?

After a minute, Nat said, "You think what?"

"I think we need to check out that outlaw hideout the old bugger at the livery told us about."

The old feller had gotten quite talkative when threatened with the law. And since the stolen Percheron was standing right there in his corral, he'd have had a hard time denying involvement. Turns out, he'd opened up pretty good.

"East," he'd said, pointing off in one direction before changing his mind and pointing another. He'd been right the first time, Yester noted. "Somewhere in those hills. I figure it's twenty miles or so. A long day's travel."

Nat gave him the eye. "Probably lying," he'd said to Yester.

"I ain't." A sneer lifted a corner of his scraggly white mustache. "He ain't anything to me. I don't like Chinks any better than I like Injuns. As for the black feller and a couple men them two usually run with, well, they got prices on their heads. They'll all be laying low for a spell."

As a reason to trust his directions, it seemed a bit less than convincing, but Yester didn't see any other option. Especially since the Chinese girl had said practically the same thing.

He looked at Nat. "Let's go," he said, so they did.

KETTA

Ketta leaned her head against Kuo's back and wept. Silently, careful not to let herself shake or make a sound, so he wouldn't know. She didn't want him to guess how weak she was. How terrified. How much she wanted to be back home with her mother and her brother. Even Big Joe, the enemy she knew. What if she never saw any of them again?

They traveled the lonely trail for several miles, through sparse woodlands and rising hills marked by dark cliffs, leaving the river behind. She missed the sound of rushing water, the coolness in the patches of cottonwoods and fresh fragrance of their sun-baked leaves. Even the birds were mostly silent as they soared through the blue, blue sky. Insects ceased their chatter when the horse's legs brushed the weeds and grasses sprouting from the poor, dry soil.

After a while, she sat straighter, horrified to see a wet spot on his shirt where her tears had soaked through.

"It's hot," she said. "My face is sweating."

"Yes. It is hot." His body gave a little shake. "There's a camping spot just ahead. We'll stop there and go on in the morning, when the horse has rested."

Ketta suppressed a snort. Evidently, he forgot he was speaking to a girl who knew a bit about horses, seeing they were the family business. This horse wasn't tired. He strode along under the combined load of Kuo and herself that still was a good bit lighter than the average-sized man. And they'd gone slowly, plodding along and never breaking out of a walk. Even so, she wasn't in any more of a hurry than Kuo to get wherever they were going.

Maybe he wasn't so sure about this hideout he'd mentioned. Not so sure about what, or who, he'd find there. The other man, Scar—or Milt, she supposed she ought to call him—who must've been the one to shoot Frank in the head, would he be waiting to do the same to Kuo? And if he succeeded, what about her?

A thought occurred to her. "Did the black man—"

"Tug," Kuo said. "He has a name. All of us have a name."

It stopped Ketta for a moment. What did he mean, *all of us*? Then, "Are you sure Tug got on the boat?"

"Yes. He sold that horse he was riding for the passage money. Had to. Milt has control of—" He cut himself off. "There was no money at your ranch," he finally continued, as though in disapproval. "Noonan must be very poor."

Ketta sniffed. At least no one could accuse Big Joe of being a thief.

"Did you see him get on the boat?" she persisted.

"Why?"

"Just to be sure he is gone. Maybe he doubled back and shot . . . that man."

Apparently, this logic made Kuo think, and think he did, until Ketta wondered what was going on in his mind.

"He got on board," he said at last. "Milt, or one of the others, shot Frank. Frank, he rubbed some people the wrong way. Whined a lot. A real complainer."

"Others?" It came out a squeak. Did he mean more outlaws? How many? How would anyone ever rescue her from a whole gang? Or was anyone even trying? Her heart felt as heavy as a block of granite.

"Milt's sons, for the most part." Kuo laughed bitterly. "A regular robbers' roost."

Ketta didn't see anything funny about it. She remembered Milt hadn't liked her. He'd thought she'd fetch a good price from some unknown man who liked young, pretty girls. Like Ah Kum, the girl in the shed. She'd said her name meant "good as gold." Ketta wondered who'd given her the name. The old woman?

They stopped long before dark, when the trail started an abrupt climb. The sun still shone above the bluff where Ketta knew the river to be. She had a very good sense of direction and figured to find her way home by herself if she got the chance. She wasn't lost. Not by a long shot, having kept careful track of their route.

Doves hiding in the brush called out, their soft sounds warning of intrusion but not frantic with fear. Somehow, they helped Ketta feel calmer, too.

Kuo chose a pleasant camping spot. Dismounting and lifting Ketta to the ground, he hobbled the horse amongst a stand of yellowed grass. A trickle of water spurted from the mountain at the bottom of one of the draws, forming a small pool.

Spurted cold and clear. Ketta washed her face and hands and drank until her belly said enough. Here Kuo finally relaxed, taking the saddle from the horse and spreading it and the blanket on the ground to dry before dark.

"Build a fire," he told Ketta. "A small one, with no smoke. I want some coffee."

The main trail was invisible from this point, which she supposed eased his mind. Perhaps he didn't want unexpected—or unwelcome—visitors anymore than she did. Their difference might be in who each considered unwelcome. Ketta would be glad to see Big Joe, even if he sneered at her. But maybe not if he beat her.

Kuo hadn't beat her. Slapped her a few times, though not so hard as to jar her teeth. An odd thought ripped through her, one that knew surprise.

Before the coffee boiled, Kuo fell asleep, and Ketta set it aside, keeping it warm until he awakened only a few minutes later.

Ketta was watching him when his eyes opened. "Do you have a last name?" She handed him the cup, blowing on her fingers because the tin cup radiated heat.

" 'Course I do." He yawned and guzzled coffee. "Why?"

"What is it?"

He frowned at her, his slanted eyes tilting downwards. "Horner."

Her mouth shaped the word—words. "Kuo Horner." It sounded strange to her, like the two didn't mesh together. Horner was an American name.

"Is my last name Horner, too?"

In the midst of taking a large swallow of coffee, he broke into a fit of coughing. "No. I don't think it works that way. You take your mother's name." He paused. "Because her and me, we're not married. So, you take hers." He sat back. "When's supper?"

Ketta figured he was just trying to divert her questions. "Does that mean I belong to her?"

"Sure," he muttered. "I guess so."

Her head lifted. "Then you should take me back to her. You stole me, and I want to go home."

Kuo stared at her for a long minute, his black eyes glittering, then said, "You think you belong to Noonan? That's what they call you, isn't it? Ketta Noonan? You like his name? I hear he beats you, little girl. Maybe," he added, "you deserve it. Do you?"

Mute now, Ketta shook her head. After a moment, she said, "My mother never beats me. And my brother Yester, he takes care of me. Sometimes he takes a whupping Big Joe means for me. Sometimes he gets between Big Joe and me."

"A regular hero, eh?"

Ketta smiled a tiny smile. "Yes."

She didn't think her answer pleased her father. Why? Did he want to be a hero? Something to ponder as she portioned out the food they'd neglected at noon.

Later, the rising wind blew dust and bits of debris from the dry countryside over their campsite, coating Kuo's blanket and Ketta's saddle pad. She just buried her face in the blanket, thoughts and images running through her head. But her thoughts were not of the wind or the dust. They were about Kuo. Her father.

Ketta had the strange idea that maybe he really did want to be a hero.

But he wasn't. He was a kidnapper.

Chapter Thirteen: Yester

Yester and Nat made good time in the cool of the morning, having departed the town early. Their horses were fresh and well fed; the boys eager to be back on the trail. The only problem was their uncertainty of whether they were on the right trail.

Along about mid-morning, they chanced upon a woodcutter headed back toward Lewiston with a wagon load of red fir cut in stove-size pieces. A heavy load, from the looks of things, with four chestnut-colored draft horses harnessed to the wagon. None of the horses, Yester observed, had quite the size of Patton's Percheron. These cross-bred Belgians had worked up quite a lather.

They met at a narrow spot in the trail, and both parties stopped.

"How do," Yester said.

"How do yourself," the woodcutter replied.

He, along with a helper sitting up top the load, were willing enough to give the horses a breather while they exchanged pleasantries. Yester crossed his wrists over his saddle horn and nodded at the wood.

"How many cords you got there? Is there a good market for wood in Lewiston?" He figured his questions were as good a way as any to get the feller talking. Men always liked to talk about their work. Leastwise, all the men he knew.

"Got around two cords, this load." The woodcutter took out his chew and gnawed off a bite. "Got to go some distance to find wood for cutting. Most of the timber's been used up around here."

Yester scanned the way ahead, to hills blue on the horizon. "You come from there today?" He tilted his head.

The woodcutter looked, nodded, and spat. "Yup."

"See anybody else on the trail?"

Shrugging his shoulders, the man spat again. "Didn't notice."

"I did, boss." The younger man, a kid not any older than Yester, grinned down from his perch. "He probably don't know I saw him, but I did. Seemed to me he tried to avoid meeting up with us. Steered his horse off the road when he saw us coming. We drove right past him."

The driver frowned. "I didn't see nobody." To Yester, he said, "Willy is a little prone to letting his imagination run away with him."

"Yeah?" Willy grinned. "And you're a little prone to sleeping and letting the horses drive their ownselves. It's a good thing the horses know what they're doing," he added to Yester with a wise nod.

Yester and Nat exchanged a wary glance. Ducky, Yester thought, as Nat snickered not quite inaudibly. A feller who imagined things and another feller who slept and drove a team at the same time.

He figured it couldn't hurt to ask his questions, even of such unreliable observers. "You get a look at the feller?"

"A little. He was pretty far off and stayed out of sight. Just a man on a horse. Wore a black hat and a black shirt. I figure he must be hot in that black shirt. Ain't no color hotter than black." Willy had on a sweat-stained chambray shirt washed and faded to almost white. He still looked hot.

Meanwhile, the description didn't do Yester a lot of good. He had only the vaguest memory of the Chinaman he'd seen in Pullman, since he hadn't wanted to get caught staring. Sure thought he'd been dressed all in black, but then, so were a lot of people.

He shrugged. "I'm looking for a Chinaman," he said.

Willy stared at him. "Well, what do you want with a Chinaman, fer God's sake?"

"First intelligent question I've ever heard you ask anybody," the driver said and spat again, the brown juice splattering onto the road and raising a dust. The raw stench of it rose to where Yester sat his horse.

"He's a kidnapper," Nat said, finally adding a penny's worth to the conversation.

"A kidnapper!" The driver shot Nat a look. "Who'd he kidnap?"

"My sister." Yester shifted uncomfortably. "Was the yahoo you saw a Chinaman?"

Willie pondered, moving uncomfortably on his seat atop the piled wood. "Don't know," he said at last. "Didn't get that clear of a look at him."

"Hell." The driver snorted. "Everbody knows you can't see twenty feet in front of you."

"Can too," Willie said.

"Can't."

Yester figured this exchange might go on forever if he didn't put a stop to it. "Well," he broke in, "could you see if he had anybody with him?"

At this, though Willie turned his eyes upward as if searching the cloudless blue sky for an answer, he had a positive answer. "Nope. One horse. One man."

Yester's shoulders slumped. Are we on the wrong trail? he wondered.

"His sister is young," Nat said. "Only twelve and small. She'd probably be riding either in front of her kidnapper or behind him. You might not have been able to see her at a distance. Do you think this might be possible?"

They all, even the driver, looked to Willie, whose eyes turned upward again.

Grateful for Nat's intervention, Yester waited for Willie to think and to answer. Finally, he did.

"Could be," he said, then more firmly, "Yeah, it's possible."

It wasn't much to go on, Yester thought as, after getting a description of just where Willie had seen the man, he and Nat rode on.

"Think Willie knew what he was talking about?" he asked Nat, a half mile farther down the road. They rode side by side, any trail wide enough for a wood wagon being plenty wide for the two of them.

Nat shrugged. "He seemed pretty sure of where he saw them. Guess we can take a look at the tracks. See if the horse is the same one we were tracking yesterday." He seemed confident.

"If we can find the place."

"We'll find it."

The sun beat down. Twists and turns took them from shadow to bright, from cool to hot. The sound of the river rang strong. Presently, they came to a sharp turn, where the road's builders had gone around a room-sized boulder.

"Don't guess Willie could've missed this," Nat said.

"Nope."

They guided their horses off the trail into a small bunch of cottonwoods on the river side. They'd gotten plenty of moisture, their leaves lush and green even in the summer heat.

Nat pointed down. "Look."

It struck Yester that his heart plumb lifted in his chest. Here under the trees, a heavy dew had collected overnight. The soil retained the ability to show tracks. Sure enough, there was a trail. But not, he saw, the hoofprints of the horse they'd been following yesterday. No bent nail marked this shoe. Disappointment—more, a kind of grief—surged through him, until Nat gripped his arm.

"No, look here," Nat said. "Ketta."

There, off to the side, was the clear imprint of a small shoe. One of a size to fit a small girl.

"Ketta," Yester agreed.

Sure now of the right direction, they slowed, taking time to watch for traces of the horse to follow. If it hadn't been for Nat, Yester knew, he would've lost the trail, especially when their prey left the road and headed off through an almost trackless cut. They followed, stopping where they saw signs that Ketta and her kidnapper had stopped. Finally, they came back to the sound of running water and the river.

Yester rose in his stirrups to ease his rear end. "Gotta take a break. Horses could use a drink, too."

Nat agreed. "Yeah. I'm about paralyzed."

Yester mustered a chuckle. "You? I thought you were born on a horse. Least that's what you told me."

Groaning, Nat dismounted. "Huh. That's what I told Ketta. She believed me."

Sobered, the boys took reins in hand and, finding a fairly level path down to the water, led the horses to drink.

Nat's sharply indrawn breath drew Yester's attention. "What?"

"What's that?"

Yester followed Nat's pointing forefinger. He squinted. "A downed tree." He looked harder and blinked. "Maybe it came out of somebody's yard. It's got—"

"Clothes on."

"No, it doesn't. It's . . ."

"It's a man," Nat yelled, causing both horses to snort and pull back.

By the time the boys had them under control again, the body had drifted farther down the river, tumbling and turning, and pausing as it whirled in an eddy. A wayward spin caught the dead man in a current that took him to the river's opposite bank, and there lodged him in the branches of a tree that had fallen into the water.

Too far for them to reach. Too far for them to see. Clearly, at any rate. But not far enough to miss that whoever he might be, he was no longer intact.

"A dead man," Yester said.

Nat swallowed. "Yes." He swallowed again. "You think it was the Chinaman?"

"No." Yester was positive. "The body is wearing a red shirt. And he's white. Did you see how white his . . . that part of his face is?" He stared across to where the body bobbed in the current as though impatient for rescue.

"Do you think the Chinaman killed him?" Appearing as though his hand moved of its own accord, Nat patted his pony's neck.

"God, I hope not. I hope Ketta didn't have to see that. She'd . . . she'd . . . well, she couldn't bear it."

"Yeah," Nat agreed. "She's pretty tough for a girl, but she isn't *that* tough."

"Not sure I am," Yester said.

"Me, neither," Nat said.

Ketta

In the morning, Kuo rousted Ketta out early. Along with a brisk wind, there'd been a spot of rain last night. What was left of it wet the sparse grass as they regained the trail, staining the horse's hooves and turning them dark. They followed the trail into a narrow valley, crossed that, then headed into another valley, this one rising higher in the mountains. The day heated under the blistering sun, humidity making it hard to breathe. They passed into spotty timber, the canopy sometimes dense enough to block the rays, and Ketta, still mindful of her sore back, shivered in relief. Yet, then, cold made the pain revive.

By then the trail had tapered down to a vague path.

"Are we lost?" she dared to ask, the susurrant voice of the trees damping her soft question almost down to nothing.

A small chuckle broke through Kuo's sober expression. "No." Evidently, he felt her shake because he asked, "Are you cold?"

Cold, hot, scared, tired, hungry. All of that and more, not that she'd ever in this world admit as much to her kidnapper. To her father.

But, "Yes," she said, because she figured it was better to be cold than scared.

"Not much farther," Kuo said gruffly. "You can last another quarter hour."

"Yes," she whispered, but, really, it didn't take that long for her to smell smoke and hear a horse's whinny off in the direction they were moving toward.

"Do you have a wife?" she thought to ask. "Or someone who takes care of your home when you're gone?"

He sniffed the air and pulled the horse to a stop. "No wife. But—" He sat motionless for what must've been a full minute before twisting in the saddle until he faced her. "When we get there, you keep your mouth shut, hear me? Don't talk to anybody. If they ask you something, you say yes or no. Only yes or no. Stay close to me."

"They?" Her voice quavered.

He sighed and turned away.

"This was a bad idea," she heard him say, but she believed he said it to himself.

One more bend around a particularly thick clump of bushes shaded by pine trees brought them within sight of a rough log cabin butted right up against the mountain. Ketta imagined that if you opened the back door—provided it had a back door—

you'd bump your nose on the hillside. Smoke rose from the plain stone chimney in a thin, gray mist.

Off to the side, a peeled pole corral held a half-dozen horses. A lean-to stood nearby. A hundred yards farther on, a rough shelter put a roof over what she thought must be a spring. And, of course, an outhouse stood beyond that.

Most discomfiting, however, was the man seated in a rickety looking rocker on the cabin's narrow porch.

Scar. Milt, the murderer. A shotgun lay across his lap, and he appeared to believe he owned this place.

Ketta, unaware of pinching Kuo's sides until he said, "ouch," recoiled as he slapped her hand away. Then he swore, although she didn't think he meant the swearing for her.

"Remember, no talking," he said softly. His lips didn't move.

She nodded, her head brushing his back. He tensed as one man stepped out of the cabin, and another appeared over by the corral. This one carried a pitchfork, but it didn't look like he intended on chucking hay. There was none to chuck. He held the tool like a weapon.

Ketta felt when Kuo sucked in a deep breath. "Don't touch my arms," he said to her, reaching down and loosening the loop holding his revolver securely in the holster. "If I get knocked off the horse, you get in the saddle and get out of here. Go fast. As fast as this horse can run."

She hiccuped and emitted something that sounded like a silent scream.

"Do you hear me?" he said.

"Yes."

But, in the end, it didn't come to that, and she didn't know whether to be glad or sorry.

"There you are." Milt rose to his feet, a smile distorting his mouth between straggles of facial hair. "What the hell took you so long? I was beginning to think you'd got yourself caught."

He peered around Kuo to where Ketta made herself small. "Still got the girl, I see. Well, that's fine."

Kuo sounded surprised. "Of course. She's my daughter. You have your sons, don't you?" He kept his attention on Milt, although Ketta had the impression he knew exactly where the other two men were standing as well. "When did you arrive?"

"Yesterday."

"And I see you're still riding a Rocking Box P horse. You think that's wise?"

Milt's chin thrust forward. "Anybody got an argument about it, I guess I know what to do."

Sliding from the horse, Kuo laughed as though he hadn't a care in the world. "You're looking for a noose around your neck, Milt. You realize that, don't you?"

"Yeah? And who's gonna put it there?"

"Might be Patton himself if you don't have a care. And I," here Ketta sensed menace in the way he talked to the man, "ain't exactly eager to have either Patton or the law coming around. Understand?"

"Yeah, yeah." More sullen than Yester sometimes got when Big Joe was ranting at him for some thing or another, Milt lost his smarmy grin. "I'll take the nag down to Ross's place and turn him loose. Satisfy you?"

"Better than nothing."

"Maybe I'll go tomorrow."

"Sooner is better than later."

By this time, the man over by the corral had poked the pitchfork into the barren ground near the lean-to and labored at rolling a smoke. Kind of awkward about it, too. He didn't look so dangerous to Ketta's eyes. With his smooth face and slicked back, brown hair, she figured he was only a couple years older than her brother. Not nearly so handsome, of course, as he'd inherited his father's prominent nose, though his bore no frightening, ridged scars.

The man standing in the cabin doorway was different. Slack-mouthed, bug-eyed, stoop shouldered, and scary-looking. It was hard to tell how old he was. Could've been either older or younger than the other one. And his nose was even worse, surely as large and flat as a bull's. She decided to avoid him altogether. In fact, Kuo gave her that exact advice as he helped her down, keeping the horse between them and the men.

"Stay away from them, child," he said, low enough she barely heard. "Don't talk to them. Don't get near them. Don't let them get near you. I don't think either one is right in the head. You got a problem, you call for me. Call me quick. Got that?"

He'd warned her already. Had he thought she didn't hear? Or did the double warning indicate he meant to frighten her into obedience?

Ketta's eyes opened wide and grew as round as her mother's, instead of tilting at the corners. "I want to go home," she whispered fiercely.

"You are home," Kuo said and turned on his heel. "Just mind me. Come along."

She followed, nearly treading on his heels going up the steps and passing Milt and the bug-eyed man. The young one's whole head seemed skewed, and she was sure there must be something awfully wrong with him. Wary, she kept an eye on him until she got inside.

The cabin didn't amount to much. A single room with a door shutting off what she supposed to be a bedroom at one end. A small stove to provide both heat, when necessary, and a place to cook. A low bench stood along one wall, with two shelves above it. Two chairs, a stool, and a table completed the furnishings.

A window looked out toward the trail into the valley. Weak light shone through the dust-streaked pane.

Dark, Ketta decided, looking around, her nose wrinkling,

would've been better.

"Phew." Kuo dropped his saddlebags on the table positioned in the center of the room. He had to clear a space first, the whole table being cluttered with filthy dishes and the remains of food. A mouse jumped and ran as the saddlebags landed almost on top of him.

Ketta wished she could do the same. Jump and run, that is. As it was, she only jumped. And squeaked.

She didn't even try to suppress the "Ugh" that slipped from her mouth. "Disgusting!"

Kuo's eyes, normally showing at least part of his half-white heritage, narrowed to dangerous slits.

"Milt," he roared, "get your ass in here."

A tremble started somewhere in Ketta's innards. Trouble coming. She knew it.

The doorway darkened. "What're you yelling about?" Milt asked. "Can't say as I appreciate being bellered at by a . . ."

Ketta knew what he meant to say. So did Kuo. *Chinaman.*

"This is my home," Kuo said, his voice very quiet. Ominously so, Ketta thought.

"Yeah. So?"

Kuo gestured. "What is this mess?"

He might've meant only the table's squalor, but his waving hand took in a pile of blankets dumped in the middle of the floor. Ketta caught the rankness of them from where she stood. A pair of grimy socks hung over the back of one of the chairs. Dirt and horse manure shaken from clumping boots made a path between door and table and, to a lesser degree, the stove.

Milt stared around, face blank. "What mess?"

Kuo stomped over to the inner door and flung it open. A bed was there. An empty whiskey bottle lay on its side beside it, while a pistol in a holster hung from a corner post. A mussed single blanket showed where the person who last occupied the bed hadn't bothered to remove his boots. A puddle of tobacco juice, complete with wad, dampened the floor.

Ketta gagged. Say what you will, at least Big Joe didn't chew tobacco. And neither, thank goodness, did Kuo.

"I don't sleep in a pigsty." Her father spoke quietly, calmly, and all the while she felt the anger seething below the surface of his words. "I don't eat in one, either. Get this garbage cleared out of here."

Milt seemed quite bewildered, as if he didn't understand plain English. "Clear it out? You mean . . ."

"I mean clean up your garbage."

The moon face of the bug-eyed man hung over Milt's shoulder. Maybe it gave Milt courage, because, shifting his feet, he stared right at Ketta.

"You need housekeeping, tell the girl to do it," he said. "My boys don't do woman's work."

Kuo's hand hovered close to the pistol on his hip. "In my house, people, men or women—or children—follow my rules. That one," he glanced quickly at the vacuous face of the man standing behind Milt and back again, "he can start by bringing a couple buckets of clean water and washing up these dishes."

Milt's lip curled in a sneer. His gaze traveled slowly around, ending up on Ketta. "Ain't much of a house."

"But it's mine. You can leave any time, you know." Kuo's chin lifted. "After you clean up after yourselves."

"Pa?" the bug-eyed man said. "What's he mean?"

Kuo answered. "I mean, fetch water, heat it up, and wash all the things you've dirtied. Which," he added, "seems to be everything in the house."

"Pa?" This time, the man whined.

Milt, watching Kuo, evidently came to some sort of conclusion. One that said it was in his best interests to follow Kuo's demand. "Do what he says, Dunce. You go on and get the water.

Guess we did make ourselves to home a leetle more free than we ought."

"Good choice," Kuo said.

Milt's grin at Kuo didn't come easy, Ketta could tell that. He hated Kuo for making him back down. What surprised her was that her father seemed to take it all at face value. And she knew she'd been proven right when she heard Milt muttering to himself as he and his addled son left.

"Might not be his house much longer," is what he said, low enough Ketta figured even the one he called Dunce didn't hear. But she did. And she was going to tell her father, too, just as soon as they were alone. She knew a threat when she heard one. But would Kuo believe her?

"After this, clean off your shoes before you come in," her father told them as they passed outside. No. He hadn't heard.

Chapter Fourteen: Yester

"Gol-dang it, Nat, where'd they get to?" Yester, red-eyed and grumpy from lack of sleep, spoke quietly, although he wanted to shout. Last night they'd been right behind his little sister and her kidnapper. Well, maybe a few hours behind, but now it appeared the pair had disappeared from the planet.

Nat, riding a couple horse lengths in front of Yester, turned, bracing himself with one hand on his cayuse's rump. "Dunno," he said. He sounded every bit as impatient as Yester.

"Thought your pa taught you to track a feather floating on the breeze," Yester said, rubbing it in a little more. This tracking business was all on Nat, and Yester had to admit he hadn't let him forget it for even a minute.

A flush turning Nat's brown face an odd rust color, he faced forward again. "Guess he didn't include windstorms in the program."

"I guess not."

Last night's wind had kept them both awake as treetops creaked and moaned, bushes whipped, and the horses stomped and shook their heads. The ponies hadn't liked the weather any better than the humans. To top it all off, they'd had to douse their small fire for fear of a blown ember setting the whole countryside aflame. At the time, they'd been glad to see the rain come down.

Anyway, this present setback wasn't Nat's fault, and Yester knew it, so he added, a bit too long after his first comment, "I don't imagine anybody could track anything after that. Maybe not even Fontaine himself."

Going by Nat's rigid back, straight and stiff as a poker, he wasn't exactly mollified. "I'll find them. Soon as they're on the move they'll be leaving traces again," he said.

Unless, Yester thought, keeping the idea to himself, they'd gotten where they were going and weren't leaving any traces for Nat to find. There'd been the campfire they'd seen in the distance, though, last night. If they could find that, maybe they'd pick up the trail again. Unless the fire had belonged to someone else.

"We should head for the campfire we saw," he started, only to have Nat turn again and glare at him.

"What do you think I'm doing, trying to find a cow to milk?" Nat huffed. "I ain't stupid, Yester."

"I know you ain't," Yester said, "I just—"

Nat cut him off again. Holding up a hand, he stopped and peered around. "Looks like somebody might've gone right through this opening here. It's worth checking."

"Here?" Yester gazed around. The "opening" Nat mentioned didn't look like much to him. Hardly enough room for a horse to pass, but when he examined the surrounding bushes closely, he did see where some small branches had been broken and leaves knocked off. "Could've been the wind. I don't see any traces of a horse."

Nat merely grunted and urged his pony through the bushes. Yester followed.

After a bit, they found a pile of horse manure, scattered, and covered with dust and leaves and twigs and such. "Looks old," Yester said.

"Yeah, but it isn't. It's from yesterday. See the way the bugs are crawling in it?"

Yester squinted down. Nat had good eyes. Better than his, at any rate. Yester could barely see the bugs, or only when they moved as they went about their business. He finally felt a little excitement. Even this much put them a hair closer to finding Ketta. He was surc of it. Well, wanted to believe so, anyway.

Pushing on, they followed a winding path, coming upon a tiny clear space surrounded by a few trees. The grass, thoroughly chewed down, was green at the nub, indicating ground water. A few charred remains of sticks showed where somebody had poured water on the fire. The soil beneath the fire was dry, that a few inches further from the center, was not. It seemed clear that, just as he and Nat had done, whoever had camped here had been cautious about their fire spreading.

Yester followed the sound of water and finally struck pay dirt. "Hey, Nat. It was them. We . . ." He stopped. Better give credit to the one who'd earned it. "You found them."

Nat pushed through the bushes to join him where Yester stared down at the small footprint in the waterlogged dirt surrounding the spring.

"Ketta," Nat breathed, his relief plain.

"Yep. You did it."

Modestly, Nat hung his head. "Got us this far, but we ain't found them yet."

"We will." Yester grinned. "You will."

Sure enough, it didn't take long before Nat found the fresh sign Kuo's horse had laid down. They mounted up and presently came back out onto the main trail. Only one set of tracks sullied the windswept path.

"I'm not a scout, but even I can see this," Yester said, excitement rising in him. "Look. This is the same horse we picked up earlier. The Chinaman's for sure."

"Yep," Nat said. Only moments later, he reined his cayuse to a stop. "Look here. See this?" He pointed down to where, as if out of nowhere, a second set of tracks joined their quarry's. Or not joined, because, as he told Yester, "Somebody besides us is following Kuo and Ketta."

Jaw dropping, Yester remarked it, too. "Where'd he come from?"

Nat shook his head. "Dunno. Made his way up from the river, I reckon."

"Maybe it's Patton."

"Doubt it. See, he wasn't tracking him. Appears to me like whoever it is knows where Kuo is going."

They looked at each other.

"How're we gonna get your sister away from *two* outlaws?" Nat finally asked.

Easy to tell Nat was worried, Yester thought. He wasn't alone in that. Yester worried, too, fear for Ketta running through him like a whole peck of rats gnawing at his innards. He had to bring Ketta home, safe and well. Ma had said so, and as poorly as she'd been when he left, he'd never be able to go home without his sister. Not and face his ma.

Never go home. He'd made a promise. Smart-mouth talk, and now he had to make good on it.

They'd gone more than a mile before Nat called Yester's attention to the fact he hadn't gotten an answer to his question. The one about rescuing Ketta from two outlaws.

"I dunno," Yester said. "I've got the rifle."

Nat snorted. "I've got a knife, which probably won't do much good. Yester, we know Kuo is armed. Nobody who robs a store goes in barehanded. Anyway, you said you saw it. I expect anybody he deals with has a gun, too."

"Yeah. I imagine so."

The horses plodded on through yet another flawless summer day rapidly growing hotter and hotter, just like Yester's temper. "Maybe I oughta sit out on the hillside and take pot shots at them from a distance."

"While you're hiding behind a rock," Nat agreed. "Ambush. That's one idea."

"Safest." Yester thought a moment. "Surest. I'm a pretty fair shot."

"Just like shooting a deer." Nat paused. "Except, Yester, they ain't deer. Deer don't shoot back."

Yester kind of got the shakes just thinking about it. "So, I gotta make the first shot count."

They rode a little farther, until they reached an area where trees grew more thickly and a smaller trail led off the larger one. Sure enough, both sets of the tracks leading them to this spot headed off into the narrow cut.

Nat drew rein. "I dunno, Yester. I got a bad feeling about this place."

The walls of the cut towered above them, blue sky showing directly overhead, but deep shade overlay most of the trail itself.

Eyeing the way the tracks led into the distance, wending around blind corners and stone outcroppings easy for ambushers to hide behind, Yester's feelings paralleled Nat's. He stopped beside Nat and pondered.

"What do you think about leaving the horses here and exploring a bit on foot? Get above the trail."

"You think somebody is watching for us?"

"Maybe not for us, but for somebody. Patton, maybe. Or maybe even my pa."

"Your pa?" Nat gave him a look. "Your pa has his horses back, and he doesn't care about Ketta."

"Yes, but the Chinaman doesn't know that. Or not for sure, anyway. Maybe he thinks . . ." Yester's lips clamped together. "Might depend on what Ketta has told him."

Opening his dark eyes wide in surprise, Nat said, "You think Ketta told him anything?"

With a sigh, Yester stepped to the ground. "She might.

Depends on what those outlaws have done to her. And I don't blame her," he added.

"I don't, either." Nat slid down beside his friend and, slipping the bit from his horse's mouth so it could graze, tied the cayuse to the spike of a branch on a downed log. He stood beside the animal. "You coming?"

Ketta

Ketta didn't care for the way that awful old scar-faced Milt watched her, inspecting every move she made. No. And not his dim-witted, bull-nosed sons, either. Even once when she went to the privy, which was located down a well-worn path about fifty yards from the cabin. Cracks in the privy's weathered boards made the little building less than private. She had good reason to fret, Ketta thought. Especially since there was Milt, a straw stuck between his crooked teeth and his lips all slack and hanging half open, waiting when she came out. He'd stood there for the whole time she was inside, legs crossed at the ankles as he leaned against a tree.

Kuo was sitting at the table drinking a cup of coffee when she returned to the cabin. She was almost running and breathless, eager to be back by her father's side.

"What's the matter?" he asked after a single glance at her face. He'd been watching Dunce mop the floor and, from the looks of all the water splashed around, making a fairly decent job of it.

"Nothing." She slipped onto a chair at his side, trembling a little.

She had all his attention now. "Nothing?" he said. "Then why are you shaking? Did one of the men say something to scare you?" His voice went cold. "Did one of them touch you?"

Mute, Ketta shook her head. Just touched her with his eyes, that's all. Bad enough.

"What then?"

She shook her head again, but this time, her fears bubbled to the surface. "He watched me. I went to the necessary, and he followed me. Just stood there. I think he can see through the cracks."

"Who can?"

"Him." Ketta glanced through the open doorway to where Milt was ambling across the yard to where Beaver—that was the name of Milt's less addled son—was whiling away the morning with a game that seemed a bit like horseshoes.

"Milt? Or Beaver?"

"Milt." She hated even saying his name.

Her father, zeroing in on the direction of her gaze, went still before shaking his head. "Not likely he can see through the cracks, child. But don't go out again without telling me. I'll watch, make sure he doesn't step out of line."

Ketta gave him a stare. "He's a horrible man. I wish he would go away."

"Yes, he is, and yes, I, too, wish he'd go away," Kuo muttered, low enough she barely heard. His mouth, which had worn a half smile only a moment before, had straightened to a thin slit. He glanced at Dunce, still swinging the mop back and forth across the plank floor. Louder, he said, "Things aren't that simple."

One of Ketta's feet kicked against a chair leg. "Why not? You said this is your place." Her gaze traveled around the cabin's dark and shoddy interior. "You could make him leave, I bet. Him and him," she pointed at Dunce, "and the other one, too." As a clincher, she added, "That's what Big Joe would do."

Kuo, his face settling into hard lines, slammed his tin cup of coffee onto the table.

Ketta jumped, wide-eyed as coffee splattered across the mess still littering the tabletop from other cups and other meals. The commotion caused Dunce to gawk their way.

"If I was Big Joe, little priss," Kuo snapped, "you'd be missing your front teeth for taking a smart-mouth tone to your father like you done. Do it again, and maybe I'll take a lesson from Joe Noonan. One you won't like."

Blinking violently, Ketta shrank into herself. She should've known. Men always took another man's part, even if he was a bitter enemy. It was just something they did, fair or not. Well, that was all right then. She knew she had only herself to depend on when it came to escaping this whole nest of evil men. She placed her father among the group. Here she'd been thinking—wishing—he was better, kinder, than she knew, but she'd been wrong. He was a thief, after all, and worse. A horse thief, which, according to Big Joe, was the worst of the worst, more despicable even than a girl thief.

Resolve hardening, a list formed in her mind. She had to pick a time to collect something to eat, saddle a horse—not always an easy task for anyone as small as she—and find her way down the trail to the main road. All without anyone catching her at it. Tonight, maybe. The sooner the better, while she still remembered how they'd gotten here.

Tonight, for sure.

Although, and here a smidgeon of worry edged into her plans, coming here they hadn't traveled at night. Everything looked different in the dark.

Meanwhile, threats or no threats, she planned on sticking close to Kuo.

Ketta settled herself and hung her head, her cloud of hair hiding her face. "Sorry," she said, hoping he couldn't tell a lie from the truth. "I won't do it again."

"Better not." Mollified, Kuo got to his feet. Raising his voice, he said, "Dunce, that's enough. It'll take two days for this floor to dry, as much water as you've slopped around. Go see if Milt has any chores for you to do."

Ketta almost laughed at the way Dunce dropped the mop right there in the middle of the floor and high-tailed it outside. Almost. Because apparently her catalog of chores now included cleaning up what everyone else left unfinished, like the mopping and the stack of dirty dishes. She was pretty sure some of them had been used more than once between washings. Thoroughly revolted, she set to work with a will.

Come noon, the outlaws piled into the cabin demanding food. Ketta, not much to her surprise, had been charged with preparing the meal, and she ranged from stove top to stew pot to table as quickly as possible. Sooner done, the sooner they'd be out of there.

No doubt it was too much to hope there wouldn't be a problem, that, it turned out, being the shortage of chairs. Although, Ketta thought, any excuse would've done.

As their right, Kuo and Milt had claimed the two chairs. Dunce, a goopy grin on his face, snagged the stool, which left Beaver gaping about.

"There's a bench over there," Kuo said, attempting to forestall the battle he saw coming. "Grab it, Beaver."

Kuo's instruction fell on intentionally deaf ears.

Already piqued, Ketta snorted with disgust when Beaver shoved Dunce out of his way and yanked the stool out from under his brother. Dunce, clumsy at best, fell backward into the table. A bowl's worth of stew spilled as Dunce landed in Milt's lap, Milt having been the first to the table. Or pig to the trough, as Ketta termed the competition to herself. Milt, compounding the foofaraw, pushed Dunce away, causing the bread Ketta had sliced into fifteen precise slices, to sway on its stack and three pieces tumble to the floor.

Without a word, she picked the bread up, brushed it off, and put a slice onto each of the three outlaws' plates.

Milt, of course, set loose an explosion of curses. "The hell. I ain't eating that."

"Why not?" Ketta said. "He," she pointed at Dunce, acting as if she didn't know his name, "just mopped. The floor's cleaner than your clothes. You'd eat the bread if it'd fallen on your shirt, wouldn't you?"

"Sass," he yelled, fist plunging through the air somewhere close to where her ear had been a fraction of a second ago.

Adept at ducking, due no doubt to Big Joe's training, she no longer stood in that spot.

Bent on going after her, Milt lunged to his feet even as Dunce and Beaver stood back. Dunce's mouth hung open as he settled in to watch the fun of a girl being beat to a pulp.

They weren't attending to Kuo, who grasped Ketta's shoulders and set her out of the line of fire.

"That's enough," he said. "Settle down, all of you. And quit your grousing. You've all eaten worse than a slice of bread that's been dropped on the floor." His lip curled. "Even on this floor. Judging by the filth you left on my table, none of you are any better than a bunch of hogs."

Gratefully, Ketta glanced at him, amazed their thoughts coincided so precisely. How odd.

"What the hell, you damn Chink? You don't talk to a white man like that." Hard-faced and showing his temper, Milt's hand moved toward the pistol at his side before seeming to think better of it. Then, smiling with what looked like evil intent, he stepped in with his fists raised to pound the smaller man instead.

Kuo, ready for him, looked almost as enthusiastic. He fended off Milt's first swing, catching the blow on his forearm. Although the slighter man by twenty pounds or so, he pushed the outlaw out the door and onto the narrow porch. They squared off there.

Beaver and Dunce followed, jumping around and Dunce yelling his support for Milt. After a pause, Ketta ventured out, too.

Milt looked to have the advantage. At first. And it was apparent he thought so, as he went into the fight with his lips pulled into a grin. The larger man by far, with a longer reach, he barreled in ready to surround Kuo in a bear hug and squeeze the life out of him.

But Kuo's first quick, solid blow to the ear changed Milt's mind about grappling. The outlaw stepped back, landing a roundhouse punch on Kuo's upper arm that made the smaller man shake out his hand like it'd gone numb.

Ketta, feeling more than a little sick, reached back inside the cabin and grabbed the carbine one of the men, she thought it was Beaver, had brought inside and left by his chair.

She didn't really trust her father much. Barely more than the others, truth to tell, but the fact remained she couldn't let Milt kill him as seemed his intention. Kuo stood between her and the outlaws. In more ways than one.

Like right now, as the men bobbed and shifted and swung about, so fast Ketta could barely follow. The carbine hung useless in her hands. She didn't want to be the one who killed her father. Unfortunately, he literally did stand between her and Milt. Holding fire, she waited for the two to turn about.

One of the two uttered a pained sounding grunt as a blow landed. Air wheezed out of someone's lungs. A second meaty thud sent both of them to the splintered porch floor. Sweat flew in big salty drops from both men.

Kuo, first up, landed a blow on Milt's mouth that made blood spurt all the way to the yard. His knuckles came away scarred and bloody.

Roaring his pain, the outlaw barreled in with a punch aimed for Kuo's jaw. It missed, instead striking Kuo in the eye socket as he ducked. Kuo dropped, falling onto his back.

Cackling his glee, Milt flung himself onto Kuo's weakened

body, only to fly backward as Kuo twisted, caught the outlaw on his feet and, with a strong thrust of his legs, sent him tumbling. Milt bucked up onto his hands and knees, breath wheezing in and out of his lungs like a broken concertina as he struggled to breathe.

Kuo rolled twice as Beaver started forward. Kuo sat up onto his rear end, spun, and, with a strong sweeping motion of one foot, took Beaver's legs out from under him. Beaver ended up stretched out beside Milt. Dunce, wisely, considering his intellect, made no moves but stood with his arms dangling.

Which was just as well as Ketta brought the carbine up into shooting position. She worked the lever, drawing a cartridge into the chamber.

"Stop," she cried. "Everybody just stop." The carbine pointed first at Dunce, the only one besides herself still standing, then Milt, Beaver, and, finally, even Kuo, who got slowly to his feet.

"Easy, child." Kuo touched the knob forming on his forehead. "We're done." He looked at Milt out of his one good eye. "Aren't we?"

Milt wiped his hand across his bloody mouth and spat a tooth attached to an inch-long root onto the ground. He grinned, even as his eyes glared with hate. "For now."

"Until next time." Kuo nodded and said to Ketta, "Put the gun down."

If Ketta'd had to make a guess, she'd have said there was a promise in Kuo's few words to the outlaw. The "until next time" part.

She didn't want to obey. Maybe this very instant was her chance to get away. But they were all watching her, each man ready to jump her if she gave him the chance. Yes, even her father, whom she felt certain she'd saved from a terrible beating, at the least. After a while, she let the carbine drop.

★ ★ ★ ★ ★

Ketta spied the horse and rider before anyone else. Easy enough to do since she was the only one not involved with a game utilizing cards, dice, and the frequent exchange of money, all accompanied by a great deal of swearing. Her father, to her dismay, appeared to have forgotten the fight. Overlooked it, at any rate. He lost himself in the game, to the point of being blind to his surroundings. Although that may have been caused by his left eye, swollen almost shut from the fight with Milt.

She had to tug three times on his sleeve in order to gain his attention. And he wasn't pleased with the distraction.

He shook her off, his good eye narrowing as he scowled. "What do you want? Don't bother me when I'm busy."

Busy? Ketta thought, disgusted. "Someone is coming," she said, also for the third time.

Apparently, this finally sank in, with Milt also taking note, as a small grin skewed his face and made his lip bleed again.

"Is it him?" Beaver asked Milt, the only words Ketta had ever heard him utter. Alert now, Kuo looked up. His gaze shifted from Milt to Beaver and back again. "You expecting somebody?" he asked Milt.

"Who, me?" But Milt's question pretty much answered itself if the grin on his ugly face meant anything.

And Ketta, glancing up into her father's face, clearly saw unease paint itself there, even masked by his black and swollen eye.

Chapter Fifteen: Yester

"Slow down, we don't want to barge into a trap," Yester said, studying the terrain in front of them. The way the path narrowed and forced anyone on horseback into riding single file worried him. He didn't like the way the tall, narrow canyon shut out the sun, either. Shadows dappled the fallen stones, perfect cover for anyone hiding in ambush. "Let's scout the way ahead for a mile or so, then come back for the horses. I don't want to leave them along the trail for long. Never know who might come along and leave us afoot."

"You think there's more of these damn outlaws coming up behind us?" No mistaking the alarm in Nat's voice.

"I don't know. But I ain't forgot there were four of the bastards that"—Yester hesitated, then went on—"that burned our ranch, stole our horses, and took Ketta."

He didn't miss the quick look Nat shot him. Figured he knew what it meant, too. Nat was wondering about Ma, but Yester couldn't bring himself to talk out loud about what had happened to her. It wasn't a thing he felt free to discuss. Not even with a sympathetic friend.

And what had Pa meant when he said "maybe the woman wouldn't be there, either." Did he mean she'd just be gone? That he'd throw her out like a used-up broom? Or did he mean she'd be dead?

He bit down on the thoughts. Not now. He had to save Ketta and only think about how to do it.

Nat, as always sensitive to the reason behind Yester's

reticence, didn't press the matter. "Yeah, and the only ones we know for sure are ahead of us are Kuo and Ketta. And now this other one. Unless he's one of Patton's men on the same trail we are."

For a moment, Yester's heart lifted. Could that be? "That'd be fine, I guess, but don't count on it."

"I'm not."

Yester lifted his rifle from the scabbard on his saddle and propped the gun over his shoulder. He made sure of the handful of shells in his pocket then, sucking in a breath, led off. The tracks that had led them here soon petered out on the hard, rock-strewn ground, but he wasn't worried. It was impossible for the riders to have taken any other way. Striding out strongly, he'd gone only a few yards when a touch on his back brought him around.

"You make as much noise as a herd of cattle," Nat said. "Watch where you put your feet. I don't want to be shot by some yahoo sitting up on the ridge using me for target practice."

Yester felt his face getting hot. Here he was supposed to be the leader and instead was acting like he'd never heard of the word *stealth*. "Sorry."

After that he made every effort to walk more softly. Couldn't help making some noise, though. No matter how hard he tried for silence, his boots on the gravelly ground just plain made more racket than Nat's moccasins. In ten or so minutes, they reached what Nat decided was about a mile from where they'd left the horses. Relieved, they stopped, puffing a little.

"You see anything?" Yester asked.

"No. You want me to go back and bring up the horses?" Nat started to turn, stopping with one foot poised above the ground. "Heh! You hear that?"

At first Yester heard nothing but his own breathing, the heaviness of which told him they'd been going uphill in a fairly rapid ascent. That and the cry of a bird as it flew overhead, gliding on still wings.

"No." But then he did hear something, and he frowned. "What the heck is going on?"

Nat put his foot down, closed his eyes, and cocked his head. "People shouting."

Yester heard them, too. "Are they laughing?"

Nat listened some more. "I think so." His eyes were rounded when he opened them. "I heard several different voices. There are more men here than we thought, Yester. What are we going to do?"

"I dunno." But he did know. The more raucous and louder those voices became, the more determined he grew. This wasn't just Ketta and her "father." He had the hope this Kuo feller was treating her right. But now, with more men in the picture, all of them apparently around the next bend whooping and hollering like a bunch of crazy drunks, well, it put a different complexion on things.

A sudden vision of his ma, lying on the ground burned, beaten, and broken swam into his sight. Ketta was just a kid. Pretty, though. He had the troubled, worse, the frightening thought of what a group of scoundrels might do to an innocent girl like her provided they got the chance. And Ketta. Hell, she'd never even been away from home before. She'd have no idea what to do against men like this. If there was anything she *could* do.

Was that the very thing going on now?

Fighting sickness away, he looked over at Nat. "What do you want to do?"

"We have to go on."

Yester's jaw set. "Well, c'mon, then. Let's see what all the commotion is about."

Grim faced, Nat nodded.

A couple minutes later, taken by surprise when the short canyon ended, they came close to walking right out into the open. Nat, in the lead again, shot out an arm to bar Yester from going any farther.

They found themselves at the entrance to a narrow meadow. A couple hundred yards farther on—give or take—a small, rough cabin edged up against the hill rising sharply behind it. Off to one side stood a privy and a corral for the horses standing hipshot in the shade of a few spindly aspens.

The only man stirring himself was unsaddling a weary-appearing spotted horse. Apparently, they, man and horse, had just arrived, not more than a few minutes before Yester and Nat. It'd been a near thing that they'd avoided catching up with whoever he might be. A shootist, Yester thought, or maybe a gunslinger, drawing the term from a dime novel he'd read as he took note of the twin, tied-down holsters low on the man's hips.

He nudged Nat, pointing toward the man with the guns.

"I see him. Crap," Nat said. "Who is he?"

"Dunno." Yester studied on the fact several men surrounded the newcomer in a welcoming and approving sort of way. He had a hunch were he and Nat to show up, they wouldn't be treated so politely.

Nat had more on his mind. "Lookit, Yester. There's five of them." He sounded dismayed.

"I can count." Yeah, but Yester almost wished he couldn't.

"And where's Ketta? I don't see her anywhere."

The omission worried Yester, too. And then he thought maybe it was a good thing. "She's probably in the cabin," he said, taking a guess, and, sure enough, the cabin door opened right then, and his sister's tousled head poked out in a cautious kind of way. Beside him, Nat drew in a sharp breath.

"She doesn't look hurt," he said.

"No, she doesn't." It was too far to see her features from this distance. All he knew for certain was that she appeared fine when she stepped out and peered over at the men at the corral. Apparently, she had use of her limbs, anyway, unbound and free. Good. She'd be able to run, when the time came.

Nat must've been thinking along the same lines, almost like he'd read Yester's mind. "Wish she knew we were here. So, maybe she could sneak outta there and meet up with us. Then maybe you wouldn't have to shoot anybody."

"I don't mind shooting one of them. Any of them. All of them that gets in our way." Yester's words came out gruff. And he meant every one.

"Goes without saying," Nat replied, then went on to say it. "They deserve a hanging, if you ask me. But if you shoot one, Yester, try for that feller packing two pistols. I wouldn't mind takin' one of his guns home with me. A keepsake."

Yester nodded. "And I'll take the leftover. I been wanting a six-shooter. Had a coyote jump out right under Flint's nose the other day. Could've used it then. By the time I got the rifle outta my scabbard he was long gone."

Some part of him was thinking, who cares? Why'd he even mention a flea-bitten coyote with this situation under way? He knew, though. Because he didn't have to put the plan in motion while he talked about something else. Anything else.

Before too many minutes passed, the newest arrival at the cabin had run a brush over his horse, watered it, and tipped a bait of grain into a wooden trough. With much elbowing and raucous laughter, the men went into the cabin, closing the door behind the last one.

Yester and Nat exchanged a look.

"We'd better move up," Yester said. "Scout the area." After a moment he added, "In case we have to make a run for it."

Nat nodded. "You and me, we can outrun those outlaws any

day of the week. Best if we know where we're running to, though."

Yester had to grin. " 'Specially if they're shooting at us."

"Huh. Had to say that, didn't you? I'm not sure Ketta can run fast enough."

"None of us can outrun a bullet."

They were silent a moment before Nat said, "We'll have to each take her by an arm and scoot her along, if she can't." His Adam's apple moved up and down as if his throat were as dry as Yester's own.

Yester found the waiting hard. Minutes ticked past. The horses in the corral, after a little fight that involved head shaking and whinnies over the oats the rider had set out for his pinto, settled down to drowsing in the sun. Birds took up their lackadaisical flight across the meadow, some alighting to peck at the earth. It grew hotter, the boys sweating as they poised to make a dash across the open.

"I'll go first," Nat said, "towards the corral. Soon as I reach cover, you go the opposite way. We'll wait until Ketta comes out." His cheeks turned dusky as he nodded toward the privy, which sat closest to his side. "She'll have to come out sometime."

He didn't bother to wait for Yester's agreement. Rising from where he hunkered in the lee of tumbled boulders, he slipped from place to place until settling down behind some brush halfway between the corral and the privy. The thing is, he didn't run. The horses remained calm, and even the birds appeared to take no notice.

Yester took a breath when Nat settled in place. The first breath, he figured, since his friend had moved. He gasped for air like he'd been socked in the gut. By a giant.

His turn now. One last check of the closed cabin door, the quiet horses, the peaceful silence. Taking a hint from Nat, he, too, went slowly, hunched over and willing himself not to run, to be invisible.

The opening of the door caught him when he was halfway to his selected destination. A man stood in the cabin doorway. He was looking over his shoulder and saying something to those inside.

Yester collapsed to the ground behind a scrawny clump of fireweed and froze, his face pressed into the earth.

KETTA

Kuo's question of whether Milt was expecting company had a quick answer. Slurping a final *glug* of whiskey, Milt left the half-empty bottle on the table and, followed by Beaver and Dunce, swarmed out the door. Abandoned cards fluttered to the floor.

"Is it him?" Dunce was saying. "Is it Heller?"

Heller. What kind of name is that? Ketta wondered. It sounded like a dog. And she didn't mean a little lap dog, like Mama had told her about. Something called a poodle.

Kuo got up more slowly and went to stand in the open doorway. Expression frozen, he watched the reunion taking place outside. After a moment, he touched Ketta's shoulder as she tried to look around him. "Stay inside, child. Don't speak. Don't do anything to draw attention to yourself."

"Who is it?"

"The devil."

Ketta glanced up at him. He meant it, she saw. He really did think the newcomer was the devil. And if he seemed a devil to Kuo, the man must be fearsome indeed. Her chest felt tight, as if she might explode.

"Has he come for me?" she whispered.

Kuo shook himself, sort of like Barney shaking off rain or worry, and smiled down at her. But it wasn't a real smile. She knew that. It looked like the ones her mother bestowed upon her about the time Big Joe was due home from his monthly toot.

"Nah," Kuo said. "I reckon he's just meeting up with Milt and came here 'cause it's out of the way. They probably have a job in mind."

"A job?" Ketta had a hard time thinking anybody in this world would want to hire Milt for anything. Beaver or Dunce, either, for that matter. Her father was lying. She knew it.

"Probably not the kind of job you're thinking of." Kuo's reply confounded her further as he prepared to join the men. Preparations that included strapping on a gunbelt and a holster with the butt end of a large revolver sticking out of it. "Wait here." He glanced around. "Sit over by the stove. Try to avoid anybody taking notice of you. Don't get in anybody's way. And don't talk to any of them."

"Should I go in the other room?" There was a small room behind the main one, which Ketta's exploration had found to contain, along with a filthy, dirty bed, bits and pieces of mining equipment, the hides of animals evidently trapped during the winter, and a few supplies.

Kuo shook his head at her question. "No. One of them is apt to think that's an invitation."

"Invitation?" she asked, but he was already explaining.

"There's no way out. At least, no easy way out. At least if you—" He shut it off. "Don't worry. They'll soon be gone. All of them."

She nodded but wasn't sure she believed him. He didn't believe it himself. She could tell.

Her father jumped from the porch and went to join the others, acting as if the newcomer was indeed an honored guest. Ketta couldn't resist poking her head around the corner and stepping out to take a long look.

After a bit, she retreated and took up the sheltered space

behind the stove. Sweat sprouted on her forehead and down her back, but she hardly felt it. There were more important things to worry about.

"Where's the girl?" Heller peered around the cabin, the interior dark to anyone coming from outside as Dunce, the last one in, closed the door.

Kuo froze, blocking the two young men behind him.

"Light the lamp, Dunce," Milt ordered his son. "Heller's of a mind to see what he's buying."

But Dunce, in shoving past Kuo, fell over the stool as he lunged ahead to do his father's bidding. Inadvertently, he bumped into Heller.

"Idiot," Heller said, pushing the clumsy kid out of the way. "Just open the damn door." He made an impatient gesture, and Beaver hastened to reopen it, sending a shaft of sunlight across the rough plank floor.

Ketta went as still as a chipmunk under a hawk's eye. Even so, it wasn't long before Milt spied her in the corner, doing her best to make herself small. He pointed at her.

"Come out of there," the stranger, Heller, rumbled.

Ketta looked at her father.

His jaw tightened, and he gave a short nod. "Get some food on the table, child," he said. "It's coming on for suppertime."

It lacked an hour or so, but who was counting? Doubting she had any choice, Ketta rose and went to the stove. "The woodbox is empty." Her voice came out breathless and . . . scared. "I'll go get some."

She'd run. The moment she got outside, she'd flee, horse or no horse. Maybe no horse was better. They'd have a terrible time tracking her on foot once she was away from the cabin, if only she could stay hidden until dark. Plans rushed through her head like water down the river in springtime. She'd—

Milt's fist came down on the table, rattling the dice and whiskey bottle still standing there. "Dunce, you go get the wood."

Heller reached for the bottle, but his eyes were on Ketta, studying her as if he, for sure, was the hawk and she the chipmunk. "Fetch me a clean glass, girl," he said.

Ketta looked at Kuo again.

"I told her to stay out of the way," her father said. "Didn't want her causing any trouble between the boys."

Heller's gaze hadn't shifted. "I can see where she might. She ain't all yellow and slanty-eyed like most of these Chink girls. Looks almost white."

"Told you so," Milt said. "Purdy as a pitcher. Gotta sassy mouth on her, though. Might take a beatin' or two to straighten her out and make her behave."

Something inside Ketta's chest fluttered and wouldn't go away. Why didn't Kuo say something? Why didn't he tell those men to skeddadle? To leave her alone. Defend himself, while he was at it, although maybe it was all right for a man to be a "Chink," but not for a girl.

Or was he scared, too?

Yes.

The realization shook her to the core.

Heller snapped his fingers, reminding Ketta of the way Big Joe called Barney to him. "You, girl," he said to her. "I said fetch me a glass. Now."

Once again Ketta looked to Kuo, at which he gave a small nod. Feet dragging, she went over to a shelf her father had affixed to the logs at some time or another and took down one of the jars from which the men had taken to drinking their hootch.

Heller watched her all the way, so that she thought sure he physically touched her, and she shivered. Setting the glass in front of him, she backed away, twisting aside when he tried to nab her wrist.

"You better get her trained," Heller snarled, staring at Kuo with eerie intensity. "I ain't shelling out good money for a sassy-mouthed brat who doesn't mind."

Ketta gasped. "I am a human being," she shouted. "I am not a slave. I am not for sale."

Heller lunged out of his chair, one hand grasping her hair and jerking her face up toward him. His other hand slammed down, catching her cheekbone a solid blow.

The pain overwhelmed. Ketta let out a short shriek before the world and everything in it went black. She was unaware until Kuo told her later, when she complained about her scalp hurting, that she'd hung suspended by her hair for a long five seconds. Until, in fact, Kuo snatched his revolver from its holster and pointed it at Heller, who finally laughed and let her drop.

Head buzzing, she came out of the blackness to hear Kuo shouting at the men. All of them, not just Heller. "Enough. She's right, she isn't for sale. Any deal you made with Milt is off. Damaging my property is not part of the agreement."

"Say, Milt," Heller drawled, "I thought you said the sale was all arranged. Don't look like it to me. I rode all the way out here to take delivery, not get held up by a misbegotten Chinaman. I don't take kindly to it, neither."

"Kuo . . ." Milt said, drawing out his name as if in warning.

Somewhere above her head, Ketta heard hissing, like an angry cat arguing with a snarling dog.

Presently, the hissing turned into words. "Get out." Kuo's whisper held double menace. "All of you. Saddle up and go. This is your only warning."

Heller chuckled. "You sure you're calling the shots, Kuo? Look around. I see four men lined up against you. You and the girl."

"But my gun is out and cocked, Heller. Even you can't beat a bullet aimed right at you. And you, you're the one in my sights."

Ketta opened one eye, the only eye, she discovered, she could see out of, to find Kuo standing, legs spraddled, above her. The barrel of his pistol was directly overhead, his fist around the grip, his finger on the trigger.

"Well then," Heller said, slow and easy. He raised his hands halfway into the air. "Looks like you've got me."

"Sonuvabitch!" Milt said. "Heller, don't blame me. I didn't know he'd renege on the deal."

"*I* made no such deal." Kuo looked as fierce as a snarling cougar, his lips drawn back over gnashing teeth.

"Well, Milt. Seems I do blame you." Heller's colorless eyes flashed like lights in the dark. "But I blame him more. He won't live through this day."

"Threats," Kuo said, as if scorning the idea. "Leave now." His gun barrel didn't waver. "Now."

Feet shuffled. "I'm going," Dunce said.

"Yeah," Beaver, the silent one, agreed.

The clomping of boots continued on out the door.

"For now," Milt snarled. "Kuo, this ain't over. You're making me look bad to my good friend Heller. That just ain't right, you being who you are. Be warned. If he don't get you, I will."

"Get out, I said!" Kuo shouted anew. "All of you."

Heller, when Ketta peeked up at him, said nothing more. Even with blurred vision she saw he had a loopy little grin on his bewhiskered face. It bothered her more than if he'd been shouting.

He and Kuo's eyes were locked. They remained that way until first Milt, then Heller, backed all the way outside.

Kuo stepped over Ketta and slammed the door shut. There was a bar to put across it. He dropped it in place, then stood there a moment, his face bleak, before holstering his revolver and reaching down to pick her up.

Ketta could barely lift her head. She cried silently, hot tears sliding down her cheeks. If only Yester were here. Or no. She wouldn't wish him mixed in this situation. Not even for her freedom.

Kneeling, Kuo gathered her to him.

And she let him.

A bullet whizzed through the small window past her father's head and plowed into the rough table. The table rocked under the impact, knocking over the whiskey bottle and spreading the raw smell of cheap alcohol as it soaked into the wood.

The first single shot was soon followed by a barrage of gunfire. The window shattered into a million pieces that flew everywhere in the room. The noise was almost enough to make Ketta pass out again. Kuo pressed her flat onto the floor, his body the weight to hold her down.

Finally, the din ended as the outlaws' guns emptied. Abrupt silence vibrated with its own echo.

Kuo lay still, Ketta locked in his arms. "Well, child." His face was pale and frozen looking as he gazed down at her. "Looks like we're in for it now."

Chapter Sixteen: Yester

Yester pressed his face into the earth. He figured he might as well get used to it seeing as how he'd probably be there for eternity. Those damn outlaws had to be looking right at him and planning to use him for target practice. How could they not? He lay in what must be plain sight. Why were they delaying?

After a minute, when nothing happened, he lifted his head an inch off the ground and parted the branches of the fireweed he'd fallen behind.

"What the hell?" His breath stirred the dust, the whole yard as hot and dry as that desert he'd read about. The one in Africa, where lions and elephants roamed.

His guts shriveled when two men stampeded out of the cabin and jumped off the porch into the yard. They were the two who hadn't been in Pullman with the rest of the gang. They weren't taking in the view, though. No, sir. They both were staring back into the cabin's dark interior like something real interesting was going on inside.

He didn't dare move, even if the two were occupied. Who knows what the others were up to. Maybe these fellers were just a tease.

Sure wished he could see what held them enthralled. Somehow, where Ketta was concerned, he doubted it was anything good.

Loud voices carried to him. Some cussing. Something that,

from the tone, sounded like threats. Finally, a man yelled, "Get out, I said! All of you," and two more men backed out of the cabin. They moved more slowly than the first two.

Yester caught a glimpse of a gun barrel gleaming in a ray of sunlight. Looked to him as if there must've been a falling out between the outlaws. What did that mean for Ketta?

The door slammed shut. The four men outside stood as if dumbfounded, staring at the door, before one of them gestured the others in closer for a hobnob. One of them stepped off to the side of the cabin, to about where Yester would've been if he'd made it across the open ground, and fired off a shot through a little window.

Yester jumped, the fireweed waving in front of his face.

He'd seen the man, a real ugly galoot, before. A scarred-up feller as homely as a hobgoblin, the feller had been with Kuo at the bar in Pullman. If Yester had to guess he'd say the two weren't such good friends now as they'd seemed then.

The crack of the shot had barely faded before the other three men drew their weapons and opened fire on the cabin. Yester could hardly believe his eyes—and his ears protested the racket. Over at the corral, horses startled by the noise commenced bucking and running inside the circle. Dust flew; one of them kicked a hole in the watering trough.

Nat, hidden practically inside the corral itself, took the opportunity to make a dash for cover closer to the cabin.

Just like Yester had to do.

Now or never, he told himself. Sucking in a mouthful of air, he jumped to his feet and ran, four, then five strides. His long body landed in a forward dive, finding shelter behind a loosely stacked pile of wood. He figured he'd never moved so fast in his life. And maybe as soundlessly. Who knew, considering the gunfire and the whinnying of several frantic horses?

Releasing his breath, he chanced poking his head around the

woodpile just in time for a "ping" to sound and a splinter of wood to pierce his cheek.

"Damn." Drawing back faster than a worm into its hole, he dabbed at blood with his shirt sleeve. A ricochet. The outlaws hadn't spotted him. If they had, the stack of wood would've been riddled by now, and his body as full of holes as a window screen.

The shooting stopped.

After maybe sixty seconds, the horses slowed their frightened pacing and went still.

The man who'd arrived just ahead of him and Nat ducked down and reloaded his firearms. The rest of the men followed suit and then stood shouting and making rude gestures toward the cabin. They muttered a little among themselves, but Yester couldn't hear what they were saying.

Weren't they afraid of being shot? Yester was torn between admiration for their nerve and disgust at their stupidity.

Why hadn't Kuo shot back at them? That's what Yester couldn't figure. And maybe the outlaws couldn't, either, because, after a minute or so, the ugly son-of-a-gun he'd recognized called out, "Hi, Kuo. You alive in there?"

"I'm alive," Kuo shouted back. "You and your boys, and Heller, too, better pack up and go. You ain't welcome here no more."

The ugly feller did an angry little dance, puffs of dust rising beneath his boots. "You're the one ain't welcome, Chink. We're taking over this here hideout."

"Yeah," a younger one shouted, shaking his fist.

The gunslinger fellow grabbed Ugly and said something in his ear. Ugly nodded and yelled, "Heller says we'll let you live, long as you're the one to pack up and go."

Gunslinger said something more, and Ugly repeated, "Do that, and he'll guarantee your safe passing. Myself, I'd just as soon kill you."

Kuo shouted back, "Like you did Frank? Shot up with the back of his head missing?"

"Found that, did you?" Ugly had a good belly laugh. "Oh, yeah. Heller says for you to leave the girl when you go. Part of the condition of your getting out of here alive."

Yester's mouth went dry.

Gunslinger elbowed Ugly and spoke again.

"Safe passage," Ugly amended, grinning, "that's what he said."

Yester had good eyesight. There was no missing Ugly's suggestive wink.

A gunshot from the cabin answered, the bullet coming near enough to Ugly's foot to take a notch out of the toe of his boot. He bounded high in the air, coming down cursing as he joined the others in a mad scatter.

None, to Yester's relief, in his direction.

They'd reached a stalemate.

A full half hour passed. Yester's throat grew drier and drier as he sprawled behind the woodpile with the hot August sun beating down on him. A scrawny jack pine shaded the other side of the pile, but none for him. He wondered how Nat was faring, if he was as thirsty as himself. Even though Yester'd seen his friend's flight from the corral, he had no idea where Nat had ended up. For all he knew, Nat had taken to his heels.

But, no. Nat would never do that. He'd be on the other side of the cabin, waiting for a break, just like Yester.

The lull didn't last much longer.

Yester'd seen the outlaws start a discussion, bandying ideas back and forth. He'd caught parts of the talk. Single words mostly, mixed with a few phrases. Words like fire, shoot, carve him up, lift her skirt, sell.

His heart thudded. Some of the threat seemed aimed at Kuo,

which didn't worry him so much. It was the last couple, about lifting her skirt and selling, that did. Those were aimed right at Ketta. Enough had happened here for him to believe Kuo was defending Ketta, risking his own life to do so. Common sense seemed to indicate he and Kuo ought to join forces to fight their mutual enemy. That'd put him and Nat and Kuo against the four outlaws. Might not even the odds, but make 'em better. If only he and Nat had more than Yester's old rifle and a couple of pocket knives between them.

The outlaws all had guns. Yester figured his next job was to get at least one of them for Nat, and maybe an extra for himself.

Yester had been studying the men he now considered targets. He figured taking Heller's guns away from him was out. For now. Likewise, Ugly's. The other two, they were different. Not much older than he was, for one thing, which he hoped meant not much experience in the outlawing business. And not to be conceited or anything, but he'd bet on his own intellect coming in ahead of theirs. Theirs put together.

He tried not to think of his own lack of experience in anything except doing ranch chores and riding herd on some half-wild horses.

The outlaw boys were excited by the action and careless. The buck-toothed feller with the pimples and sweated-through holes in the armpits of his shirt was getting real antsy. He kept putting his carbine down, then having to look around to find it. His reason for setting the carbine down was not reassuring, since he had a whetstone he used to hone the blade of a large hunting knife every few minutes.

The other young one—Yester heard him called Dunce—apparently lived up to the name. His eyes were vacant as he gazed around, and his jaw hung slack most of the time. He shambled when he walked, so Yester thought he'd have walked in circles if somebody, mostly Ugly, didn't call him to order every now and then. He did, however, keep a pretty good grip on a small handgun.

So. One or the other.

The waiting ended when Heller said, "You, Dunce, fetch some wood over here. We're going to start us a fire."

"A fire? What for?" Dunce looked around. Bent over and picked up a couple twigs from the ground.

Yester tensed. He thought he knew what for.

"Not them little bits," Heller snapped. "Dumb shit. Over at the woodpile. Bring four or five good-sized chunks."

"But it's hot, and we ain't got any food to cook." Dunce whined like a little kid.

Heller snorted. "Jesus. Ought to shoot you myself. Tell this kid what the fire is for, Milt."

"Gonna burn them out, Dunce. You hustle now and do what Heller says. Get that fire built right here in the yard. Let Kuo and that girl see what's coming."

"Oh," Dunce said, apparently enlightened. "We going to burn the house down like you did at that ranch?"

"That's right," Milt said.

Dunce grinned. "Fun. I wish I'd been there."

Removing a rock from under his elbow, Yester hefted it in his hand. Not as heavy as he'd like. But there was a branch, maybe three feet long, the wind had blown off the pine in the not too far distant past. It all depended on how close Dunce came.

Turned out he came real close, and, even then, it took two thumps on Dunce's noggin with the branch to knock him out. The job didn't go cleanly, either, with Dunce having time to yowl, "Ow" before the second blow put him down. And then Yester had to snatch up the pistol and rummage in a pants pocket for ammunition before making his escape.

Could be it didn't take more than five or ten seconds all told, but each second felt more like a minute to Yester. The greatest surprise was that nobody came running to see what had happened to Dunce. Not until Yester had turned the corner around the cabin and paused for a glance back. Even then it was only the buck-toothed one and not Milt or Heller.

The boy leaned over his brother, if that's what he was, and called out to the others, "Dunce ran into a tree and knocked himself out. What do you want me to do?"

Heller cursed. "Leave the dummy lay. You bring the wood. We gotta get the fire going."

Yester gave a sigh. Sure was clear they didn't have a care about being interrupted or even overheard. But a fire. He couldn't let that happen.

First thing, he had to find Nat.

Turned out, Nat found him.

KETTA

When the crack of gunfire faded, and chunks of lead quit flying through the air, Kuo rolled aside from Ketta's rigid body.

She lay as if frozen, thinking that nothing could touch her as long as she stayed still. But her eyes . . . she couldn't seem to close her eyes. The one that wasn't already swollen closed, she meant.

Kuo's face swam into view above her. He sat her up and folded her into his arms.

"Are you hurt?" he asked.

She thought maybe it wasn't the first time he'd spoken to her. Not even the first time to pose that question.

"No. Yes." Her lips barely formed the answer. Finally, she blinked both eyes open and looked directly at him. Of its own volition, her hand came up and touched his cheekbone. "But you. You're bleeding." A drop ran down his chin and plopped onto her face. That particular wound on his cheek wasn't the only one. Two or three splinters stuck out from his skin like stiff pig bristles. One was ghastly, just missing his eye. Or did it?

Quickly, she closed her own eyes, shutting the vision out.

"We're a lucky pair, child. Both of us," he said as if amazed at the discovery.

"We are?" She blinked again. His left hand, which he'd used to cover her face, looked like a rat had been chewing at it, and even his shirt bore several new holes.

Men's voices came through loud and clear now that the windows were shot into honed shards and glittery dust.

"Kuo," Milt shouted. "Hey, Kuo. You alive?"

Grunting, Kuo set her aside and crawled toward the window. She saw him wince as pieces of broken window pane cut through the knees of his britches and bit into his hands. His revolver had fallen from the holster when the shooting started and he'd dived to cover her up. The pistol had skated under the table. Spying it, he snatched up his gun as he went.

"I'm alive," he called back, and something more besides, something rude and insulting. Bracing his back against the cabin wall, he fumbled for more cartridges to reload the gun.

She started to get up, but he waved her back. Did he expect another attack? Ketta didn't know if she could stand one. But she couldn't stay sprawled in the middle of the floor, either, amidst all the broken glass.

Stooping, she went over to join Kuo at the window. Copying him, she stayed at the window's side and peered out. Positioned opposite him, her perspective was different from his, but it seemed to her the outlaws, though they'd taken cover, weren't all that well hidden.

"Why don't you shoot them?" she asked. "Milt. Why don't you shoot Milt? He's right there." Her forefinger pointed.

Kuo sighed. "If I shoot, they'll shoot back. At some time, they'll shoot us. Me or you. Or both."

Ketta set her hands on her hips. "Not if you shoot them first."

"I am one gun; they are four. And I don't think it's escaped you that my sight is somewhat impaired."

Glaring at Kuo, Ketta finally understood what his wounds meant to their safety. "Oh," she gasped.

"Yes." His voice was dry.

Before, when she first snapped out of the strange blankness she'd felt when under fire, she'd known Kuo had several nasty splinters in his face and that his blood dripped onto her. She hadn't noticed the effect one of the splinters had on him though. Now she did.

"Oh," she said again.

One of those slivers pinned his eyelid to the brow bone. Blood filled the eye. Blood he couldn't blink away.

"I need you to pull the splinter out," he said. "Now, before they start shooting again."

Only then did she realize the din had stopped.

"You want me to pull it out?" she squeaked, her hands coming up and covering her mouth. In truth, she felt sick at the notion.

His good eye fixed on her. "Who else?"

Could she do it? Was she even strong enough? Ketta set herself. Well, she had to be, that's all. There was no one else. Impossible to leave him like this. Besides, she baked bread, didn't she? Kneading and pummeling the stiff dough into a silken mass. She milked the cow. Her hands were strong for all they were tiny, and her fingers nimble.

Ketta drew in a deep, deep breath. "Come sit," she said. "I can't reach you from here."

The whisper of a smile touched his lips. "Good girl."

They crept from their post by the window to the part of the room Kuo deemed safest, seeing it was protected on two sides by cabin walls. Ketta, righting a chair, dragged it over and gestured Kuo into it.

The first try resulted in her fingers slipping from the blood-soaked wood, but not before moving it enough to start new bleeding. Yes, and a harsh-drawn grunt that rocked her to her soul.

Ketta snatched her fingers from the splinter. "I can't do it. It's in too deep and slippery. I can't get a grip on it."

"Try again. Pull straight out."

"Oh, but . . . I'm hurting you."

"Try again," he insisted. He reached in a pocket and drew out a small wash-leather pouch filled with some heavy substance. "Use this."

Filled with misgivings, she received the bag and, without even thinking, shook the contents onto the floor.

Kuo snorted. "That's gold, you know. From my own claim. You're mighty careless."

"Gold?" Ketta frowned. The little pile didn't look like much. Certainly not the glittering mass she expected of something as valuable as gold. This had almost as much black grit in it as yellow.

Anyway, why wasn't Kuo angry? Big Joe would've knocked her from here to heaven's gates if she'd done such a thing.

But then an idea struck her. He probably didn't figure he would live long enough to spend the gold, that's why.

This time, fingers covered by the bag and dry, when she pulled on the inch-long piece, it came free. Fancying she heard a small sound as suction around the wound released, Ketta fought the awful churning in her belly. More blood rushed down Kuo's face, spreading into a red mask. His eye closed now, but showed through a hole in the lid. Ketta nearly cried.

Nearly. But not quite.

Kuo took the pouch and pressed it against the wound. It

didn't do much toward stemming the flow of blood. And probably nothing to stop the pain, as he lurched from the chair and went to sit with his back against the wall. There, he closed both eyes, quivering with reaction.

To stop her own tears, she took Kuo's place in observing the outlaws in the yard. They milled around, ducking behind cover where they found it, shaking fists in the air and yelling. Finally, in plain sight, they grouped together and appeared to be having a discussion. Gleeful at its conclusion, Dunce headed over to the woodpile, while Beaver built the foundation for a campfire.

"Why are they starting a fire?"

She didn't realize she'd spoken out loud until Kuo answered.

"Gonna try to burn us out, I expect."

"Burn us out? You mean start the cabin on fire with us inside?"

Kuo gave a short huff of laughter—or something like. "One of Milt's favorite things to do."

"Like he did at our . . . Big Joe's place."

"Yes."

"What are we going to do?" she asked, deep worry in her soft voice. "I don't want to burn up."

"No. Me, either." Kuo raised a slight smile at her admission. "You watching them?"

Horrified by the thought of being burned alive, she'd forgotten for a moment, but at his reminder, she glanced out the window again. There were Milt and Heller, standing together and letting—no, demanding—the two younger outlaws do the work of starting the fire. Beaver was over close to the trees, gathering a light armload of brush, while Dunce . . .

Ketta peeked around the window again, catching just a glimmer as Dunce, in his filthy green shirt, seemed to sink into oblivion behind the woodpile. When a figure rose and darted around the corner of the cabin, the shirt was blue.

Ketta blinked.

Blue?

Yes, the same funny color of blue a shirt of Yester's had turned when it inadvertently got washed with a new red neckerchief belonging to Big Joe. Anyway, Yester's shirt was now a color more intense than spring lilacs but on the same order. A color Mama had smiled over, saying it a good thing the shirt had turned color and not the neckerchief.

Ketta agreed. Yester wore the shirt without complaint. Big Joe would've stomped his neckerchief into the ground.

Could there be two shirts of that color? Ketta didn't think so.

All of a sudden her stomach turned a somersault, and what felt like a bubble rose up in her throat. She barely suppressed an excited squeal.

Yester was here. He'd come for her.

This time her stomach turned upside down and stayed that way.

Was Yester alone? She sure didn't see anybody else. And what could her brother do all by himself? What if Heller or Milt, or even that awful Beaver, shot him? Her beautiful brother?

"Kuo?" she said in a soft, quavering voice.

He sat pressed against the round log walls of his cabin. His hand held the little cloth bag against his eye although the wound still bled. "What is it, child? Are they coming? Maybe you'd better take my pistol." His upper lip quirked. "I remember you tried to shoot Milt once before. This revolver will fire. Just be careful where it's pointed."

"Kuo?" she said again, hearing his words but not making sense of them.

He opened his good eye. "What is it?" He sat a little straighter.

"I think . . . I think my brother has come for me."

At this, Kuo went so still it was as if he stopped breathing.

"Your brother? That handsome boy?"

Ketta's insides trembled. With fear? With joy? "Yes."

Chapter Seventeen: Yester

Yester ran straight into Nat as he rounded the corner. Literally. Nose to nose. He skidded to a halt, Nat's knife, unsheathed and at the ready, just missed poking him in the gut.

"Yester! Damn. I almost cut you." Nat's face had turned a shade or two paler than its usual light brown.

"Yeah, I noticed." A shaky grin twerked Yester's lips. "Glad you're here, but I gotta say I'd just as soon not get stuck."

"You didn't."

"Luck. Anyway, I've got a present for you."

"A present?" Nat started, but Yester was already proffering the revolver he'd taken from the outlaw he'd heard the others call Dunce. "Where'd you get it?"

Yester nodded back from whence he'd come. "One of the outlaws. Here. I got some extra cartridges for it, too."

Nat stared at him, then at the pistol. "Did you kill him?"

"No. Should've, probably, but I just clubbed him over the head a couple times." Yester gave his own head a rueful shake. "It might've been three times. I think his skull is like a petrified dinosaur."

"Huh." Nat took the handful of cartridges and, like Dunce, stuck them in a pocket. "Thanks. From the looks of things, I might need this."

"I figure so."

"The thing is," Nat said, "how many of these galoots do we have to fight? These four for sure—or maybe three, on account of you taking care of one—but what about whoever it is in there with Ketta?" He nodded over his shoulder at the cabin.

The same thing Yester had been asking himself. "Don't know about him," he said at last. "About her . . . her father. But I think he's trying to keep Ketta away from the rest of them, so maybe we're fighting on the same side."

"Wish he knew it." Nat's face puckered as the information sank in. "I'd hate for him to shoot one of us by mistake."

"Well, yeah, but you and me, we've got an advantage. We ain't penned up inside a cabin that some folks are fixing to set on fire."

Like a man settling in on a hard job, Nat clubbed his hair behind his head and tied it with a string from his pocket. "We can't let them do that."

"Didn't plan on it. Least not until Ketta is safe. Let me think a minute on how to get her out."

Nat was peering around Yester to where the outlaws were hooting and hollering and dancing around like a bunch of wild men. "Better think fast. Looks like they got the fire kindled, and they're piling on the wood."

Yester turned and studied on the men building the fire to dire heights. A column of smoke rose in the air. He didn't like what he was seeing. Not one bit. "Think they're just gonna leave Dunce laying there?"

"I don't care one way or another," Nat said, shrugging.

"Naw. Me, either."

He wasn't very good at this thinking business, Yester reflected. He couldn't for the life of him figure on how to get Ketta out of the cabin without either him, or Nat, or Ketta herself being gunned down. Nat reported that he'd already scouted behind the house, squeezing himself between its walls and the rocky bluff. No door there, he informed Yester. Nor window. No way out at all as far as he could see.

"Hell," Yester said and kept on pondering. "Nat, what we ought to do is take down the gunslinger. Do that, and I figure the others will give up."

Nat wasn't so sure. "I dunno, Yester. The old man looks like he's the one giving most of the orders."

Yester grunted. Nat had a point. "So, we take him down first. Then the gunslinger."

But how? They couldn't depend on luck. Nat, though, had an answer for that, too.

"I recollect you saying—bragging—what a good shot you are, Yester. Why don't you just shoot him from here? Shoot them both? You've got good cover."

"You mean, from ambush?" Yester could hardly believe this was Nat talking.

"Why not? They'd ambush you."

Yeah, he knew they would. The idea of an ambush stuck in his craw even though he'd put the idea forward earlier.

Puffed-up talk that had turned serious, he acknowledged.

He noticed his shirt was wet, sweated through and through, and the hand holding his rifle slippery. Standing here in the shade, it felt kind of chilly when a breeze stirred.

Breeze or fear? He didn't like where this was going.

A spate of gunfire from the cabin took the thought from his mind.

"What . . ."

Nat flopped onto the ground and crawled forward until he had a decent view of the happenings out front.

"The guy holed up inside, he's the one shooting," he reported to Yester. "Looks like he might've nicked the young one in the leg. I see blood." He paused a moment. "Not much. Too bad. Made him drop his firebrand in the yard, and now they've got some dry weeds flaring up." He laughed. "The old one is making the young one piss on them. Guess they don't want to set the woods on fire."

"Not until they get what they came for," Yester said sourly. He knelt down behind Nat. Sure enough, there was the buck-toothed one, standing with a twisted look on his face. Guess he didn't like exposing himself, there in the open.

As Yester debated taking a shot, more gunfire erupted. The outlaws, this time, laying down a covering broadside into the cabin until the grass fire was extinguished and Bucktooth darted back to cover. Sure enough, he was limping, proving Kuo was on the job inside the cabin.

Excitement over for the moment, Nat retreated and sat up. "What are we going to do?" he asked Yester.

"We've got to get Ketta out. I don't care about those men, aside from hoping they kill each other off. But if we don't work fast, Ketta is apt to die right along with them. All that shooting they're doing . . . well, they can't keep on missing forever."

"Right." His brow puckered, Nat pondered. "What if I go back to where the meadow opens into the canyon. When I get there, I'll yell. Draw the outlaws off. Then you can call out to Ketta. See if her father will let her go. If not—"

"If not, what?"

"Shoot them."

Yester kind of liked the idea, except for one thing. It put Nat in too much danger. If either of them tried such a half-baked stunt, it should be him putting himself on the spot. And if the plan worked, drawing some of them away, even this group of outlaws couldn't be stupid enough to leave the cabin unguarded.

He shook his head. "Not you. I'll do it. You see if you can contact Ketta. Besides, you've scouted the area better than me. Once you have her out of there, you can get her away without getting caught."

Nat looked like he wanted to argue but finally nodded. "All right. Let's get started, then. And, Yester?"

Yester swallowed down on his fear. "What?"

"Be careful."

Yester forced a grin. "Now you sound like my ma."

"Yes. Mine, too."

Dreading the dash between cabin corner and woodpile, Yester spent a few seconds working up his nerve. He'd done it once, he could do it again, he told himself. Watch for a moment when all the outlaws were looking the other way. They seemed to do that quite often. All it'd take was a little unexpected something to draw their attention.

He waited, breathing like he was already running. Finally, the chance came. The flight of a few birds, as it happened, a small flock set in motion by the stone Nat judiciously tossed into their midst.

Then Yester dashed into the open, five, six steps, until he hunkered down behind the woodpile where he'd left Dunce. Unseen and unheard. He wiped sweat from his brow with a hand that shook.

Dunce still lay there, a small trickle of blood oozing from a gash at the back of his head. Yester knew he was alive by the way his chest rose and fell. Relieved not to be hobnobbing with a corpse, he cocked an ear towards the outlaws.

"On three," the one called Milt said, "each of you boys grab a torch and run up close to the cabin. Beaver, you take one side of the window. Heller, you take the other. I'll stay right here and shoot if I see anybody moving inside. That'll do'er. They either come out or they fry. Don't matter all that much which."

"Okay, Pa," the buck-toothed lad said, "but I hope they come out. I want me that girl."

"Stand in line, sonny." Dismissing Beaver's concerns, the gunslinger stared hard at the ugly, older man. "Plan is all right. Up to a point."

"What point?"

"The one where two run up with lighted torches. Ain't gonna be me. Has to be you and Beaver, here."

"Well, say, Heller, I ain't so young as I used to be. Getting crippled up. You do it. You're young and spry."

Heller leaned forward. "And a helluva lot better shot."

Right here, Yester thought. This was the best place for him. He had clear shots at all three of them. Provided his old rifle didn't jam up like it did sometimes. Wait until two of them had torches in hand. That'd put a damper on them fighting back. For a few seconds, at least.

His mind raced, telling him what to do. It had him so stirred up that, at first, he failed to notice the sounds behind him. Right up until hands like a vise grabbed onto his ears and mashed his head right down into his neck bones.

"Pa, Pa," Dunce yelled, happy as a skunk in a henhouse. "I got me one."

"Dunce? That you?" Ugly didn't sound all that happy his son had awakened. "You got one what?"

Idiot, Yester mournfully answered for him. Just before he started fighting back.

Ketta

"I really did!" Ketta jumped to her feet and broke into an excited little dance. "I saw him. My brother is here. He'll save me. Save us."

Why didn't Kuo look happier? They could depend on Yester's help. She knew it.

"How did he find this place?" Kuo demanded, maybe talking to himself.

Ketta answered, anyway. "Yester is smart," she said proudly. "And he's stubborn. He keeps after things until they turn out right." It was true. He did, but she didn't know as he'd ever done anything like this before. Most of his experience involved finding lost stock or chasing down game.

Kuo made some kind of funny sound deep in his throat. Disbelief? Surprise? Anger? But why should he be angry? "Smart, eh?" he repeated.

Ketta's joy faded. Silly girl. Of course, her father wasn't pleased. After all, he'd stolen her away from her family in the first place. He'd probably rather she *died* or got *sold* into slavery than be rescued by her brother.

With all her heart, she wished she could snatch those revealing words back. Keep Kuo in the dark as to Yester's presence. If he and Yester were to come face to face, how would they react? Friends or mortal enemies? Better, perhaps, if they didn't meet. If she were able to—

"We don't need smart," he said, interrupting her soaring thoughts as he rose to his feet. "We need somebody good with a gun. Maybe several men good with a gun, given that is Burk Heller out there. Not one half-grown boy who thinks he's an avenging angel."

"Another outlaw?" she said, even as she wondered if Yester did think of himself as an avenging angel? It didn't sound much like her brother.

"An outlaw who's fighting on my side." Kuo's correction sounded a little bitter.

"Like Tug, I suppose."

"Yes. Like Tug."

Outside, the outlaws were prancing about like schoolchildren on a cold winter morning instead of this hot summer day. Beaver kept darting to the front and shooting off his gun as if he had all the bullets in the world. And although the fire itself was out of her line of sight, Ketta smelled it well enough and observed smoke spreading across the clearing.

Moment by moment, her fear grew. She hadn't forgotten the way the outlaws had set her home afire. Not by a long shot.

And left Mama to burn up.

Why, oh, why didn't Yester do something?

Standing beside the window, the glass all shot out by now, Ketta kept her eyes peeled for another glimpse of her brother. And for the outlaw attack, too. She doubted Kuo's ability to twist himself far enough to see, given his damaged eye. But he, she knew, heard them well enough. The catcalls and the promise to burn them out.

A sudden burst of curses resounded. More, Ketta realized, than before. What was happening?

Kuo, his expression grim, reached down a box of ammunition from a shelf and set it beside him. "You know how to load a gun?"

Ketta looked around at him. "Yes." She'd seen Yester and Big Joe do it often enough. When she'd tried to use Big Joe's broken pistol back at the ranch, her failure hadn't been because of ignorance. Or not entirely, at any rate.

"Well, then," Kuo said, "get ready. They'll start shooting any minute. I have my rifle and this revolver. When one is empty, I'll hand it to you to reload, and I'll use the other. They won't be expecting that."

A long shiver started in Ketta's belly and didn't let up. "All right."

"They'll be shooting their guns at the same time they're trying to throw a fire brand into the cabin. If they succeed with a torch, you see if you can put it out. Got water in a bucket. Use that first. Then smother it with the bear hide off the bed. If that don't work—"

He stopped at that and fired a shot. Someone, Milt probably, laughed and yelled, "Missed, Chink."

Ketta saw Beaver, running fast, pass in front of the cabin and give a flaming torch a hefty toss. Whether his aim owed to skill or to luck, the torch sailed in through the open window and landed on the floor beside her, near enough to burn a hole in her skirt.

Shrieking, she started forward, only to have Kuo holler, "Don't be stupid, child. Stay back. Don't give 'em a target."

Ketta barely heard, ignoring his advice as she beat out the torch with a wet towel. He left her to it, firing until his revolver was empty, then handed the gun to Ketta. Methodically, she ejected the spent cartridges and inserted new ones.

"Good girl," Kuo said, smiling at her.

He looked awful; his eye swollen shut, his face bruised and bloody. She knew he hadn't hit anyone with the shots. Wasted ammunition.

"Wahoo!" Somebody outside gleefully yelled, and a whole lot of shooting forced Kuo to keep his head down.

The next fire brand thudded against the door on the outside.

"Sonuva—" With a glance at Ketta, Kuo cut off the expletive. It didn't matter, she thought. She knew just as well as he that there was nothing they could do about it. The fire was bound to catch eventually, and then they, if they were even still alive, would either burn or be forced out.

Where, oh where, had Yester gotten to? Why hadn't she heard anything from him? Self doubt grew. Had she been mistaken in that quick glimpse? Was Yester a figment of her imagination?

Smoke seeped under the door, rising to flow through the cracks where the door met the casing.

"Kuo," she cried. "Look!"

He barely spared the smoke a glance. "No surprise." Snapping off a couple rifle shots, he passed the weapon to her, taking up the revolver in its stead.

Ketta's hands shook as she forced cartridges into the rifle's breech. She felt Kuo watching her.

Finishing her task, Ketta crawled over to where Kuo kept his ammunition. Maybe ten rifle cartridges remained. All the revolver shells were already at her station. It wouldn't be much longer before all was spent, their defenses gone. She held up the ammunition box for his inspection. Face impassive, Kuo nodded.

"Guess it's time," he said.

"Time for what?"

"For you to get out of here."

Chapter Eighteen: Yester

Yester didn't know but what Dunce was trying to wrench his head right off his shoulders. That's what it felt like. Or maybe Dunce thought he had caught himself a chicken and planned on wringing its neck.

Truthfully, the idea didn't sit all that well.

What Dunce hadn't taken into account was Yester's height. While Dunce, though strong and massive, was built along the lines of a sawed-off tree stump, Yester was just the opposite. Whereas a bit on the skinny side, along with being a six footer, he was still whipcord strong. Enough so that when he rose to his feet in an attempt to shake Dunce off, Dunce lost his grip on Yester's ears.

Freed up Yester's ability to fight back, is what it did. After all, he was considered the best wrestler in the county, unless you counted those university boys over to Moscow. And he didn't. Yester didn't figure they had much real experience. Not like him, who'd gotten quite a bit of practice in taking down steers and the cowboys who rode herd on them. And they were a rough bunch.

Yester knew how to fight dirty, and he didn't hesitate.

Dunce stood directly behind him. Yester propelled himself backward, slamming hard against the clumsy fellow and forcing him into stumbling over his own feet. The downward pressure on Yester's neck gave way, and Yester jerked his head backward. He knew he'd connected when the spray of blood from Dunce's broken nose sent droplets flying everywhere.

"Ow!" Dunce yowled. "I'm a-gonna—"

Whatever he intended, the threat was lost as Yester spun around, shoved his knee between Dunce's legs, and not only tried to emasculate him, but tripped him as well. Dunce fell heavily, with a few more "ow, ow, ows" added in.

"What the hell?" Milt bellowed. "Beaver, fer God's sake go see what's ailing your brother now."

Evidently, none of them had actually caught sight of Yester. Not yet. Yester thought he wanted to keep the miracle going. Getting one last lick in, he thrust his boot in Dunce's belly, which curled the man into a wooly-bug ball. He scooted off into the nearby woods just before Beaver came around the corner.

"Pa says to shut up," Beaver was saying. "What the hell's the matter with you?"

"Ow, ow," Dunce replied, clutching at the front of his pants.

It wasn't until Yester got around to checking to see if his neck was broken that he remembered his rifle. Somewhere along the way, he'd lost it.

Goddamn.

KETTA

"Get out of here?" Ketta's mouth dropped open. Had Kuo's mind gone sideways, due maybe to breathing the smoke curling up from around the door? "They'll shoot us the minute we step outside."

A small smile touched his lips. "Not if they don't see us. See you. You're going first."

"What do you mean?"

"I mean there's a bolt-hole. An alternate route. You know what that means, don't you? Seems like for a girl who's never gone to school you're plenty smart."

"Of course I know what a bolt-hole is." She had one of her

very own at home, after all. Her very own cave. "Mama is a good teacher," she added. "She was the school teacher for the district until she married Mr. Noonan."

He waved this off. "Listen, child, this is what we're going to do. First of all, I'm sending you out the bolt-hole." He stopped and touched his swollen eye. "You sure you saw your brother? You weren't just daydreaming?"

Ketta gave him a glare fit to peel paint off a wall. "I don't daydream. Especially when the house is on fire and people are shooting."

Kuo chuckled. "Good girl. Be best then if, as soon as you're out, you go to where you last seen him. Try to meet up. I'll give you what cover I can. When you're clear, I'll give those boneheads out there a volley and then get out myself. We'll meet up over by the spring. You know where it is?"

She nodded and pointed, but he shook his head. "Not that one. There's another, one Milt and his boys don't know about. When it's safe, you cross the meadow. The spring is about a half mile up the canyon. You can't miss it. The green stuff will show you. Got it?"

"Yes."

He turned to fire his rifle out the window. A yip of pain rewarded the effort. "Pinked him, by God," he said.

Kuo's attention came back to Ketta. "You stay at the spring until I come for you. You and your brother both, if he's really out there. Or . . ." Narrowing his good eye, he stared hard at her. "Or, if I don't get there, you wait either until Milt and the others leave, or you skedaddle under cover of darkness. Figure out the route beforehand so's you can creep out without making a lot of noise. Understand?"

It sounded to Ketta an awful lot like he thought he might not make it out of the house. The burning house.

"I understand," she said, her voice wobbling.

YESTER

Where the devil had Nat gotten to?

That was the question on Yester's mind as he slipped into the woods behind the corral full of horses. It was the place he'd last seen Nat after giving him the pistol. To tell the truth, he kind of regretted the generosity. Nat at least had his long knife. All he had was a pocketknife with a blade as dull as one of his ma's butter knives.

"Nat," he called softly when a flurry of shots provided a diversion. "You here?"

He got no answer.

Disturbed by the smoke and gunshots, the horses milled about the corral in a mostly counter-clockwise direction. Every once in a while, one changed around, which set them all to neighing and biting at one another. Yester cast his eye over them, choosing his moment before sliding between pole rails into the enclosure.

Over at the fire, the outlaws took no notice of the horses, being inured by now to their restlessness. The gunslinger and Milt had taken up a position almost out of Yester's sight. The beaver-toothed fellow sped between one place and another, evidently to wherever he thought he had a clear shot. Or any kind of shot, come to think on it, considering Yester didn't know if any of them had made a useful shot yet. Not even the gunslinger.

Meanwhile, Dunce was stretched out at the woodpile still nursing his private parts. He wasn't seeing much of anything just now. Every once in a while, his feet drummed the ground as if enduring a surge of pain. "Ow, ow, ow," he'd yell.

Yester had a hard time raising any sympathy, especially whenever he tried turning his head.

"Dunce," one of the other outlaws yelled, "shut up that caterwauling."

It worked for maybe ten seconds, then the "owing" started up again.

Yester ducked behind the pinto as the beaver-toothed feller approached. He came over and stared down at his brother.

"Pa says to shut the hell up. You're getting on Heller's nerves," Bucktooth said. "And you know what that means." Having delivered the message, he spun around and went to join the others.

There must've been a true threat in the words somewhere, because the yelling stopped. Even so, Dunce continued to writhe.

Disgusted, Yester trotted alongside one of the horses as it made a circuit of the corral. The outlaws, except for Dunce, were out of sight as Yester and the horse came even with the gate. The horse stopped, as if assessing his chance for escape.

Not so good, Yester figured, without a little help. He stepped around the horse and flipped up the wire holding the top of the gatepost. Then he ducked back under the horse's chin and made another circuit of the corral.

This time when he got to the gate, he saw it sagging. Nothing more he could do at the moment, though, because Milt came into sight with another lighted torch just as Yester prepared to loosen the bottom catch of the gate. Jumping backward, Yester about got trampled underfoot by the outlaw's pinto, stumbling between horses as, the firebrand tossed into the cabin, Milt turned and headed back to the fire.

Yester thought for sure his heart was failing him, it thumped so hard.

Determined now, Yester stuck with it. The way clear on the next round, he stomped down on the wire, releasing the gate bottom. At the same time, he grabbed onto the gatepost and yanked it around with him. He was in plain sight now, but he kept right on, dragging the gate back until it caught on higher ground.

He ran for cover, diving once more into the woods beyond the corral. He felt a little dizzy, like maybe he hadn't had a full lung of air since he'd started this business. He gasped as the first horse found the way to freedom. Then another and another.

Over at the woodpile, Dunce had seen Yester clear the gate, and he called out.

"Hey."

A change from his "ows," but nobody seemed to be listening.

Yester faded farther back into the woods.

KETTA

Kuo fired off a couple shots "just to keep their heads down for a minute" and led Ketta into the bedroom. It was dark as night in there. Smoke swirled around their heads in great clouds. Both she and Kuo were coughing, and she, for one, had a hard time catching her breath.

"There's no window," she gasped out, her throat raw.

"Nope. No window." Kuo found the handle of an old broom and started poking at the ceiling, a couple feet from the wall edge. Harder and harder, he thrust, finally saying, "Oof. There it is."

"What?" Ketta asked.

"Come here," he said. "Let me lift you up."

"Wh—?" She had no chance to finish. Under the final thrust, a line of daylight appeared, and a trapdoor onto the roof dropped down. "Oh."

"Hurry, child," he said, and, as she came near, he scooped her up, holding her aloft until she could grab the edges of the opening and heave herself through. She gave a kick to propel herself all the way through. Beneath her, she heard him cough again.

"Is the roof on fire?" he called up to her.

"Yes, but not this corner."

"Good. Edge on down to the eaves, where the cabin meets the hill. There are trees. Climb into one and use it as a ladder to work your way down. Run, then. Remember where I told you to go. We will meet at the spring." He went into another spasm of coughing.

She lay on her belly and looked down at him. "You come, too," she said impulsively. "Come now. You'll burn up in there." Tears filled her eyes. Silly girl. Hadn't he kidnapped her, stolen her away from her mother, from her brother? Said he'd sell her to the highest bidder? Why should she care?

Ketta heard him wheezing, trying to breathe and choking on the boiling smoke. For herself, she sucked her lungs full of smoke-free air, which served to clear the strange dizzy feeling that had overtaken her.

"I'll be right behind you. Go now. Hurry," he said roughly and turned away. She heard him coughing even harder as the trapdoor slammed shut, hiding him from sight.

"Kuo?" she said. "Father?"

He didn't answer.

Heat pierced through the rough shingles Kuo had told her he'd fashioned himself. Belly burning, Ketta squirmed to the edge of the roofline. She disliked heights, and the steep pitch of the roof threatened to roll her off. Being up this high frightened her. But not, she decided, as much as the thought of the flames licking at the wood beneath her.

Inside the cabin, the bark of Kuo's cough carried to her. And then a couple gunshots. At least he was still alive. But for how much longer?

At the roof's edge, she reached out—the distance between herself and the tree looming large—stretching until she finally grasped a limb and tugged it closer.

The limb, a whippy branch with a mind of its own, resisted. When she let up, it pulled her forward until her whole body, fingertip to toe, stretched across the span between her and safety. Maybe safety. As long as she could hold on. Ketta gritted her teeth, determined not to let go.

But then, probably because of the way her palms were chafing against the rough bark of the tree, rubbing her raw, she went into a slide. Her body dropped from the roof, slamming hard against the tree's trunk.

Crying out, Ketta hung now by one hand, and that one was slipping.

"Ketta, let go. I'll catch you."

Was that God speaking to her?

No. The voice came from below.

CHAPTER NINETEEN: YESTER

Yester wormed his way between some bushes with fuzzy, pale-green leaves the moment he cleared the corral. Grinning, he watched it finally dawn on the outlaws what was happening.

"Hey," Dunce yelled. "Hey." The gasping tone of the last "hey" indicated one of the horses had probably stepped on him.

The idea didn't break Yester's heart, that's for sure.

Neither Dunce's family nor the gunslinger paid any attention to the man's cries. Not until the pinto sped past in a flash of brown and white, and the gunslinger—what had Milt called him? Heller?—looked up from reloading his pistols again. Cartridges dropped from between his fingers.

"What the hell?" he said, then louder, "Who opened the corral gate?"

"Huh?" Beaver gave up his cavorting around the fire and watched, mouth open, as another horse trotted past. "Dunce?" It may have been an accusation.

"Where is he? I'll kill the stupid son of a bitch myself." Heller started toward the corral, which caused Yester to put his head down and flinch backward. The realization struck him that he had no weapon. Sadly, he figured he knew where his rifle had disappeared to, and it wasn't where he could lay his hand on it.

Milt took the firebrand Beaver had nursed into flame and deftly tossed it atop the cabin roof. "What's the matter with Dunce? What did he do now?"

"Let the goddamn horses loose."

"You sure about that?" Milt started toward them. "Beaver said Dunce knocked hisself out. What if—"

Heller, with Beaver trotting along right behind, didn't stop. "You don't see anybody else, do you?"

A shot came from inside the cabin, tearing a hole through Milt's filthy black hat. He ducked down and scrambled back to the fire.

"Sure wasn't Kuo, nor his little girl. Got them penned up just fine." Heller rounded the corner of the woodpile where Dunce, who'd finally stopped moaning, was just getting to his hands and knees. "Which means it had to be this one."

He stared down at Dunce, who stared blankly back at him. Heller's face twisted. "Witless good-for-nothing," he said and shot him, a neat round hole in Dunce's forehead.

"Hey." Beaver's jaw dropped. "Hey." He sounded remarkably like his late brother.

Yester hardly believed his own eyes. A roaring in his ears, like the river in springtime as the ice went out, smothered all sound and sort of fogged his mind.

The gunslinger had just murdered Dunce. Shot him down like an animal for meat, without a care for the poor idiot's family or bothering to find out if Dunce had done what Heller accused him of.

Dunce wasn't a good guy, Yester reminded himself. He probably would've shot Heller the same way for the same reasons if he'd thought of it or if his pa had told him to. And only a few minutes ago he'd been ready to kill Yester. But still—

A fight wasn't the same as this cold-blooded execution.

"Milt," Heller bellowed, and Yester thought maybe he'd tried to get the older man's attention before.

After a minute, Milt looked up. "You killed my son."

"Waste of good food, keeping him alive."

"That weren't for you to judge. I'm the one paid for his food."

Heller shrugged. "A load off your mind. You oughta be thanking me."

"Well, I ain't." Milt appeared to think. "But—"

Shoving his pistols into the holsters, Heller took charge. "Milt, you keep Kuo penned up inside. Tell him to send out the girl. Tell him we'll let him live if he does."

"Will we?"

Heller grinned. "What do you think?"

"I think we won't." Milt cast one last glance at Dunce's body. "Why am I doing the talking? What are you going to do?"

"I'm taking your other boy, and him and me are gonna round up these horses." Heller toed Dunce, the body moving with a queer, slack motion.

Milt turned a hard look on the gunslinger. "Don't you shoot Beaver down. He's a good boy."

"Yeah? Then you tell him he better not give me any trouble."

A rope hung looped over one of the corral posts. Heller picked it up on the way by, even as he yelled for Beaver to come help with the runaway horses. "And bring a couple bridles," he added.

Yester kind of thought Beaver's footsteps lagged as he obeyed. If it were me, Yester thought, I wouldn't be wanting to get anywhere near the man.

He was lucky his runaway horse idea had worked, Yester thought. As soon as Beaver and Heller passed out of sight along the trail back to the main road, he shifted from his hiding place. Truth to tell, he was a little dismayed at how helpless he felt. And he sure enough hoped the two would catch up the horses before they got to where he and Nat had left theirs. Just not too soon. So far, none of the outlaws had any idea they had company.

This looked like the best chance he'd ever get to rescue Ketta. But, first of all, he had to put Milt out of commission. And maybe Kuo, too, if the fire didn't take care of him first. 'Cause chances were Kuo would just as likely shoot him or Nat, or both, as soon as the others. Which reminded him, just where had Nat gotten to? He hadn't seen a sign of him for what seemed like hours.

Keeping his eye peeled to avoid any nasty surprises, Yester made his way over to the woodpile and Dunce's body.

There wasn't a lot of blood. Not like he'd been expecting. Nevertheless, Yester gulped down whatever it was trying to churn a way out of his stomach and set to searching for his rifle. He'd been about . . . here . . . when Dunce grabbed him. So, his rifle should be—

He found it stuck in between a couple chunks of wood. Low down to the ground, he figured it'd been scooted there as he and Dunce wrestled and halfway covered with wood chips and the like. At least, he thought, shaking dirt out of the barrel, Beaver hadn't spied it when he talked to Dunce. And neither had Heller, when he fired a bullet into Dunce's tiny brain.

Yester had no more than satisfied himself the rifle was safe enough to shoot than he spotted Heller. The outlaw had already captured the pinto and was riding him bareback.

"Dammit. Lazy dang horse didn't even get as far as the meadow." Yester stared at him.

Oblivious, the outlaw was twirling a rope as if he imagined himself a top hand. Beaver must've still been hunting horses, because he was nowhere in sight. As Yester watched, Heller turned the pinto in the direction the other horses had gone as if intending to help Beaver.

Dangerous? Or a relief? Yester wiped sweat from his face.

Just around the corner, his back turned to the woodpile, Milt was passing the time by pinging shots into the burning cabin, though not as if he had any ambition about it.

No response came from the cabin. Maybe, Yester thought,

because Kuo and Ketta were burned up.

Rage swelled up like a red curtain behind his eyes. Without a second thought, Yester stood up. He brushed dirt from the rifle's rear sight and propped the barrel on the topmost piece of wood on the stack. *Perfect.*

The figure atop the pinto bobbed at the top of the vee. No matter. He had a good sense of timing. And when the proper time came, he squeezed the trigger like he was caressing a girl. Or like he dreamed of caressing a girl.

The noise surprised him. And the recoil. And the evidence of good aim.

Out in the meadow, the outlaw sagged to one side before he fell, sprawling amidst the grass and almost hidden by its tall height. Snorting, the pinto crow-hopped a time or two and trotted away. Behind him, the grasses threshed for a few seconds, then stopped.

Milt had spun around. "What the hell?" He surveyed the scene for a few seconds, spotting the riderless pinto. As if sensing danger, he emptied his six-gun, firing one shot into the meadow grass and startling the horse into racing away again. Another shot went through the cabin window, where flames were bursting forth; yet another into the woodpile, missing Yester by scant inches. A fourth try ended on the revolver's empty click. Milt sprang into shelter behind a nearby rickety three-wheeled cart and hunkered down.

As for Yester, he let out a shaky breath. *My God,* he thought, hardly aware of the bullet that'd passed over his bowed head, *I killed a man.*

And he wasn't sorry. Not one bit.

His head came up when Milt yelled.

"Kuo, hiya, Kuo. You burned up yet? You and the girl?"

Ketta

Ketta hadn't realized it before, but she'd been hanging by her fingertips from the tree branch with her eyes closed. Now they opened, and she looked down.

"Nat!" Her fingers slipped. "Oh, Nat."

Her grip failed then, along with her strength, and she dropped, sure she'd have a broken ankle upon landing. She didn't. All due to Nat following through on his promise, catching her before she hit the ground.

He stood her upright, and let her go as if she were hot. Ketta, wanting nothing so much as to cling to him, flung her arms around him in a flash of exuberance.

"Dang, Ketta, you're getting heavy." Nat appeared discomfited by her behavior, but maybe not exactly displeased. He detached himself, smiling down at her with a self-satisfied expression before tilting his head toward the burning cabin. Heat eddied through the log walls as smoke drifted from the roof. "Where's the Chinaman?"

Ketta frowned upward. "He's supposed to be following me out."

"He'd better make it fast." Shaking his head, Nat took her hand and pulled her along behind him.

Ketta looked back. Kuo should've escaped by now, but the roof vent remained closed. She dragged behind as Nat did his best to hurry her. In consequence, they moved slowly. Nat insisted on silence, both of them crouching almost double until they were somewhere beyond the corral and he stopped.

"Duck," he said, lifting up some brush and gesturing her into a low, narrow opening.

"What is it?" Ketta bent and peered ahead.

"A hideyhole carved into the hillside. Just like the one you have at home, only smaller. Somebody dug this one with a pick and shovel. Like a cache. It's a good place for you to hide."

She looked closer. "How did you ever find it?" It was well concealed, and almost invisible. Even if you knew it was there you might have to search.

"Luck." Nat's chest puffed out, just a little. "One of those outlaws about walked up on me, and I had to get out of sight quick. Good thing he was noisy and I heard him coming. I'm a pretty good scout."

"You are, Nat," she breathed. "A really good scout. I'm so glad to see you. But tell me quick, where's Yester? I spotted him, you know, a while ago. Before the shooting started. I could hardly believe my eyes."

Without warning, tears flooded into those eyes. "He came for me. You both came for me. I didn't . . . I was afraid . . ." She couldn't go on.

A blush turned Nat's tan cheeks a dusky red. "Well, sure," he said, as if it were the most ordinary thing in the world for two sixteen-year-olds to come to a girl's rescue and take on a gang of outlaws in the bargain. He turned from her, escape obviously on his mind.

But Ketta wasn't done with him yet. "Where is he?" she persisted. "Where's Yester?"

Nat put his finger to his lips. "Shh. Not so loud. We don't want—"

"Is he shot? Is he dead? Please, please, don't let him be dead." It was a wail of despair.

"Hush, Ketta. No. Heck, no. He was shooting just a minute ago. I heard his rifle."

Though for the life of her Ketta didn't see how he could tell one rifle from another just by the sound, she was willing to take his word for it. More than willing. Needful.

"Oh." It came out on a sigh. "Oh."

"Crawl on into this cave and wait while I go round him up. Don't you move. I'll be right back. We got to get out of here before the outlaws spot us."

"All right." Ketta didn't have it in her to argue. She didn't want to see those evil men ever again. Not Heller, not Beaver, not Dunce, and especially not Milt. As for Kuo—

What about Kuo? What about her father?

Yester

Two down, two to go, Yester thought. Or make that three to go. He couldn't discount the Chinaman. Even if the other outlaws had taken against him, and it appeared they were out to kill each other, it didn't mean Kuo wouldn't be happy to shoot either him or Nat at first sight.

Speaking of Nat, Yester itched to meet up with him. If they banded together, maybe they'd be in a good enough bargaining position to talk to Kuo. Have him send Ketta out.

If she was still alive in that burning cabin. Worry had Yester's heart jumping around in his chest. She could be dead by now, shot or smothered by smoke. She was so small, didn't have the lungs on her that a fellow did. Or her Chinaman father.

But first, he had to do something about Milt, strutting around the perimeter of the cabin and thinking he sat in the top spot. Or was before he hid behind that cart. From what Yester could tell, all his attention centered on the cabin. Pure luck he still seemed to think Kuo the only enemy he faced. He wasn't expecting Yester Noonan to take a hand, that was for sure, but time was running out.

Yester fumbled in his pocket, found the last three shells for his rifle and, although the rifle wasn't empty, loaded them. He went cold thinking about the lack of ammunition. What did he have, five shots, maybe six? Not many when he counted off the outlaws remaining. Milt, Beaver, Kuo. Their names echoed in his mind.

Movement over at the cart drew his attention. Milt, stirring around, trying for a more open position. His rifle barrel still pointed at the window, where razor sharp shards of glass prevented a safe exit, in case Kuo and Ketta had thoughts of escaping through it.

But he should've been watching the door.

Yester received bare warning, alerted by the squeal of hinges. The door creaked open, revealing a narrow line of black. Smoke boiled out in an enveloping fog. A pistol barrel poked through the smoke.

Milt noticed the movement at last. He rose up in a crouch, the cart wheel not doing much to hide him. His rifle pointed at the door where the crack widened. Almost as if he couldn't help himself, the outlaw fired off a shot, then two or three more. Pieces of the door casing splintered away at the height of a man's head.

All movement halted. Milt and Kuo. Each waited on the other.

Yester waited, too. From his angle, Kuo was just visible. A cough wracked the man, bending him almost double. As soon as it was over, he yanked the door all the way open and plunged outside, staggering as he raced toward the cart where Milt rose to his feet. He went faster than a person might think possible.

Yester stood up, too. Wrenched to his feet without thought of being seen as the two outlaws each banged off a few more shots at each other. Neither man, he observed sourly, could hit a grizzly bear if it was standing right in front of him. Both missed. It looked like a standoff. Kuo flopped down on his belly on one side of the fire, while Milt knelt behind the cart wheel again. Both men were visible to the other, as well as to Yester.

Go ahead, he thought, kill each other. But, inexplicably, they both held off.

He wasn't watching them anymore, anyhow. He was watching the cabin door yet again. Watching for his sister to come running out.

He held his breath, as if willing her to do the same against the smoke. He willed her to run as she'd never run before, although she was always fleet of foot.

"C'mon, Ketta," he muttered. "C'mon."

But the doorway remained empty as flames burst through the cabin roof and shot upward into the darkening sky.

The narrow, irregular area between the bluff and the burning cabin proved hotter than Hades as Nat darted through the shortcut in search of Yester. He shaded his eyes with a forearm and his mouth with his hand as he passed the fire, which now burned fiercely.

Sweat poured from him when he came out the other side.

Yester, his back turned to Nat, was visible from the corner of the cabin. The bumbling dumb fellow lay dead at his feet.

Nat whistled, the high pitch of it lost as more gunfire erupted.

Yester didn't hear. He crouched with his rifle propped between chunks of wood, and, as Nat watched, he fired. Out in the meadow, a man fell from a horse.

Nat tried the whistle again as Yester calmly reloaded his rifle, but this time, his mouth gone dry, no sound came out.

Over at the other side of the cabin, Milt fired off a few rounds, apparently without aim, and reloaded. Maybe Kuo had been watching for the chance, because he burst out the cabin door as though poked with a sharp stick and raced toward the other outlaw, firing his pistol as he came.

He flopped down on the near side of the fire Beaver had tended, and, for a few seconds, Nat figured for sure he'd been hit. And maybe he had, but then Kuo stirred and, like a snake, slithered toward Milt.

"Filthy yellow bastard," Milt yelled. "I got you now, by God."

Kuo, lying flat, snapped off a shot. The bullet hit Milt in the thigh, and, although he didn't go down, it sent him staggering backward, away from the wheel's scant cover.

Nat, with the heat from the burning cabin about to set his shirt on fire, took the opportunity to run for the woodpile and Yester. The two outlaws traded shots again as he slid in beside his friend, barely avoiding Dunce's body.

Yester whirled, rifle aimed straight at Nat.

Nat threw up his hands. "Don't shoot."

"Nat." Yester's face appeared a little green under his tan, but relieved at the company. The rifle barrel dropped. "I was afraid you were dead, too. And Ketta." Mouth tight, he glanced toward the cabin. "We're too late. She's still in there."

"Oh, no, she ain't." Nat grinned at his friend. "I've got her safe."

"Safe? You do?" An astonished, but hopeful, look passed over Yester's face. "How?"

"She got out through a roof vent on the backside of the cabin." Nat gestured toward Kuo. "He boosted her through and told her to run."

"He did? The Chinaman?"

"Yeah. Well, he is her pa. Right? Guess he thinks something of her."

"He should," Yester said fiercely, facing toward the two outlaws again.

Nat thought there might've been a trace of moisture in his friend's hazel eyes. Yester's sharp elbow in his ribs diverted his attention.

"Look," Yester said.

Kuo was on the move again, and leaving a blood trail as he squirmed toward Milt.

"Where's he hit?" Nat asked.

Yester shrugged. "Don't know, but it appears as if he's slowed down some."

"Yeah. It does. He has."

Once or twice they saw him brush at his eyes, like he had a hard time seeing what lay ahead.

As for Milt, he'd collapsed into a sitting position, with his legs straight out in front of him. He bled even more copiously than Kuo. A good-sized puddle had formed under his thigh even as the thirsty ground sucked in the moisture.

"Kuo must've hit Milt's artery," Yester said. "Looks like he's bleeding out."

Maybe, but Milt found the strength to lever another cartridge into the rifle chamber and fire at Kuo. Careless aim or no, Kuo jerked as it hit. His left arm dragged uselessly at his side. Blood poured from the half-severed limb.

"You're a dead man, Kuo," Milt hollered. Tried to holler anyway, his voice failing.

Kuo raised up. "So are you." The wavering barrel of his pistol spat. A fresh spatter of red adorned Milt's shirt at the gut.

Blood spooled from Milt's slack mouth. "Burned that yellow daughter of yours to a black crisp. Too bad. I'd've liked to use her."

"Gah. You're wrong. She lives. She is too good for the likes of you." Kuo smiled, and, from their place, both Yester and Nat could see his teeth were red and his mouth filled with blood.

"Lung shot," Yester said.

Milt fired again, a bullet that plowed into the earth and cast dirt over Kuo's head, now flat against the ground.

But that was all. Except for the snap of the fire, it went silent.

Minutes passed.

Nat stood up. "Guess we'd better see if they're dead."

"Yeah." Yester arose, too, stepping around Dunce, but Nat stopped and pointed down at the body.

"Did you kill him, too?"

"Me? No. Heller, the gunslinger, did. Just pointed his gun

and shot him like it didn't mean a thing." Yester shook his head.

For some reason, Nat was relieved.

Yester

Kuo breathed his last as Yester turned him over. He was pretty far gone, but his eyes met Yester's for just an instant, and Yester could've sworn he saw relief there before the light died out.

Milt, dead as last year's birthday, was even uglier and stunk worse in death than in life. If such a thing were possible.

"Suppose we ought to bury them?" Nat stood beside Yester with his hands behind his back.

"I suppose."

"It's a lot of graves." Nat sounded a little overwhelmed. "Four men."

"I know. But it don't seem right to just leave 'em lay for the bugs and the beasts."

Nat nodded, then his lips twisted. "They wouldn't bother if it was us. You can lay money on that."

"I know." Yester looked up. "But we ain't them."

"We can lay them out under this tree. They must have bedrolls. We'll wrap them in their blankets."

"You're fussing like an old woman, Nat." Tired to the bone, Yester dreaded touching the bodies and he knew it went against Nat's grain.

Nat brushed aside the slur. "Do you want me to go get our horses? I can drag Heller's body here on the way back."

Yester started to agree, but stopped himself. That wasn't fair to Nat. "I'll do it as soon as we tidy these three up and throw a tarp over them. Then you can spring Ketta. I don't want her to see all these dead men. It'd scare her to death."

"All right."

A small voice spoke from behind them. "I'm not scared. I'm glad they're dead. Except for—"

Yester spun around. "Ketta!"

"Thought I told you to stay put until I came for you," Nat grumbled.

Not that Ketta heard him. Heard either of them. Just as she'd done earlier with Nat, she flung herself at Yester, hugging him like she'd never let him go. He shook with the force of her trembling.

"You came for me," she cried. "You really did."

Yester stood there and let her hug. "Well," he said when he got his own voice back, "yeah."

Heller's pinto wandered into camp just as Yester finished helping Nat throw a filthy square of canvas over the bodies. Except for Kuo's. Ketta insisted he be set apart.

"Why?" Yester asked, to which she simply replied, "He was my father."

Nat stood there shaking his head in bewilderment. "Yes, but, Ketta, he kidnapped you. Put you through hell. Lookit what else happened. You almost got shot. You almost got burned up."

"I almost got sold, like a slave." Hands on narrow hips, she set her mouth, a stubborn look that echoed her mother, truth be told. "But I didn't. He didn't sell me. And he protected me from them." Her gaze settled on the lumpy tarp. "Best he was able."

"Didn't do a very damn good job," Yester muttered. "None of it needed to happen, anyway. He should've left you alone. He should've left Ma alone."

Ketta didn't bother to deny it. "I know." She drew in a deep breath. "Is Mama all right? I've been so worried." Words seemed to fail her.

Yester gritted his teeth. "Nat's ma is with her. The day we left home, she said Ma would live, although she's torn up some. And scared for you."

"And Big Joe?"

Yester only shrugged.

He went to catch up the pinto then, almost glad to get away from her. Long enough to gather himself. To be strong. This still wasn't over. It wouldn't be over until they all got home safe and in one piece, and heard what Big Joe had to say.

If he had two cents to rub together, Yester thought, he'd leave and set out on his own. Maybe take Ketta with him. And Ma, if she made it through.

The pinto was a good horse. Didn't fuss at all with a new rider on his back. Even bareback, they made good time through the meadow to the canyon's entrance. About midway he marked where Heller's body had fallen, determined to fetch it on the way back.

His horse and Nat's pony were still where they'd been hitched, standing hipshot and patient. Without taking time to dismount, Yester put the horses on a lead and started back. He wanted to get this next part over with.

Mid-meadow, he found Heller sprawled face down in the grass. Cautiously, making sure there were no surprises, Yester circled the body. Yeah, the man was dead all right. Flies had gathered and were fornicating on the outlaw's open eyes. A neat bullet hole was centered in his back, and, for a moment, Yester regretted the way he'd died.

He didn't have time to think much on it. As he swung his leg over to dismount, the crack of a rifle echoed across the meadow. A fraction of a second later he felt a fiery sting in his arm, and his hand went numb. What the hell?

The sight of blood pouring down his arm sent him diving into the grass on his belly beside Heller's body. A shot slammed into Heller, jolting the corpse into a caricature of lifelike movement. Yester huddled behind the outlaw, making himself low and small. Or as small as a six-footer can get.

Goddamn. Who was shooting at him?

The bucktoothed feller, Beaver, that's who. How had he forgotten Dunce's brother? Careless.

Worse, his rifle, which he'd dropped when the bullet hit, was out of reach, the pinto having shied off at the sound of gunfire. Yester's own horse, as well as Nat's cayuse, had followed the pinto. Afraid to raise his head above the grass to see what had become of them, he listened hard. Back at the cabin, Ketta was screaming his name.

Hell! She probably figured he'd been killed, fast as he'd gone to ground.

Hell! Beaver was probably sneaking up on him right now, and him without a weapon. But even as he thought it, those revolvers of Heller's he'd coveted drifted through his mind. Taking care not to stir the grass, he fumbled at the holster on Heller's hip. And swore. It was empty, the gun having most likely fallen out when Heller went down.

But he'd had two.

This time Yester had no choice but to risk a look. Maybe the other pistol had remained in the holster.

Staying as flat as possible, Yester reached over the outlaw's hip with his good arm and rolled the dead outlaw up onto his side. He was in luck. Yester snatched the pistol from the holster even as a second slug rocked Heller's body.

This time the bullet went right on through the corpse and clipped Yester's side. The shock of it forced a hoarse cry from him.

Hell! Now he had another hole in his shirt—but at least he was armed.

Yester figured he'd be dead as a mackerel if he reared up and tried to find a target. Whereas Beaver probably had his gun trained right on the spot just waiting for Yester to do something dumb. So, he'd better be smart. Which meant he'd have to wait for Beaver to come to him, as he had no doubt Beaver would. To spit on his dead body, if nothing else.

After a minute or so, the flies settled back on Heller. Some, drawn by fresh blood, landed on him. Determined not to stir, to make Beaver think he was dead, he forced himself to lie still.

Yester hadn't felt much pain until now. The numbness in his arm went away to be replaced with a world of hurt. His side burned like he'd been branded. The wait seemed to go on and on. He'd begun to feel a little woozy by the time a whisper of sound reached his ears.

A horse stepped closer to where he lay against Heller. As if they were unholy lovers, he thought distastefully.

A tongue clicked, urging the unwilling animal closer.

Yester kept his eyes closed as he felt a shadow pass over him, hoping he suppressed a telltale flinch.

The man on the horse stopped a few feet away, the horse being unwilling to get any closer. It pranced and snorted, spewing slime over Yester's face. This time he knew his flinch was visible.

And Beaver caught it. "Not dead yet? I can fix that."

Yester knew he didn't have time to wait. He rolled toward the horse, only stopping when he reached its legs. The startled horse jumped sideways, fighting the rein as Beaver jerked its head up.

Eyes wide open now, Yester jumped to his feet, his head bumping the horse's nose on the way up. This time the horse shied backward, and Beaver, perhaps not the finest of horsemen at his best, slewed half on, half off. His rifle, held in one hand, shot into the sky.

Yester opened fire. The revolver bucked in his hand, missing his target, he figured in disgust, by a half-dozen yards. Damn. Unable to raise his wounded arm, he had nothing to brace his hand and correct the aim.

"Point your finger and shoot." Big Joe's voice echoed in his mind. "That's all there is to it. You got to learn how to squeeze off your shot. Be gentle on the trigger."

Yester didn't see any choice but to follow his pa's advice, seeing that Beaver had regained his seat on the horse and yanked it back around.

As if the pistol were an extension of his hand, Yester pointed his finger and squeezed.

Double reports echoed across the meadow.

Beaver's mouth opened in a scream, exposing his unfortunate teeth. His rifle dropped to the ground. The horse stepped on it and ducked away, at the same time that Beaver lost his seat. The man thudded to the ground and lay moaning.

"Pa," he cried. "Pa?"

Yester plodded forward and stood beside him, his own blood dripping down on the man who'd shot him.

"Your pa is dead," he said. "All the rest of them are dead."

Beaver stared at him. "Dead?" It was as if everything that had happened in the last few hours—minutes—had flown from his memory.

"I reckon you will be, too, soon enough," Yester said.

"No. I—"

But he was.

Abruptly, legs unable to support him, Yester sat down.

Surrounded by dead men, he thought, just before the world turned black and he sank into oblivion.

Chapter Twenty: Ketta

"We should go see what's taking Yester so long." Ketta fretted, staring off into the growing darkness. "It's been a half hour since we heard those shots. Thirty minutes. At least thirty minutes. Maybe an hour." She stood with her arms wrapped around herself as if she were cold. No matter that the mostly burned cabin still radiated heat, the fire used to ignite the torches still glowed, and, though dusk had finally come to the canyon, it retained the warmth of the day. A pall of smoke overlay everything else.

"What if . . ."

"I'll go," Nat said. He'd been pacing the open ground in front of the cabin, as restless and anxious as she.

"I'll go with you."

"No," Nat began, but Ketta ignored him.

"Maybe he's bleeding. Maybe he needs our help. Maybe—" She stopped, swallowed, then went on, "Yes, he probably needs our help."

"Possible, I guess," Nat said, which didn't soothe Ketta in the least.

The pinto, followed by Yester's horse and Nat's cayuse, had wandered up to the cabin a few minutes ago, along with another that one of the outlaws had been riding. There was blood drying on the pinto's flank. Fresh blood, which Nat had taken care to rub away.

"We've waited long enough." Ketta started toward the horses, choosing the one from home that Yester had ridden on his quest. Queenie. Ketta had ridden the black mare before, when Big Joe wasn't around to notice. She did a graceful little leap, her left foot landing in the stirrup, and dragged herself aboard. "Let's go."

Nat, helpless to stop her, mounted his cayuse and, leading the other horses, followed.

With night falling, it was getting hard to see. A horse, bridled but not saddled, so it must've been Beaver's, loomed out of the gathering darkness as it grazed in the middle of the meadow. It threw up its head and nickered as they approached. The other horses answered as Ketta reined in the mare and listened.

Nothing. Only the rattle of the bit and crunch of teeth as the grazing horse chewed around the metal.

"Nat?" Ketta whispered.

"I'm here." He stopped beside her and surveyed the area. "There." He pointed to a circle cleared in the tall grass.

Three dark lumps stood out against the straw-yellow vegetation. Body-sized lumps.

A sob broke from Ketta's throat.

Nat swore. "Don't cry."

Ketta gulped. "I'm not crying."

"Yes, you are."

"Not." As if to prove her toughness, she slid to the ground and led the horse over to the first body, yanking roughly at the rein when the horse threw up its head in protest.

"It's Beaver," she said, sighing her relief. The farthest body she recognized as Heller, his black clothing blurring the outlines. That left the one in-between.

"Ketta, stop," Nat said, catching up to her. "Let me check first."

"No. It's my job. He came for me."

Yester lay on his side, knees curled, head bent. He'd fallen with his wounded arm up, revealing a wound for Ketta's and Nat's inspection. The gash went all the way to the bone, which showed white through the blood.

"Yester," Ketta whispered but got no response. She looked at Nat. "Is he dead?"

Nat drew a shaky breath. "No. See. He's still bleeding. Dead men don't bleed."

In proof, Yester let out a moan. His eyelids fluttered. "Damn," he said. ". . . hurts."

Ketta was never so relieved in her life to hear somebody complain.

"I'm here, Yester," she whispered to him. "Nat and me. We'll help you. You're going to be all right."

Although she loved and admired every inch of her tall brother, before too many minutes passed, Ketta had cause to rethink her admiration. She and Nat had all they could do, straining and sweating as they loaded Yester on a horse. They chose the cayuse because he was the smallest. Inches counted when it came to manhandling a six-footer unable to help himself.

"I'll come back for the other two," Nat said, sweat beads rolling down his face when they finally had Yester astride. "Only I'm not loading them. I'll loop a rope around their feet and drag them."

Ketta applauded this plan. Anyway, outlaw bodies hardly counted in comparison to her brother. She led the cayuse back to the camp while Nat walked beside Yester and held him steady.

They got him down on a blanket back at the smoldering cabin. It was fully dark by now, and Ketta rebuilt the campfire for more light. In the work of a moment, she'd stripped Yester of his ragged and bloody shirt and bent to inspect his wounds.

"The one in his side isn't bad," she told Nat, even though he could see as much for himself. "It looks clean." Nevertheless, she hunted up a pot from some camping supplies, filled it with water, and put it over the fire to boil.

"Probably leave a nasty scar."

"Uh-huh." Ketta sighed, bending again and peering closely at Yester's side. "Needs stitches but I don't have anything to sew him up with." Truthfully, she wasn't any too sure she could've done it even if she'd had the wherewithal. "Come help me." Gathering her strength, she ripped her brother's faded shirt into strips to bind the wound. After washing the worst of the grime from it, that is.

Scars didn't concern her, but nerving herself to attend his arm did. One look and she averted her eyes. "He needs a doctor."

"We'll get him to one." Nat glanced around the clearing. "We'll leave tomorrow morning at daylight. It's too dark to travel tonight."

"You could find a doctor and bring him here," she said, quelling an inward shiver.

"I'm not leaving you alone here with Yester shot up and five dead bodies in need of burying." Adamant, Nat's soft voice took on a hardness she'd never heard before.

"I'll be all right. I'm not afraid." But she was. Haunts were sure to attach themselves to those men. All of them, even Kuo, her father.

"And I'm not digging that many holes tonight," Nat said, as if she hadn't spoken. "That's if I could find a shovel."

Carefully, Ketta ripped a piece off her already torn and shoddy apron, rinsed it out, and dipped it in the hot water to bathe Yester's wounds.

She got to thinking as she worked. "You don't need to bury them, Nat. In fact, you'd better not."

"Not?"

"Not if you want the reward."

"What reward?"

When she was finished cleaning and covering Yester's arm, she sank onto her heels and looked up at Nat.

"The reward on Heller and Milt. They were bragging"—she emitted a little hiss between her teeth—"about who had the most reward money out for them. Heller won. He showed everyone a wanted poster that said there's a $1500 bounty on him."

Nat's dark eyes widened. "That's a lot of money. What did he do?"

"According to the poster he's wanted for train robbery. And murder."

Nat swallowed. "And you—" He stopped. "What about Milt?"

"He's only worth half that. He robbed some banks. And killed a man while he was at it, of course." She said it like it was old hat. "The other two, Beaver and Dunce, they weren't mentioned by name, but there's an extra hundred for Milt's two accomplices. I expect that means them."

Staring at her in wonder, Nat had one more question. "And Kuo? Is there a reward for him as well?"

She looked away, finding it hard to meet his eyes. "Yes, him, too. But . . ." she hesitated.

"But what?"

"I hate turning him in. He is . . . he was my father."

"How much bounty on him?"

"Five hundred. He went along with the bank robberies. But he didn't kill anybody." She hoped.

Nat stared off into the dark beyond the fire. "You'd better claim it," he said, but Ketta shuddered.

"I don't want it. I don't want anybody to know he's my father."

She'd thought Yester still unconscious, or asleep. Unaware, at any rate. But he wasn't.

"Take the money," he said. "He owes you. Think on it as your inheritance."

Nat having made his point, and, with Yester concurring, they waited until morning to set out for Lewiston. They made quite a cavalcade then, on the trail at daylight. All the living were hungry, having only a sip of coffee and a stale, crumbly biscuit apiece to still their rumbling bellies.

Yester's arm hurt so damn bad he barely kept from crying like a little girl. Or maybe a baby. Every move sent agony jolting through his entire body, including his horse's plodding stride. He tried to think only grateful thoughts. That he was alive, for one. And he knew he'd use his arm again, because his fingers moved. In fact, they twitched in reaction to the pain.

He settled into his saddle and concentrated on staying on the horse.

Nat led a string of five horses. Each held a body bundled in their respective bedrolls. Except for Kuo. Heller'd had a spare blanket, which served for Kuo, his goods having all burned up in the cabin.

Ketta and Nat'd had quite a time loading the corpses, until Yester suggested using a pulley he'd observed anchored in a tree. Kuo had probably used it for hanging game. Whatever, it worked equally as well for one man, that being Nat, to haul a body high enough to lower onto a horse's back. Ketta had helped, using a system where even a girl could hold the package steady and guide it into place.

Not that it had been easy.

Still, they'd managed, Yester by staying out of the way and letting the other two work. He smiled, thinking of the way easygoing Nat lost his temper and yelled at his helper, and Ketta, the aforementioned helper, yelled right back. She would never have done such a thing before. Never. But then, Nat wouldn't have, either. Which of them had changed the most during this adventure?

Or was it Yester himself who'd changed most. He'd killed a man, now. Two men. Most people never dreamed of taking another person's life.

They hadn't been good men, he told himself. Best not to think of it.

So, he didn't. Not too much.

They traversed the canyon and came down to the trail beside the river, backtracking the way they'd arrived yesterday. The trail became a road, where passersby surveyed the bundles aboard the horses and, eyeing the grim caravan, thought better of asking questions.

Eventually the town of Lewiston opened up before them. Late afternoon found them drawing to a halt in front of the sheriff's office.

Yester was slumped in the saddle by this time, barely able to lift his head. Which elected Nat spokesman, calling out to the sheriff by name. A crowd gathered.

Thankfully, the sheriff was in. Poised for trouble, he came to stand in the doorway, his hand on the butt of his pistol. Taking a moment, he surveyed the group.

"Whatcha got here, boys?" he said, although, judging by the gathering crowd, anybody who had eyes could and had guessed the contents of the horses' loads.

"Dead outlaws," Nat answered laconically.

"Who killed them?"

"Me." Yester found it in himself to raise his head and speak. "Two of them. The rest got to fighting and killed each other."

The sheriff stared. "Who are they?"

Ketta spoke up. "He told you. Outlaws. Thieves. Murderers." She paused. "Kidnappers."

Narrow-eyed, the sheriff said, "Who'd they kidnap?"

"Me." To all appearances she didn't even hear the crowd's murmur. "Please, is there a doctor here? My brother has been shot."

As it turned out, Lewiston not only had a doctor, it had a hospital. A hospital in which, over his strong protests, Yester spent the next couple days while his wounds healed. To his disgust, the staff was plumb set on feeding their patients nourishing broths. Then came a bath, a badly needed bath. Yester's problem was the pretty nurse not much older than he who was put in charge. Yester figured he'd feel better about it if he could just die. Yep. Right there on the spot.

Meanwhile, due to the good will the sheriff promoted, Ketta and Nat were installed in a rooming house that had agreed to shelter them for as long as necessary. Maybe it wasn't the best rooming house in town. What high-toned establishment wants to take in a Métis and a mixed-blood Chinese girl? However, the two found the meals filling, the rooms adequate, and, causing Ketta to squeal with delight and almost fracture Yester's ears when she told him about it, the place boasted a modern bathroom. After some fuss and bother and an extra fee, hot bath water ran into a deep, claw-footed tub. She reveled in a bath. Two baths—she held up two fingers to show him—as if she could never be clean enough.

Even Nat tried out the indoor tub.

"Beats this hospital, for sure," Yester said gloomily.

They had money. The sheriff, once he got a look at the outlaws' bodies, extended them a few dollars credit on the basis of the pending rewards coming through. Which they did, on the day after Yester joined Nat and Ketta at the rooming house.

Finally, it was time to head home. Money in their pockets, or, more precisely, after some argument, wrapped in a bandana and buried at the bottom of a container of flour. Ketta's idea.

"In case somebody tries to rob us," she said.

Yester gave her a look, wondering how she'd gotten so wise.

Nat flourished one of Heller's six-guns, a pearl-handled .44 caliber Smith and Wesson Russian, a share of the spoils. "We got protection. Nobody is going to rob us. Nobody knows we have money."

Ketta's nose wrinkled. "Do too. Don't you think people are talking about us? About your and Yester's exploits? Bet everybody in town knows. Bet everyone in the whole country!"

"Better listen to her, Nat," Yester advised, grinning at their argument. Ketta had been a whole lot more forceful in stating her opinion these last few days.

"Yes. We bought all these supplies, didn't we?" she was saying. "I got a new dress—two new dresses—and Yester and you both got some clothes. We bought gifts, too, and we paid cash. Of course, people know we have money."

"Well, maybe we spent it all."

"Huh."

The sheriff proved amicable to Yester's insistence that they be the ones to return Patton's horses to him. Especially the Percheron. Yester felt duty bound, considering the rancher's help in their quest. The sheriff had decided to keep Heller's pinto for his own.

Once gaining the top of the long, steep hill up from the Snake, they ambled slowly through the countryside, taking care for Yester's wounds. On the second day, they passed through Patton's freestanding gate, making sure to close it after them.

Ketta laughed.

Warned by the dog, Patton and his wife emerged from their house and watched them come. Patton's right leg was splinted from hip to ankle, five dirty bare toes exposed to the elements, and he was leaning on crutches. Hatless, his head bore a thick white bandage wrapped around it. He was pleased to accept the animals and congratulated the three, shaking hands all around.

"Young lady, I'm glad to see your brother got you back in one, whole piece." Patton's mouth curled under his mustache into a smile. "And you, lad, you done good." His nod included Nat. "Both of you boys done good. And you're both alive to talk about it." He sounded a bit surprised at that, something Yester didn't consider too complimentary.

Yester had to shake hands using his left. "That we are, sir. We wondered, though, what happened to you. Last Nat and me saw, you and your hands took off after those outlaws. We hoped to meet with you again, right up until they all got together at the Chinaman's cabin. By then we figured something had gone wrong."

Patton's face turned a ruddy hue. "Horse stepped in a gopher hole, broke both his leg and mine. Had to shoot him. The boys almost had to shoot me, too. I'd bumped my head on a rock, and they carried me home on a travois. By the time I regained my senses, we figured the tracks were wiped out, and there was no use setting off again."

Yester couldn't figure how the old man had ever imagined to fork a horse in his condition, let alone chase outlaws.

"You still ain't regained your senses, old man," Mrs. Patton declared, "or you'd've invited these young folks into the house for a bite to eat."

Something other than trail food appealed to the three. They dismounted, Mrs. Patton taking Ketta under her wing.

"Why, you seem a little older than I thought," the lady said, her arm around Ketta's shoulders. "I understood you were just a child."

"I'm small for my age," Ketta replied shyly. "But I'm almost grown up."

"Yes." The old lady looked deeply into Ketta's eyes. "Yes, I see you are."

Their tale told in detail, they mounted up and headed out again, Patton's insistence on paying a reward adding to their wealth.

They camped that night, and sometime along midnight Yester woke up when he heard the animals stirring. He poked Nat, who lay nearby, in the ribs.

"What?" Nat didn't move, although his open eyes showed he was wide awake.

"Got company."

"I heard."

The matched Smith & Wessons were drawn from beneath their pillowing saddles. Yester rolled into the cover of a tree stump, cursing as his arm took a knock, and when he looked back, Nat had disappeared.

"Move on, you," Yester roared. "We got you covered."

Ketta popped up, eyes wide.

"Over here!" Nat yelled from the shadows.

A shot rang out, the report loud in the night, which caused Ketta to dive beneath her blanket. Running footsteps retreated, then hoofbeats sounded.

A minute later, Nat came back and resumed his bedroll.

The other two stared at him.

"Guess you didn't get him," Yester said.

Nat shrugged. "Never even saw him."

Ketta scowled at him. "Then what were you shooting at?"

"A tree. Got a dead tree." Grinning, Nat lay down.

"Told you people knew we have money," Ketta muttered, and then, on a note of complaint, "The sheriff told everybody who'd listen about the three of us bringing in all those outlaw corpses. After that, you'd think people would be more cautious around us, wouldn't you? Who'd ever guess there are so darn many thieves in the world?"

This disturbance was the most exciting incident of the trip.

The next day they rode into the Noonans' ranch yard, and Barney, once he'd identified the riders, limped over to greet them on his three good legs, his tail wagging frantically enough to create a minor windstorm.

Horses grazed in the meadow beyond the corrals. The outhouse was back in place, the barn in the process of being repaired, and chickens strutted in and out of the coop.

Except for an attempt at fixing the step by laying a whole board over the burned part, as far as repairs went, the house hadn't been touched. Not that Yester could tell.

Alerted by Barney's baying, Yellow Bird Fontaine appeared in the doorway. She held a broom in her hands as if wishing it were a rifle until she saw who they were. Then a broad smile lit her face.

There was no sign of either Big Joe Noonan, or Magdalene. A chill swept Yester's euphoria away. It was left to Nat to lead them to the hitching rail in front of the scorched house.

"Mother," Nat announced, "we are home."

Yester and Ketta exchanged looks. Mrs. Fontaine had told Yester she'd stay with Magdalene until they returned. That she was still here seemed a good sign.

Ketta jumped from her horse without bothering with the stirrup.

"My mother," she said, rushing up to Mrs. Fontaine. "Is she . . ."

"In the bedroom." Mrs. Fontaine soothed her. "Resting. She'll be fine now that you and Yester are home. Though she will be worried by that," she added, indicating Yester's arm, still supported by a sling.

She set aside the broom and gathered Nat into her arms for a brief hug. "My son," she murmured, "I'm glad to see you."

"And I you." Nat smiled. "Told you I'd be fine. And I am."

Magdalene was sitting up in her bed peering toward the door

as Ketta and Yester tiptoed in. Her face and arms still bore traces of the bruising she'd endured at the outlaws' hands. Pain lines marked her expression, lines that cleared as Yester and Ketta approached. A frown touched her face at the sight of Yester's wound, but when Ketta skipped with excitement, it faded away.

"I brought her home, Ma. I told you I would. Me and Nat." Yester's grin stretched wide.

"They didn't hurt you?" Ma asked, catching Ketta to her. "*He* didn't hurt you?"

"No. He—" Ketta stuttered over this part. She plumped down on the bed beside her mother. "Kuo protected me from the others. He *died* protecting me." She sounded like she still had trouble believing it herself.

Magdalene's eyes, hazel like Yester's, opened wide as she stared up at her son. "He's dead?"

"Yes. All of them are."

"Tell me," Magdalene said, clapping her hands together. "Immediately." Nothing would do but she hear the story of her offspring's victory over a whole gang of outlaws.

Yester took a deep breath afterward. He'd been dreading this next question, but he had to ask. "What about Pa? Where's he?"

Ketta, he noticed, watched their mother anxiously as she shrugged.

"Out working, I suppose," Ma said, her face expressionless.

"No, I'm here," Big Joe said from the doorway.

They hadn't heard his approach. Not a one of them stirred. It was as if they all were frozen in place.

Ma had changed while they'd been gone, Yester thought. Maybe because she'd been near death. Maybe because of him and Ketta and what they'd been through. But, for whatever reason, Ma didn't seem to care one way or another about Big Joe. In the past, she'd have jerked around and shied away and acted all nervous.

And Ketta, too. She would've run for her hideyhole at the mention of Big Joe's name, let alone having him right there in person. Now she didn't even look up as he entered the room.

The silence held.

Then Big Joe said to Yester, "I see you made it home in one piece, son. And you brought her with you."

The "her" clearly meant Ketta.

Yester didn't know what to say. That he was glad to be home? That he'd stay? But he wasn't any too sure whether he would or whether he wouldn't. A lot depended on Big Joe and his attitude, but mostly on himself. And on Ma. And Ketta. Especially Ketta.

He didn't say anything, his gaze fixed on his sister.

Just then Barney stuck his nose into Ketta's hand, and tears spurted into her eyes. "I thought you were dead, Barney," she said, scratching his ears. "And you, too, Mama. I thought . . ."

She took a sustaining gulp of air and looked right into Joe Noonan's eyes. "I'm glad to be home."

As for Big Joe?

He didn't rant or rave or shout or stomp. He didn't call her names.

He didn't tell her "Welcome home," either.

But he nodded.

Yester figured that was enough for now.

ABOUT THE AUTHOR

C. K. Crigger lives with two feisty little dogs in Spokane Valley, Washington. A big fan of local history, all of her books are set in the inland Northwest and make use of a historical background. She is a two-time Spur Award finalist, in 2007 for Short Fiction, and in 2009 for Audio. She reviews books and writes occasional articles for *Roundup* magazine. Contact her through her website at www.ckcrigger.com.

The employees of Five Star Publishing hope you have enjoyed this book.

Our Five Star novels explore little-known chapters from America's history, stories told from unique perspectives that will entertain a broad range of readers.

Other Five Star books are available at your local library, bookstore, all major book distributors, and directly from Five Star/Gale.

<u>Connect with Five Star Publishing</u>

Visit us on Facebook:
https://www.facebook.com/FiveStarCengage

Email:
FiveStar@cengage.com

For information about titles and placing orders:
(800) 223-1244
gale.orders@cengage.com

To share your comments, write to us:
Five Star Publishing
Attn: Publisher
10 Water St., Suite 310
Waterville, ME 04901